The Perfect Present

The Perfect Present

ROCHELLE ALERS
CHERIS HODGES
PAMELA YAYE

Kensington Publishing Corp.

www.kensingtonbooks.com

DAFINA BOOKS are published by

Kensington Publishing Corp.
119 West 40th Street
New York, NY 10018

ISBN-13: 978-1-4967-1018-5
ISBN-10: 1-4967-1018-5
First Kensington Mass Market Edition: October 2017

eISBN-13: 978-1-4967-1025-3
eISBN-10: 1-4967-1025-8
First Kensington Electronic Edition: October 2017

10 9 8 7 6 5 4 3 2 1

Printed in the United States of America

CONTENTS

A Christmas Layover

ROCHELLE ALERS

Chapter 1

Waiting in the aisle for several passengers to store their bags in the overhead bins, Sierra Nelson shifted her carry-on in an attempt not to bump those already seated in the aircraft. It was days before Christmas, and when she arrived at the airport, she was slightly taken aback at the throngs waiting in line to check luggage, obtain boarding passes, and go through security checkpoints. Not only had the flight been delayed two hours and overbooked, but there were a few passengers that were willing to give up their seats to be put up in nearby hotels, along with vouchers for future flights. Sierra had decided within seconds of the announcement that she would *not* be one of those amenable to taking a later flight.

She had booked the trip to fly from San Diego to Chicago more than three months in advance, had enrolled in TSA precheck, packed light, and printed her boarding pass, but the prior preparation did little to quell her impatience to be in the air and on her way to Chicago for a weeklong stay with her extended family. She found her seat in the middle of the aircraft, stored her bag, sat, secured the seat belt, and stared out the window at baggage handlers loading luggage onto a conveyor belt.

She saw a shadow out of the corner of her eye and looked up to find a man dressed in blue navy fatigues. Their eyes met for an instant, both sharing a hint of a smile, before Sierra refocused her attention on the activity going on outside the jet. His warmth and the clean scent of his cologne swept over her when he sat and secured his belt. A flight attendant, checking and closing overhead bins, stopped at their row.

"Captain Crawford, a gentleman in first class has offered to exchange seats with you."

Noah Crawford smiled. "Please thank him for me, but I prefer sitting here."

She gave him a warm smile. "I'll let him know."

Waiting until the woman continued down the aisle, Sierra turned to stare at the navy captain, her breath momentarily catching in her chest. To say he was gorgeous was an understatement. His deep-set, brown eyes glowed like smoky quartz in a complexion that reminded her of golden-brown autumn leaves. A bold nose, strong mouth, and high cheekbones made for an arresting face that garnered a second glance.

"There's a lot more legroom in first class," she said softly when he attempted to shift into a more comfortable position to accommodate his long legs.

He smiled, displaying a single dimple in his left cheek. "That's okay. I like where I'm sitting."

Sierra lowered her eyes, chiding herself for being presumptuous—something about which she occasionally lectured her fourth grade students whenever one tried explaining what another meant. "I'm sorry for intruding."

"There's no need to apologize, Miss . . ."

"Sierra Nelson," she said, introducing herself.

He took her hand, which disappeared in his larger one. "Noah Crawford."

She smiled, bringing his gaze to linger on her parted lips. "It's a pleasure to meet you, Captain Crawford, and thank you for your service to our country."

Noah released her hand, angled his head, and studied the woman less than a foot away. There was something about her round face that reminded him of a doll's. He found her flawless nut-brown complexion, delicate features, and sensual mouth mesmerizing. His eyes lingered on her short curly hair before moving down to large, slanting brown eyes with flecks of gold. He found them to be strangely beautiful; they reminded him of cat's-eye marbles.

"You're quite welcome. Are you going to Boston?"

"No. I'm getting off in Chicago." The flight was scheduled to make a layover at O'Hare before continuing on to Logan Airport.

"Is Chicago home for you?" he asked.

Sierra shook her head. "It was when growing up. How about you? Is Boston home for you?"

Noah nodded. "Yes. My mother and sisters still live there. I've tried to get Mom to move to the West Coast, but she doesn't want to be that far from her grandchildren. She also claims she loves the change of seasons."

"I'm just the opposite, because it took me one season to get used to not wearing a winter coat. However, I always keep one or two in my closet whenever

I travel back east because the last time I was in the Windy City, it snowed. And I was there on spring break."

"You're a teacher." His question was a statement.

"Yes."

"What grade do you teach?"

"Right now, I'm teaching fourth graders."

"Do you like it?"

She smiled. "I love teaching."

"Why do you live in California rather than in Illinois?" Noah asked her.

"I came out here to go to college, found a position, and then stayed. Why did you join the navy?" she asked Noah.

He stared at the seat in front of him. "I went to the Naval Academy at Annapolis."

Her eyes grew wide. "Congratulations. Should I assume you're a lifer?"

Noah paused, wondering how much he wanted to divulge to a woman who was a complete stranger. However, there was something about Sierra that made it so easy for him to talk to her. "For now, I am."

"Then you have a lot in common with my father and brothers."

"They're lifers?"

"My father was, and now my three brothers are following in his footsteps. Dad gave the army thirty years before he retired. Daniel is active army, Mark is a marine currently deployed in Afghanistan, and Luke is an army reservist. This is the first Christmas in years, with the exception of Mark, that we'll be all together."

"Are they married?"

"Yes. So I'm auntie to quite a few nieces and nephews."

His eyebrows lifted questioningly. "You don't have any children?"

Sierra shook her head. "No. I still have time before I add to my parents' ever-increasing number of grandbabies."

"Are they putting any pressure on you to give them a grandchild?"

"Not really. My parents know that I don't do well with pressure. As the only girl, I've always marched to the beat of a different drum. Even as young boys my brothers were obsessed with anything military," she said, smiling. "My grandfather was stationed in Korea, while my father fought in Vietnam, so when growing up all they heard were war stories. They all went to military school and from there it was ROTC, and eventually they became commissioned officers."

"So, you were an army brat?"

"Only for the first six years of my life. My mother was of the mind that a military base was no place to raise a girl, so she was able to convince my father that she should move back to Chicago before he was transferred to a base in Alaska."

Their conversation ended when the captain's voice came through the cabin, informing the passengers and flight crew they were preparing for liftoff. Sierra stared at the back of the seat in front of her and gripped the armrests as the aircraft picked up speed. She closed her eyes and sucked in a lungful of air as the jet went airborne.

"You can open your eyes now," crooned a deep voice in her ear.

She opened her eyes and let out an audible breath.

"You can let go of my hand now." Noah had placed his left hand over her right.

"You're afraid of flying?"

A smile parted Sierra's lips. "No. I just don't like liftoffs and landings."

"Do you want me to hold your hand when we touch down at O'Hare?"

She narrowed her eyes at him. "That's not funny, Captain America."

Noah affected a wide grin, exhibiting a mouth filled with large, straight, white teeth. "Captain America is a comic book action hero."

"And you're not?"

He sobered quickly. He couldn't reveal to Sierra that he was a Navy SEAL who had been involved in several Middle East maneuvers, and now at thirty-seven had spent more than half his life in the military. "No. I'm someone who has taken an oath to protect our country from all enemies foreign and domestic. That makes me a member of the US Armed Forces, not a hero, who just happens to be on my way to Boston to celebrate Christmas with my widowed mother, sisters, and their families."

Sierra felt properly chastised. "I'm sorry—"

"This is the second time you've apologized," he said, cutting her off. "And something tells me it's something you don't do very often."

"Not with men."

"Speaking of men," he drawled.

"What about them?"

"Will you be spending the holiday with your man?" Noah asked Sierra.

A beat passed. "No, because right now I'm not seeing anyone."

"I find that hard to believe. You're a beautiful and

obviously intelligent woman, and men should be falling over themselves to become involved with you."

Sierra chewed her lip for several seconds. "Thanks for the compliment, but it's been several years since I've been in a relationship."

"Relationships are like grains of sand on a beach, they're too numerous to count," he drawled glibly.

She went completely still. "Are you always this facetious when it comes to talking about relationships? Or could it be you don't believe in love?"

Noah chuckled, the sound rumbling in his broad chest. "Oh, I believe in love."

"If you do, then why do you sound so cynical?"

Crossing his arms over his chest, he angled his head. "Most of the women I meet aren't willing to put up with me being shipped out at a moment's notice."

"It appears as if you're meeting the wrong women. Maybe you should look for women who grew up as military brats."

"Like you?"

A soft gasp slipped past Sierra's parted lips. "No! Not like me, because I told you I'm not an army brat."

Noah turned to look at her. "Have you ever dated someone in the military?"

She nodded. "Yes."

"What happened?"

"We went out for nearly a year, and then we decided to stop seeing each other because all he talked about was going back to Texas and taking over his father's dairy farm. At the ripe old age of twenty-three, I just couldn't see myself getting up at four in the morning to milk cows or muck out barns."

"I can definitely see your point. Farming isn't for the faint of heart."

"Are you speaking from experience?" Sierra asked.

He nodded. "I used to spend the summers on my grandfather's farm in North Carolina. Grandpa raised chickens and hogs. My job was to slop the hogs and then clean out their pens. The first time I did, I almost passed out because I tried holding my breath. I literally sucked it up, and after a few days I got used to the smell."

Time passed quickly as Sierra entertained him with accounts of the children she'd taught over the years, as flight attendants distributed soft drinks, cocktails, and coffee and tea along with snack boxes. Once all of the trash was collected, the cabin's lights were dimmed and minutes later everyone seemed to be of one accord when they settled down to sleep before the jet touched down in Chicago.

Noah watched Sierra remove a shawl from the tote she had secured under the seat, wrap it around her body, and then recline the seat back. "Wake me when we get to Chi-Town."

He nodded. He knew if he didn't try to get some sleep, jet lag would play havoc with his body's circadian rhythms. And knowing his mother, she would keep him up talking when he needed to sleep. Shifting, Noah tried to get into a more comfortable position, while silently cursing the airlines for decreasing the legroom when people were growing taller, not shorter. The last thing he saw through the windows were the jagged tops of the Rockies before he finally fell asleep.

Sierra woke with a start when she felt someone shake her shoulder. "What's the matter?"

"The pilot just announced that all airports along

the East Coast from Maine to DC have been shut down because of blizzard conditions."

Her eyelids fluttered wildly. "Where are you going to stay?"

Noah pressed his mouth to her ear. "I'll try to get a room at a hotel or bed down in the airport until flights resume."

A shadow of alarm swept over her features. "No, you're not. There's no way I'm going to allow you to sleep on the floor in an airport when there's room at my folks' house. You can come home and stay with us until you can get a flight out."

"I've slept in worse places than an airport floor."

"That's not the point, Noah. You risk your life every time you put on that uniform, and I'd like to believe someone would offer to put my brothers up, given a similar situation."

"I can't impose on you like that."

"Yes, you can. Now, please don't argue with me, Captain Crawford. If I were to tell my father I didn't make the offer, he would disown me."

Noah's dimple winked at her when he smiled. "Not his precious baby girl."

Sierra felt a wave of heat in her face with his taunt. She lowered her eyes. "What's it going to be? Yes? No?"

Their gazes met and she saw something in his eyes that sent her pulse spinning. Had he thought she'd invited him to come home with her during the layover because she'd come on to him? If she was honest, she would openly admit that she found him incredibly attractive, but that's where it ended. Not only had she found him kind on the eyes but also easy to talk to.

"Yes," Noah said after a pregnant pause. "But I have to call my mother to let her know I'll be delayed."

Sierra hadn't realized she had been holding her breath. "I'll call my brother as soon as we're on the ground, to let him know I'm bringing company." When she'd called her mother to give her the time of her arrival, Evelyn Nelson reassured her one of Sierra's brothers would pick her up. Days later, Evelyn returned the call to confirm that Daniel, who'd been granted a ten-day leave, would meet her at baggage claim.

Chapter 2

Noah held Sierra's carry-on as they wended their way through the terminal to baggage claim. Those awaiting connecting flights had claimed any solid surface to sit or recline. Mothers were attempting to comfort their fretful children, while those traveling on business were barking demands into their cell phones to book them into nearby hotels until flights resumed. Meanwhile, Daniel had sent Sierra a text that he was on his way and would meet her outside the terminal.

She realized she'd sounded a tad heavy-handed when coercing Noah to come home with her until flights were resumed, but after seeing the overcrowded terminal she felt vindicated. She stared at Noah's ramrod-straight back. He stood, hands clasped behind him, as he waited with the others disembarking at O'Hare for his bag to come around the conveyor belt. Stepping forward, he grasped a bag when an elderly man attempted to retrieve it. He lifted it with minimal effort and set it on the floor, nodding when the man thanked him.

Nearly fifteen minutes later, his large duffel appeared

and Noah joined Sierra near the door. "My brother said we should wait outside for him."

Noah covered his head with a cap and, reaching for her carry-on, shouldered the door open. He glanced up at the steel-gray skies. It had begun to snow. "It looks as if the Northeast isn't the only area to get a white Christmas."

Sierra shivered as icy-cold wind stung her cheeks. "Let's hope not. If Chicago gets snowed in, then it's going to be a knockout punch for those waiting to leave the city." She took a quick glance at her watch. "Barring traffic, my brother should be here soon." The words were barely off her tongue when an SUV maneuvered up to the curb and the driver got out, dressed in desert fatigues. It was Mark, and not Daniel, who had come to meet her.

She gasped, as her heart pounded a runaway rhythm against her ribs. If his goal had been to surprise her, then he had, because Sierra felt her knees buckle slightly before she was able to regain her balance. She tried to make her feet move, but they refused to follow the dictates of her brain.

Once her brother was deployed to Afghanistan, she had made it a practice to stop every day at the church a block from her condo to say a prayer and light a candle for his safe return. Now seeing him in person was proof her prayers had been answered. One moment she was standing, and the next she found herself lifted off the ground as Mark crushed her against his body.

"No one told me that you'd come home."

Mark chuckled. "And no one said anything about your bringing your boyfriend home for Christmas," he countered, setting her on her feet. "I got in a couple of hours ago."

"He's not . . ." Her words trailed off when Mark's cell phone rang.

Mark stared at Sierra as he answered the call. "Yes, Dad. Sierra's here with her boyfriend, and you should expect us in about an hour. Yes, I'll drive carefully." He rang off. "That was *your* father. It's apparent he's worried about his little princess."

Sierra curbed the urge to roll her eyes at her brother. She'd wanted to tell him that Noah wasn't her boyfriend, but it was too late because he'd announced to their father that she hadn't come home alone. "Mark, I'd like you to meet Noah Crawford."

Mark came to attention and saluted Noah. "I'm honored, Captain Crawford."

Noah extended his hand. "It's just Noah."

Mark shook the proffered hand. "Then Noah it is. And I'm Mark. Daniel told me Sierra was bringing company, but I never would've imagined her boyfriend would be military."

"It looks as if this is truly a night for surprises," Noah said, as Sierra opened her mouth to refute Mark's belief that they were romantically involved.

Reaching for Sierra's carry-on, Mark motioned with his head. "Let's get home before it really starts coming down. Noah, you can put your duffel in the back."

Noah opened the passenger-side door and then cupped Sierra's elbow. "Let's go, girlfriend," he crooned. There was just a hint of laughter in his voice.

"How long do you think we'll be able to keep up this charade?" she asked.

"As long as it takes for me to get a flight out."

"That may not be for a couple of days."

"Come now, girlfriend, we should be able to keep it going for a couple of days. After that, we'll never have to see each other again. You can always tell your folks that it didn't work out," he said in her ear.

The last thing Sierra wanted to do was lie to her parents; however, it was now too late because she hadn't been given the opportunity to refute the pre-conception. "Okay," she said, further perpetuating the ruse.

Mark came from the rear of the SUV, picked up Noah's duffel, and rested it over his shoulder. "I hope you guys aren't having a lover's spat before Mom gets to meet him."

"No."

"Of course not."

Sierra and Noah had spoken in unison. She did not want to believe inviting a stranger to her parents' home had backfired on her, when her family were under the impression she and Noah were a couple. She smiled. "I'll sit in the back, because I know you and Mark will want to trade war stories."

Noah's eyebrows lifted questioningly. "Are you sure?"

"Yes."

He opened the door behind the front seats, assisted her up, and then sat next to Mark when he came around to sit behind the wheel.

Sierra settled back in her seat and tried to anticipate her parents' reaction to her bringing a man home with her—even though it was for only a day or two. She half listened to the conversation between her brother and supposed boyfriend as they left the airport in bumper-to-bumper traffic.

The falling snow intensified, quickly covering the roadway as wipers, turned to the fastest speed, worked to keep windshields from freezing and obscuring visibility. Forty minutes later, Mark maneuvered into the driveway leading to the sprawling Colonial in a Chicago suburb. A large live Christmas wreath decorated with miniature imitation pinecones, red and green apples, and red velvet bows had been hung on the front door, while tiny white lights ringing the house shone through the veil of heavily falling snow. Electric candles had been placed in every window, a practice her mother had begun with her children, and revived as a grandmother.

And judging by the number of vehicles in the driveway, Sierra assumed her brothers, along with their wives and children, were in attendance. Daniel lived in a Kentucky suburb near Fort Campbell, while Luke and his pediatrician wife, who was expecting their second child within weeks, had recently purchased a loft in downtown Chicago.

She inhaled as the front door opened and her father walked out. There was no doubt Philip Nelson was anxious to meet the man who had impressed his daughter enough to introduce him to her family. And she knew she had no one to blame but herself for not telling Daniel she'd met a serviceman during her flight and had invited him to stay with their family until Boston's Logan Airport reopened. However, when she'd mentioned she was bringing company, her brother drew his own conclusion, and announced she was traveling with her boyfriend.

Noah got out of the car and helped Sierra down, his arm going around her waist with her father's approach. It had only taken a single glance to know what Mark would look like in thirty years. The younger man had inherited his father's height, khaki-brown complexion, rawboned face, and features.

Philip extended both arms and Sierra moved into his embrace. "Welcome home, baby girl." He smiled, his eyes going from his daughter to Noah. He released Sierra and enveloped Noah in a bear hug. "Philip Nelson. Welcome to the family, son. And thank you for your service to our country."

"Noah Crawford. Thank you, sir, for allowing me to stay in your home for a few days."

Philip, dropping his arms, waved a hand. "None of that sir stuff. I left that behind once I retired."

"Daddy was a colonel," Sierra said.

"I was a lieutenant colonel," Philip corrected as he patted Noah's shoulder. "Come inside and meet the family. After that, you can get into your civvies and relax with the rest of us."

Noah nodded. "I have to get my duffel."

"Don't worry about that." Philip motioned to Mark. "Put Noah's bag in Sierra's room."

"That won't be necessary," he countered. "I don't mind staying in a spare room."

"There is no spare room, son. No one's going to judge you if you and my daughter share a bedroom."

"But, Daddy—"

"But nothing, Sierra," Philip said in a quiet, no-nonsense tone. "Every bedroom in the house is occupied, so this is no time for you to pretend that you and Noah aren't sleeping together." He rubbed his arms. "I don't know why I'm standing out here in the snow jawing about nonsense. Come on in the house, where it's warm."

Noah exchanged a look with Sierra, who lifted her shoulders and at the same time shook her head. It looked as if the decision for them *not* to share a bedroom had been taken out of their hands. He had never been good at lying or even bending the truth, but it was as if he had to go along with Sierra's father's ultimatum because, at the moment, he did not have a choice.

Reaching for her hand, he tucked it into the bend of his elbow as he followed Philip. "I'm sorry to put you on the spot," he said sotto voce.

"It's me that put *you* on the spot," Sierra countered. "Even though we'll sleep in the same room, we don't have to share the bed. You'll see once we get inside."

Noah experienced a modicum of relief. He wasn't a novice when it came to women, yet he also had not made it a practice to sleep with women who were complete strangers. And even after spending several hours talking with Sierra, she was still a stranger. His life in the military hadn't lent itself to forming lasting relationships, because he never knew when he would be called up for a mission that would take him away for weeks at a time—missions he was forbidden to talk about, even to those closest to him: his mother and sisters.

He patted her hand. "Don't worry about it, *darling*."

Philip glanced over his shoulder. "I'm glad you're telling her not to worry. When she was a little girl she used to get upset over nothing."

"I had every right to be upset, Daddy, when Daniel used to pop the heads off my Barbie dolls."

"And your mother punished him for it."

Noah smiled hearing the interchange between Sierra and her father, because he'd done the same with his sisters' dolls. After a while his sisters had begun hiding them, and he'd had to find something else with which to annoy them.

The instant he stepped into the entryway he was enveloped with warmth and the glow of recessed lights running the length of the hallway that opened up into a great room with a towering live spruce. Noah unlaced his boots, leaving them on a long rubber mat with dozens of other outdoor footwear.

Sierra's fingers tightened on his arm as she held on to him to keep her balance as she kicked off her shoes. "I forgot to tell you that tonight we'll have a tailgate-type buffet dinner. Christmas Eve is when we decorate the tree, while the women in the family spend the day cooking. We usually sit down to eat around eight, and those who manage not to succumb to a food coma stay up until midnight to open gifts."

"What happens Christmas morning?"

Philip smiled at Noah. "It's the dudes' turn to cook. We make up a buffet brunch for everyone, along with the requisite mimosas. Can we count on you to help us out?"

Noah smiled. "Yes."

He gave Sierra a sidelong glance, wondering if she realized how lucky she was to have both her parents with whom to celebrate the holiday. He never knew his father, who died suddenly when Noah was still a toddler, leaving his mother to raise three young children under the age of eight.

"Where is everybody?" Sierra asked Philip.

"They're all on the back porch. Why don't you go and change before everyone descends on you."

Mark joined them. "I'll take your luggage upstairs, and then I'm also going to shower and change before joining the others."

Noah relieved Mark of the bags. "I'll take those." He and Sierra followed her brother up the carpeted staircase to the second story of the expansive house with gleaming parquet floors. Sierra led the way down the hallway to her bedroom, opened the door, and waited for Noah to enter. Bedside table lamps were turned to the lowest setting, built-in window blinds were partially open, and two electric candles on the window ledge cast long and short shadows on the walls and pale bed covers. Rag dolls, colorful sock monkeys, and stuffed teddy bears claimed space on the cushioned window seat.

She flipped a wall switch, turning on the overhead light. "You can take the bed."

Noah set down the bags and turned to face her. "Where will you sleep?"

She walked into a spacious alcove that contained a white wrought-iron daybed, desk and chair, bookcases, and a table with a television and audio components. Once she was old enough to have sleepovers, Sierra's mother had a contractor remove the doors, rods, and shelves to the walk-in closet and convert it into an alcove for a daybed with a trundle. It was her favorite space in which to nap or do homework, and many nights she had fallen asleep there rather than get up and get into the queen-size bed.

"I'll sleep here."

"I don't mind taking the daybed."

"Forget it, Noah. You're my guest, and I'm certain you'll get a better night's sleep in a larger bed. Besides, I don't want to be responsible for you waking up with pains in your neck or back."

"But I don't want to put you out."

She curbed the urge to roll her eyes at him as she walked over and opened the door to the bathroom. "You're not putting me out. You can use the bathroom while I unpack and find something to wear. I'll clear a drawer in the armoire for you to store your clothes. There're also some hangers if you need them. I want to remind you that everyone is casual. Jeans, running shoes, and T-shirts and hoodies are the norm."

He gave her a snappy salute. "Yes, ma'am."

This time Sierra did roll her eyes upward. "I don't like lying to my parents, but we're going to have to come up with a story as to how we met and now are supposedly involved with each other."

Noah's eyes bored into hers. "I don't like lying either, but we have to be on the same page if we're questioned. Where do you live?"

"San Marcos. Why?"

"Have you ever been to Tijuana?"

Sierra nodded. "I went there a couple of times with a few of my colleagues when we celebrated someone's birthday."

Noah smiled. "And I've been there more than a few times with my buddies. I could say we saw a group of American women in a club and decided to offer our protection against several locals who were trying to hit on you. We made certain everyone got back across the border safely and you and I exchanged phone numbers. After that we started dating."

She angled her head, smiling. "That sounds plausible. How long have we been seeing each other?"

"I fabricated the lie, so I'll leave it up to you to determine the time frame."

Sierra mentally counted back to the last time she'd been in Tijuana. "Seven months."

"Okay. That means we met in May. And in seven months you should know that I was raised by a single mother and I have two sisters. I was just two when my father was killed in the line of duty. He was a US marshal. He was transporting a fugitive from

New York to Boston when the van in which they were riding was hit by a driver who'd lost control of his tractor trailer. Everyone in the van died instantly, while the driver of the big rig walked away with only a broken leg."

A shiver eddied over Sierra's body with this disclosure. She could not have imagined growing up without her father, despite the fact he'd spent a lot of his time away from home. However, his homecomings were likened to a celebration that went on for days and sometimes weeks on end, until it came time for him to return to his base.

"I'm sorry, Noah."

Sadness flitted over his handsome features for several seconds before it disappeared. "My mother went back to college to get a graduate degree in social work and eventually became the executive director of an agency for the elderly. She has two more years before she retires."

"What's her name?"

"Sylvia."

"She never remarried?"

"No. My mother claims she found herself comparing every man she met to my father, and because he was her first love she said they could never measure up."

"She sounds like my mother. She met my father when she was sixteen, he eighteen, and both claim it was love at first sight. Even after thirty-eight years of marriage, they still act like newlyweds. Now that we have our story together, it's time we change so I can introduce you to everyone."

Sierra busied herself unpacking her carry-on while Noah opened his duffel and removed several articles of clothing and a toiletry bag before he disappeared into the bathroom, closing the door behind him.

Once her mother decided she no longer wanted to live on base, Evelyn Nelson had a Realtor conduct a search for a house with at least six bedrooms with en suite baths, which eliminated the problem of her four children having to share one or two bathrooms. Sierra had been a month shy of her third birthday when her mother gave birth to another son, and the instant Sierra saw Mark she treated him as if he was one of her dolls instead of a real baby. They were inseparable until it came time for Mark to go to the same school where his older brothers were students. Her parents enrolled Daniel and Luke in a nearby military academy, while she had attended a private all-girls school.

Sierra had just celebrated her seventh birthday when her family moved into their new home and she claimed the bedroom that overlooked the front of the house so when she sat on the window seat she could see everyone coming and going.

She realized she was wasting time reminiscing about the past. She selected a pair of black leggings, an oversized sweatshirt stamped with her college logo, and a pair of ballet flats. She left the bedroom and made her way to the hallway bathroom.

She turned on the radio on a corner table, tuning it to a local all-news station. A special weather bulletin focused on the storm ravaging the Northeast and a new storm that was sweeping across Illinois, Indiana, and Ohio, with predictions of another foot of snow in the region, which had just dug out from under eighteen inches two weeks before. It appeared as if Noah's layover would have to be extended until the weather cleared not only on the East Coast but also the Midwest.

After brushing her teeth, she stood under the spray from the shower, thinking about the man with whom she would have to pretend involvement. Noah was someone she could possibly fall for, because he had a commanding manner she found extremely attractive. Her mother claimed Sierra was being unreasonable when she said she had no problem remaining single for the rest of her life if she never met the man with whom she could envision sharing her future. Evelyn complained that she was much too picky and no man could possibly meet her standards. That was when Sierra deliberately changed the topic of conversation to something other than marriage and children.

After her last relationship ended badly, Sierra had sworn off men. She'd declined her brothers' offers to introduce her to their friends and/or coworkers, and any man who demonstrated even a remote interest in her, she quickly deflected with what she had perfected as her screw face. And pretending that she and Noah were in a relationship was certain to thwart the Nelsons' matchmaking schemes.

Chapter 3

Sierra reentered the bedroom to find Noah dressed in a pair of relaxed jeans, a black cotton, waffle-weave, long-sleeved T-shirt, and running shoes. He held out his hands at his sides. "Is this casual enough?"

Smiling, she nodded. "You'll definitely pass inspection." She didn't want to tell him that he appeared larger, more imposing, in civilian clothes. The fatigues had concealed a rock-hard physique of a man in his prime and in peak condition.

He smiled. "I'm ready to face the inquisition."

She returned his smile with a warm one of her own. "I don't think it'll be too intense now that we've gotten our story together." Sierra flicked off the light and waited for Noah to precede her before she closed the bedroom door. "We'll take the back staircase," she said.

Noah reached for her hand. "This house is huge."

She nodded. "It didn't seem that big when we were growing up. After everyone moved out, Daddy wanted to downsize and buy a smaller house. But then his parents sold their home, and he convinced them to move into the in-law suite."

"How many rooms are in this house?"

"There are six bedrooms and seven bathrooms upstairs, and one in the in-law suite with another bathroom on the first floor. The basement is fully finished and there are two more bedrooms and two bathrooms down there. Whenever the entire family gets together, my nephews sleep in one bedroom and my nieces in the other. Daddy had the contractor put in a kitchen and a wet bar. That's where everyone hangs out until it's time for Christmas Eve dinner, which is always held in the dining room."

"How often does everyone get together?" Noah asked.

"It varies. During the summer months, my nieces and nephews like to hang out here because they're spoiled by their grand- and great-grandparents. They call this place Camp Nelson because it has become an unofficial summer camp for them. They swim in the inground pool, and my grandfather, who is a retired caterer, prepares healthy meals for them because their mothers don't want them to eat fast food. My grandmother, who was an elementary school principal, also gets into the act when she sets aside time for storytelling. She selects a book, reads the story, and then they discuss it. And whenever it rains they usually spend time in the basement watching age-appropriate movies or playing board games. It turns out to be a win-win for everyone. My parents and grandparents get to see the kids during the week and the kids' parents save money because they don't have to pay for a day- or sleepaway camp."

Noah gave Sierra's fingers a gentle squeeze. It

appeared as if he'd been invited to spend several days with the perfect family. Again, he wondered if she knew how blessed she was to have not only her parents but also her grandparents, while he had his mother, sisters, several nephews, and a number of cousins he didn't get to see often enough. Only his mother and sisters were privy to his role in the military, because as a Navy SEAL, he and the members of all SEAL teams were America's secret warriors. And because he never knew when he would be called up for another covert mission, he found it impossible to form a lasting relationship with a woman when he would disappear for weeks on end and not know if he would ever return to the States in the same condition in which he had left.

Sierra had asked if he was a lifer, and now at thirty-seven he could say he was. The question was how long he would remain a SEAL. There were parts of his body that silently told him that he was approaching forty and that there would come a time when he wouldn't be able to physically push his body beyond limits better suited for those in their twenties. He loved the military, the members of his team, and would willingly forfeit his life to save any of them.

He and Sierra stepped off the stairs and entered a kitchen that was a chef's dream. Noah noted cooktops, grills, double microwaves, wall ovens, twin dishwashers, a wine cooler refrigerator, and a side-by-side refrigerator/freezer with through-the-door ice and water. "You guys must do some serious cooking in here," he said, glancing around at the top-of-the-line appliances.

Sierra smiled up at him. "If you're still here Christmas morning, you'll get the opportunity to demonstrate whether you have any cooking skills. I must warn you that the Nelson men are very competitive when it comes to throwing down in the kitchen."

Noah grunted under his breath. "I can reassure you that I've been known to burn a few pots in my time." He wanted to tell Sierra that breakfast was his specialty and he had perfected chicken and waffles and omelets for taste and elegant presentation.

"We'll see," she said. "I told you before that my grandfather was a caterer and he taught all of us to cook."

He smothered a chuckle. "I'm not scared, nor do I cut and run."

"Oh, you bad?" Sierra drawled teasingly.

"Hell yeah! Bad to the bone." Noah laughed and Sierra's tinkling laughter joined his. They were still laughing and holding hands when they walked through the kitchen and into the enclosed back porch, where Nelsons, ranging in age from octogenarians to toddlers, were seated at a table with seating for sixteen. Pale vertical blinds spanning the width of the house were open, giving everyone an up-close-and-personal view of the falling snow. Covered chafing dishes sat warming atop buffet servers at opposite ends of the expansive space.

Philip stood up. "I was getting ready to send out a search party for you two."

The words were barely off his tongue when Sierra found herself surrounded and besieged with hugs and kisses from the members of her family. Even David Nelson scrambled off his mother's lap and screamed for his aunt to pick him up.

Sierra met Noah's eyes when she peered over her

nephew's head as she kissed his forehead. "How's Auntie Cee Cee's big boy?"

The young child tightened his hold around her neck. "Good."

She cradled the boy on her hip. "Noah, I'd like to introduce you to my family." Extending her free hand, she took his and pulled him over to an elderly couple. "I'd like you to meet the matriarch and patriarch of the family. Grandpa and Nana, I'd like you to meet my boyfriend, Noah Crawford."

Noah shook hands with Sierra's grandfather, and then leaned over to press a kiss to her grandmother's cheek. "I'm honored to meet you both." He suspected both were in their eighties, but appeared at least a decade younger. They had only a few wrinkles around their eyes, and it was obvious they monitored their weight because they were still quite slender.

Sandra Nelson gave him a shy smile. "I'm so glad my grandbaby girl finally met someone who makes her happy."

He nodded his head. "That's because she makes me happy." The revelation had rolled off his tongue so quickly and smoothly that Noah realized he had spoken the truth. Sierra was the first woman with whom he felt so natural and relaxed. He'd only met her earlier that morning, yet he felt as if he had known her for days, or perhaps even weeks. And at that moment it did not matter if they were actors in a role better suited for a made-for-television movie plot, because he planned to enjoy every minute of it until the curtain came down.

Sierra steered him over to a woman Noah knew was her mother. If her brothers were clones of their father, then she was a clone of her mother. The older woman's salt-and-pepper curly hair was stylishly coiffed for her age and face shape. He took her hand and dropped a kiss on her fingers. There was an audible gasp from several women.

"I know you're Sierra's mother and I want to thank you for raising an incredible young woman."

Evelyn lowered her eyes. "Thank you, Noah."

He shook his head. "No, thank you, Mrs. Nelson."

"It's Evelyn, but everyone calls me Evie."

Noah kissed her fingers again. "Then Evie it is." He ignored Sierra when she surreptitiously elbowed him in the ribs. She probably thought he was coming on too strong, but he had to make it good or someone would no doubt see through their ruse.

She flashed a smile. "If you're through flirting with my mother, I'd like to introduce you to my brothers and their wives."

"What about us?" chorused two young girls who were obviously twins.

"I didn't forget you, Emily and Abigail," Sierra said. "I'll introduce you two to Noah after he meets the grown folks. Darling," she drawled effortlessly, "this is my brother Daniel, and his wife, Naomi. Noah Crawford."

Daniel stood, pumped Noah's hand, and then gave him a rough embrace. "Welcome to the family. Mark told me you're military."

Noah nodded. "I'm active navy."

"Good for you. I'm also active army." He patted Noah's shoulder. "We'll talk later and compare notes."

Sierra adjusted the boy on her hip as another Nelson brother rose to his feet. "Noah, this is Luke, and the very pregnant lady next to him is Delia. She's the mother of this little munchkin clinging to me and in another month will make him a big brother."

Noah exchanged a rough embrace with Luke. "Congratulations on your impending arrival."

Smiling, Luke nodded. "Thanks, man."

Sierra moved along the table. "You've already met Mark, and the woman sitting next to him is Pilar, and as she likes to refer to herself, his better half."

Pilar blushed, the added color darkening her light-brown complexion. "Well, I am," she said with a wide grin.

"You are shameless, but I love you anyway," Mark countered, as he planted a noisy kiss on his wife's forehead. The gesture garnered a chorus of expressions of disgust from the younger Nelsons, who were clearly embarrassed by the open display of affection.

Noah couldn't stop laughing as several of the boys made faces. He wanted to tell them it wouldn't take that long before they became interested in girls and that kissing wasn't as abhorrent as they would like to believe. He still could remember his grandfather's advice that girls were to be respected, and if they didn't want him to do something with them, then he had to heed their warning. Even though he didn't have a father to talk to about what it meant to be a man, fortunately his grandfather had lived long enough to become his role model. And because he had wanted to get into a military academy, Noah was careful not to do anything that would negatively impact that possibility. It had taken his politically savvy mother, and the fact that he was a child of a deceased veteran and a federal law enforcement officer, to convince several members of Congress to approve his application to attend the US Naval Academy.

One by one Sierra introduced him to her nieces

and nephews, Noah carefully watching their reaction to his being with their aunt. One of the boys reached out to squeeze his bicep, and quickly jerked his hand away.

"Do you lift weights?" he asked.

"Yes," Noah replied. He had made it a practice to work out in order to maintain peak conditioning.

"What do you do in the navy?" Delia questioned.

"I'm assigned to intelligence," Noah said without missing a beat.

"Like NCIS?" Pilar asked.

"Not quite."

Evelyn stood up. "Enough questions. Now that everyone's here we can begin to eat."

Sierra set her nephew on his feet. "Grandpa and Nana, don't get up. I'll bring you your plates."

Noah pressed his mouth to Sierra's ear. "Did I pass?"

She nodded. "You were spectacular. In case you haven't noticed, my sisters-in-law are quite taken with your gallantry. What's up with you kissing hands?" she whispered.

"What's the expression? If you can't dazzle them with intelligence, then you baffle them with BS."

Sierra made a sucking sound with her tongue and teeth. "If you graduated from the naval academy, then you're definitely not lacking in intelligence. I don't know about you, but I'm hungry enough to devour a whole hog and half a cow."

Noah wanted to agree with her. He'd only had a cup of coffee and bran muffin before boarding the plane, and the snack box lunch was just that—a snack. Standing six-two in his bare feet and weighing two hundred fifteen pounds, he needed more than a sandwich, cookies, and an apple to keep him alert.

Evelyn removed the lids to the chafing dishes and

mouthwatering aromas wafted in the air. There were trays filled with bite-size barbecue ribs, chicken wings, sweet-and-sour meatballs, potato skins with bacon and chives, steak fries dusted with parmesan and minced garlic. There were bowls of potato and macaroni salads, a tossed vinaigrette salad, along with baskets filled with differing types of breads. A large glass bowl was filled with fresh strawberries, red, green, and black grapes, and blue- and blackberries, along with a dish of fresh cream in a pan filled with ice cubes.

Philip stood at the table on the opposite end of the porch, filling plastic cups with punch for the younger children and wine, beer, soft drinks, or bottled water for the adults. Once everyone was seated, he bowed his head and blessed the table.

There was minimal conversation as everyone concentrated on eating what they'd put on their plates. Delia handed Luke her plate for him to serve her some fruit. It was the cue for a couple of the preteen boys to jump up and refill their plates.

Sierra pressed her shoulder to Noah's. "They're not even teenagers and already their mothers are complaining about how they're eating them out of house and home."

Noah gave her a sidelong glance. "How old are they now?"

"Isaiah is ten and Caleb is twelve."

"Is it a coincidence that all of the men in your family have biblical names?"

"No, it isn't. Grandpa is Stephen, my dad is Philip, and if my mother had had another boy he would've been Matthew or John."

"Why not the girls?"

She lifted her shoulders. "I don't know. My mother told me she wanted to name me Samara, but then changed her mind and decided on Sierra."

"I like the name."

"Who decided to name you Noah?"

"Both my parents decided to name me after my grandfather."

"Is he the one who owned the hog farm?"

"Yes. He became an integral part of my life after my father passed away. He was both father and grand-dad, and he taught me what it meant to be an honorable man. He died last year and I still can't accept that he's gone."

Sierra rested a hand on his. "You have every right to miss him, Noah. I know I'm blessed to still have my parents and grandparents, but there's going to come a time when I come home and one or both won't be here. What I try to do is not dwell on the inevitable but try and enjoy every moment I can share with them."

Noah stared at his plate. It was apparent Sierra did acknowledge that she was blessed to celebrate the holidays with four generations of Nelsons. He did not want to believe he was becoming maudlin when he should be appreciative of the woman who had welcomed him into her family, when the alternative was ordering room service in a hotel, or attempting to sleep on a cot or the floor of an airport terminal.

"Sorry for being a Debbie Downer."

Resting her arm over his shoulders, Sierra leaned in and kissed his ear. "Losing someone close to us is never easy. And stop beating up on yourself because you're human."

He turned his head and their noses were only inches apart. Noah stared at her mouth and wanted to know how it would be to kiss her. However, that wasn't possible because they were sitting in a room with more than a dozen people, and even if they were in a place where they wouldn't be seen, he still would not cross the line to assuage his curiosity.

"You're right. There are times when I forget that." Once he had completed the training to become a SEAL, he had believed himself invincible, that he was physically and mentally up to accept any challenge presented to him. He'd become part of an elite brotherhood of twenty-five hundred big and buff spies and commandos who had earned the right to wear the trident pin with pride.

"Who cooked? Because this food is incredible," he said, deftly changing the topic.

"My parents. Daddy made the meat dishes and my mother the sides and salads."

Noah picked up his glass of beer, raised it in the direction of Philip, and then Evelyn. "My compliments to the chefs."

"The food is good, Grandpa and Grandma," chimed in Emily, one of the eight-year-old twins.

Philip nodded. "Thank you."

"Grandpa, can we go and watch videos now?" Isaiah asked, at the same time he wiped his mouth.

"I don't think so, Isaiah. It's getting late and you guys have to get up early tomorrow morning to decorate the tree."

"Your grandfather is right," Naomi said in agreement. "You kids should get ready to go to bed. I'm going to come down later and check to see if you brushed your teeth and are in your pajamas. And if I find anyone playing with their electronic devices, then everyone's grounded. Does everyone understand the words coming out of my mouth?"

Throwing back his head, Caleb laughed loudly. "That's from *Rush Hour!*"

Noah hid a smile when the children pushed back their chairs, picked up their paper plates and cups, and deposited them in a large plastic-lined can. It was apparent they had been taught to pick up after themselves. He pushed back his own chair and came to his feet. "I don't know about anyone else, but I'm ready for seconds."

"I'm ready for seconds, too," Delia announced. "What are y'all looking at?" she asked when everyone stared at her. "I'm eating for two."

Noah walked over and took her plate. "What do you want?"

Luke snatched the plate from Noah's hand. "I'll take care of my woman, while you do the same with yours."

Noah held up both hands. "Sorry about that."

"Watch it, little brother," Daniel drawled as he tried not to laugh. "Brother Noah happens to be built like a Sherman tank, so I think you'd better slow your roll."

There came a swollen silence before Luke doubled over in laughter. "Gotcha, Brother Noah. You should've seen your face."

A hint of a smile tilted the corners of Noah's mouth. "No, I got you, Brother Luke, because I'm going to give your wife what she wants." He bowed from the waist. "Now, what can I get you?"

Delia flashed a white-toothed grin. "I'd like a few more meatballs with the tossed salad."

He bowed again. "Consider it done."

"Mess with the bull and you get the horns," Mark said to Luke.

Laughter erupted in the room as Noah strolled over to the table to fulfill Delia's request and refill his plate.

Chapter 4

Sierra kissed her grandmother and grandfather as they announced they were going to bed and the men huddled at the far end of the table to talk. She sat down next to her mother and wrapped an arm around her waist.

"Everything was delicious."

Evelyn patted her daughter's head. "It looks as if your brothers really like Noah."

"I like him, too."

Evelyn's eyebrows lifted a fraction. "You only like him?"

"Yes." She couldn't tell her mother that she'd just met Noah, so it was impossible for her to feel an emotion that went beyond liking.

"How did you guys meet?" Pilar asked.

Sierra repeated what she and Noah had discussed earlier that evening. "And before you ask, we've been seeing each other for about seven months."

Delia rubbed her rounded belly over a navy-blue knit smock. "Are you serious about him?"

"Of course she is," Pilar interjected. "Why else would she bring him home to meet the family?"

Evelyn smiled. "I must admit I like him a lot better than that idiot you were dating a couple of years ago."

Sierra agreed with her mother. "That was the reason I never introduced him to the family. Once I told him it was over, he had a hard time accepting the fact that I didn't want to see him anymore. If Mark hadn't gotten involved, I believe I still would have a problem with him."

Pilar's eyes grew wide. "Is that when Mark told me he had to go to California to take care of some personal business?"

Sierra did not want to believe her brother hadn't told his wife why he'd asked his commanding officer for emergency family leave to confront a man who had continued to stalk her despite her having a court-issued restraining order. "I believe so."

"What did he do?" Pilar's voice was barely a whisper.

"It's not so much what he did but what he said, and after that I never saw or heard from Derrick again. And when I asked Mark about it, he said it was settled and not to ask him about it again."

Naomi whistled softly. "Daniel says Mark has always had a short fuse when it comes to nonsense."

Evelyn shook her head. "Stalking is not nonsense, Naomi. It's a crime." She gave each of the four young women a long, penetrating stare. "When Philip and I were first married and we lived on the base, I was content to be a military wife and follow my husband whenever he was transferred. Even when I had Daniel and Luke, I still was content to live on base. It was only after I gave birth to a girl that I began to think differently. I know a lot of girls grow up as military brats, but that was something I didn't want for my daughter. I suppose I'd become somewhat paranoid because there were just too many men, and as she grew older she could easily become a target for some pervert. But little did I know that she wouldn't have to live on a military base to meet some lunatic who would threaten her life."

Reaching over, Pilar patted Evelyn's hand. "I doubt if anyone is going to mess with Sierra now that she's with Noah. I thought Mark was ripped, but Noah is jacked!"

"Word," whispered Naomi. "The man has to be Special Ops to be in that kind of shape."

Delia nodded in agreement. "Is he, Sierra?"

Sierra stared at her sister-in-law. What did Delia expect her to say? Even if she knew Noah was Special Ops, she still wouldn't tell them. That admission would have to come from him. "He's in intelligence, Dr. Nelson," she said, repeating what Noah had said earlier.

Naomi narrowed her eyes. "He looks and smells like Special Ops. I'd dated Daniel for a year, and then married him, before he admitted to me that he was a Night Stalker and made me swear never to tell anyone outside the family."

"Why don't y'all stop trying to figure out what Noah is, and accept the man at his word," Evelyn admonished softly.

"Thanks, Mom," Sierra said, smiling.

Her sisters-in-law were as different in personality as in their physical appearance. Red-haired, green-eyed Kentucky native Naomi was born in a coal-mining region where the men in her family had mined coal for generations. Her brother, also Special Forces, introduced her to Daniel, and after a whirlwind romance Daniel married the nursery-school teacher, and now they were parents of two preteen boys.

Delia's grandparents had emigrated from Puerto

Rico and settled in Chicago before World War II. Her parents doted on their only child, who had graduated at the top of her class in high school and college, and then went on to study medicine at the University of Illinois at Chicago with a specialty in pediatric medicine. She was driving home one night when her car blew a tire. She managed to pull off onto the shoulder to wait for road service. Luke spotted her car and stopped to help change the tire. Delia offered to pay him, but Luke said she could repay him by giving him her phone number. Three weeks following her graduation from medical school she married Luke, and two years later they became parents of David, a bright, energetic little boy.

Pilar and Delia were second cousins *and* sisters-in-law who married brothers. Delia, the consummate matchmaker, badgered Luke to host a little get-together for Mark when he returned from his first Middle East deployment. Pilar, who'd met Mark for the first time at Delia and Luke's wedding, claimed she wanted nothing to do with the brash young marine. However, she saw him differently when he returned as a war veteran. Maturity had replaced the cockiness, and she saw the highly decorated first lieutenant in a whole new light. Pilar married Mark before his next deployment, unaware she was pregnant at the time. Mark returned to the States in time to witness the birth of his twin daughters.

The conversation segued to Delia, who didn't want to know if she was having a girl or a boy because she liked being surprised. She had just begun a six-month leave from the medical group she had formed with several of her medical school classmates. Six months would give her time to decorate her loft and bond with her new baby. She updated everyone about Luke becoming partner at his law firm, and she would have celebrated with a small gathering at their home if she didn't have to deal with the furniture deliveries and the impending birth of her baby.

"You can always have it here," Evelyn volunteered.

Delia shook her head, as a profusion of braids swayed with the motion. "No, Evie, I don't want to impose on you like that."

Evelyn waved her hand. "It's not an imposition. There's only me, Philip, and his parents rattling around this house day after day, so I look forward to Christmas, Thanksgiving, and the summer when the kids come over to liven it up. There's going to come a time when I know I'm going to have to sell it, because it's much too big for us. You and Luke have the loft. Pilar, you and Mark have your condo, but if you decide that you want to have more chil-dren, then you can have it. I'm not going to say anything to Daniel because, like his father, he plans to put in at least thirty years before he retires."

"Where are you and Dad going to live?" Sierra asked.

"There are a lot of senior communities where we don't have to concern ourselves with shoveling snow, making repairs, or even cooking if we don't want to."

"That's not going to be for a while," Sierra stated firmly.

"You're in denial. Philip and I are sixty-five and sixty-three, and I can't see myself ten or even twenty years from now trying to take care of this house, even if I hire someone to come in to clean every week. Now, if you marry Noah and decide to move back here, I would seriously consider willing you the house once he decides to leave the military."

Sierra's jaw dropped. She couldn't believe her mother was making plans for her and a stranger who was uncertain whether he would become a lifer. "Mom, I think you're getting ahead of yourself."

Evelyn stared at her with wide eyes. "Am I? You bring a man home with you to meet your family and you have no intention of planning a future with him?"

"We haven't talked about marriage."

"What do you guys talk about?" Naomi asked.

"Politics. Sports, and whatever else is trending. We really don't get to see that much of each other because he's either assigned to a base or a ship. We only reconnect when he's on leave."

Sierra didn't know why she found it so easy to perpetuate Mark's misconception as to her and Noah's relationship. It would have been so easy to tell everyone that they'd sat next to each other during the flight from San Diego to Chicago and that Noah's connecting flight to Boston was cancelled because of the weather, but after telling one lie they would be forced to continue the lies until someone uncovered the truth.

Groaning slightly, Delia stood up. "This child is definitely going to be a gymnast, because it doesn't kick like a normal baby but does somersaults and backflips."

"Leave your plate," Evelyn said when Delia reached for it. "Go to bed and get some rest. And don't you dare think about getting up early, because now that Sierra's here we'll have enough hands in the kitchen."

Delia came over to kiss her mother-in-law. "Thanks, Evie."

Evelyn stood. "The rest of you can also go to bed."

"I'll stay and help you, Mom," Sierra volunteered. "I'll put away the food."

She went into the pantry to retrieve plastic containers and made quick work of filling them with leftovers. She had just finished storing them on a shelf in the refrigerator when Noah entered the kitchen carrying an ice chest. He frowned as she attempted to smother a yawn with her hand.

"Why don't you go upstairs and turn in. You've had a long day," he said in a quiet voice. "I'll help Evie clean up the kitchen."

Sierra looked at her mother, who nodded. "Okay." She hugged her mother and kissed her cheek. "Good night."

Evelyn patted her back. "Good night, baby."

Sierra turned on her heel to walk out of the kitchen, but then found herself in Noah's arms as he lowered his head and brushed a light kiss over her parted lips. "Don't wait up for me," he said in her ear.

She was so stunned that he had kissed her, and in front of her mother, that all she could do was nod. She managed to make it upstairs to *their* bedroom, still glorying in the warmth of Noah's body against hers, the firmness of his mouth on hers, and the sensual, masculine scent of his cologne.

Why, she mused, did he have to be so damn attractive? It would have been easier for her to go along with the pretense if he were the exact opposite of everything she would want in a boyfriend or lover. Physically he was perfect, and having impeccable manners merely added to his overall charismatic personality. There was no doubt he had charmed the women in her family, and judging from his interaction with her father and brothers, he had bonded quickly with them.

Sierra brushed her teeth, washed her face, applied a moisturizer, and then pulled a nightgown over her head. Walking on bare feet, she made her way to the alcove, pulled out the trundle, and made up the daybed with linens and several blankets and a quilt. Before climbing into bed, she opened the four-paneled screen decorated with Chinese calligraphy that provided a modicum of privacy between the alcove and the rest of the bedroom.

Jet lag swept over her like a weighted lead blanket, but her brain refused to shut down. Leaning over, she turned on the bedside lamp and picked up the magazine she had left on the table during her last visit. Sierra found herself totally engrossed in an article about a woman who had defied the odds to become a medical doctor at the age of fifty-six, when she heard Noah come into the bedroom. It was as if every sound in the room was magnified: his closing the door to the bathroom, water running in the sink when he brushed his teeth, and his return to the bedroom and removing his clothes.

"Thank you for helping my mother," she called out.

Noah stuck his head around the screen. "I thought you'd be asleep by now."

She smiled. "I guess I'm a little too wound up to sleep."

"Come get into bed with me."

With wide eyes, she looked at him as if she had never seen him before. "Why?"

"So we can talk."

The seconds ticked. "Okay." Noah was already in bed, the blankets covering his lower body, when she slipped in beside him. Sierra hid a smile. Thankfully he hadn't removed his underwear. She went still when he placed an arm over her shoulders and pulled her close to his length. "What do you want to talk about?"

Noah pressed his mouth to her hair. "First I want to apologize for kissing you in front of your mother. Even though I agreed to go along with the charade that we're a couple, I feel very uncomfortable fooling your family, because I like them—a lot, Sierra."

She smiled. "And it seems as if they like you." She sobered quickly. "And if I could turn back the clock and correct Mark when he assumed we were romantically involved, I would do it. This hasn't been easy on me either. I hate more than anything to lie to my parents—my mother in particular when she assumes because you came home with me that we're planning a future together."

"You've never brought a man home to meet your family." His question was a statement.

"No." Sierra sucked in a lungful of air, held it, and then let it out slowly. "A couple of years ago I met a man—"

"Was he the soldier you dated?" Noah asked, interrupting her.

"No. When I look back, I wish he was. One of my colleagues introduced me to her cousin because we both liked black-and-white movies, documentaries, and art museums. It wasn't until we were dating for about six months that I realized we did everything together. And I do mean everything. If I went grocery shopping, then he wanted to go with me. I couldn't go to the drugstore to pick up feminine products without him shadowing me. Although I'd convinced myself that I was in love with him and accepted his marriage proposal, I knew there was something unhealthy about our relationship. And I kept putting off his request to meet my family because I was beginning to have second thoughts about sharing my life with him.

"When I finally got the nerve to end the engagement, he turned on me, screaming that if he couldn't have me, then he would make certain no man would. That's when I got a restraining order, but he ignored it. I'd find him lurking outside my school and my apartment building. I was forced to change both my home and cell phone numbers because he would call and hang up. I called the police to inform them he was stalking and harassing me, but they said they couldn't arrest him until he came within two hundred feet of my home or place of employment. That's when I finally called Mark to tell him that I feared for my life."

"What happened after that?"

Sierra felt the tension in Noah's body when his fingers tightened on her shoulder. "Mark flew out a couple of days later, and I gave him Derrick's address. My brother went to see him, and when he came back he told me he had taken care of everything."

"What did he mean by that?"

"I don't know, Noah, because Mark refuses to talk about it. It took almost a month before I stopped looking over my shoulder or screening my calls whenever my phones rang." She closed her eyes for several seconds. "I haven't dated anyone since, because there must be something about me that attracts the crazies."

"There's nothing wrong with you, Sierra. It's just

that some men don't do well with rejection. They may feel it's all right to walk away from a woman, but not the other way around."

"I can't imagine a woman leaving you."

He chuckled softly. "Why can't you?"

"I don't know. Call it women's intuition, but there's something about you that most women look for in a man."

"And what's that?"

"You have home training."

Noah laughed. "Is home training that important to you?"

"It's everything to me. Whenever I used to act up, Nana would remind me that I was raised better than that. What really hit home was when she said I was a descendant of survivors and I should never do anything to disgrace my ancestors."

Noah pulled Sierra closer. "My grandparents would tell me the same thing. I can still hear my grandfather's voice when he'd say, 'Boy, your mama sent you down here so I can help you grow up to see what it takes to go from a boy to a man. Making babies don't make you a man but a reckless fool, because you have to be able to take care of your woman and your seed. And if you can't, then don't make no baby. A real man is respectful, hardworking, and most of all trustworthy.' He drummed that into my head year after year, until I realized how right he was.

"My grandfather had to drop out of school in the eleventh grade when his daddy died and he had to step up and take over running the farm. He was close to seventy when he went back to night school to earn his high school diploma. He'd proven himself a successful businessman when he sold his hogs to local restaurants, but claimed earning that piece of paper was a personal achievement."

"He sounds as if he was a remarkable man," Sierra said.

Noah ran his fingers through her short hair. "That he was. What time do you plan to get up in the morning?" Soft snores answered his query and he realized Sierra had fallen asleep. Under another set of circumstances, he would have welcomed the soft crush of her breasts and the subtle scent of the perfume on her silky skin, but he found Sierra too much of a temptation for them to share a bed.

Untangling their limbs, he slipped off the bed and carried her to the alcove. She stirred slightly when he placed her on the bed, but she did not wake up. Noah smiled as he pulled the blankets over the slender figure. He could not have imagined her fear when she had had to deal with a stalker ex-boyfriend. However, she was lucky that her brother was able to defuse the situation, or it could have ended tragically. He'd watched too many television crime shows featuring women who had become victims of stalkers and jealous lovers. Leaning over, he kissed her forehead.

"Sweet dreams, beautiful." He flicked off the table lamp and returned to his bed.

When he'd boarded the plane he never would've anticipated sitting next to a petite slip of a woman with whom he would bond enough for her to invite him to stay with her family for a Christmas layover. Noah knew without a doubt he would spend Christmas Eve with the Nelsons, because all flights in and out of O'Hare were cancelled because of the storm. At first he'd believed the weather had conspired against him when he couldn't get to Boston to celebrate the holiday with his family, but if he had to be stranded, then he was fortunate to spend it with Sierra's family.

They had welcomed him like a long-lost relative. He instantly connected with her father and brothers. It helped that they all shared a military background, but that was only a small part of why he felt so comfortable with them. They epitomized to Noah what it meant to be a family unit: They loved and protected their wives, children, siblings, and parents.

He closed his eyes and within minutes he succumbed to a deep, dreamless sleep.

Chapter 5

Sierra woke Christmas Eve morning, got out of bed, and peered through the blinds to find it was still snowing, though not as heavily as it had been the night before. She managed to gather a change of clothes and slip down to the hallway bathroom to shower and dress without waking Noah.

Her sock-covered feet were silent as she descended the staircase that led to the kitchen. The distinctive aromas of brewing coffee and grilling bacon wafted to her nostrils. Her mother, Naomi, and Pilar were busy seasoning and prepping a large turkey, a fresh ham, and two beef rib roasts.

"Good morning!"

Three heads popped up at her greeting.

Evelyn smiled. "I thought you'd still be asleep because of jet lag."

Sierra walked into the kitchen and sat on a stool at the cooking island. "If I feel myself crashing, I'll take a nap later this afternoon. Is there anything you want me to do?"

"You can finish grilling the bacon," Pilar suggested, "while I slice up a few melons."

Picking up a pair of tongs, Sierra tested the doneness of several strips. A platter of sliced ham steaks sprinkled with cinnamon and brown sugar, and sausage links, muffins, toast, and eggs cooked to order would be put out for breakfast, along with bowls of fresh fruit, juice, coffee, and tea.

Whenever she returned to Chicago, Sierra did not feel as if she really was home unless she heard the childish voices of her nieces and nephews and/or joined her mother and grandmother in the kitchen. She rarely cooked for herself, although she enjoyed it when she did, because she usually called her favorite gourmet shop to place an order for enough food to last her for several days.

She placed the cooked slices in an aluminum tray lined with paper towels. "Mom, do you think we have enough bacon?"

Evelyn peered into the tray. "Four pounds should be enough, because we'll also have ham and sausage."

She gave her mother a sidelong glance. "Now you know the Nelson men are carnivores."

"I think a lot of them are hungover from last night. Philip admitted he had at least three beers, while Luke, Mark, Daniel, and Noah had twice that much."

Naomi rested her hands at her waist over a bibbed apron. "Now I know why Daniel didn't wake up when I got out of bed, because he's always up before me."

Pilar grunted under her breath. "I hope they get up in time to take care of the kids, because we're going to be busy cooking most of the day."

Evelyn nodded. "They'll have to babysit and shovel snow once it stops."

Over the next two hours, Sierra busied herself scrambling and frying eggs as, one by one, family members strolled into the kitchen declaring they were ravenous. They retreated into the enclosed back porch, where a variety of breakfast foods were on display.

She sang and hummed along with traditional and contemporary Christmas music coming from the radio on the countertop next to a small television with a built-in DVD, and managed to fix a plate for herself of scrambled eggs with several strips of ham, and a mini blueberry muffin.

Her father, Mark, and Noah still hadn't appeared, and she wondered if they were hungover or just exhausted.

Noah reached for the phone when he recognized his mother's ringtone. He peered at the screen and groaned. It was nearly ten. It was close to midnight when he finally went to sleep, but he rarely slept more than six or seven hours.

He tapped the phone icon. "Hello." His eyes went to the alcove and the daybed. It was empty. Sierra had gotten up without waking him.

"Did I wake you?"

Pushing to sit, he adjusted several pillows around his shoulders. He'd lied so much over the past twenty-four hours that he couldn't continue with his mother. "Yes."

"Are you all right?"

Noah registered the concern in his mother's voice. "I'm good. I was up late last night and I'm still a little jet lagged."

"You're lucky you got a hotel room, because I saw

news footage of people sleeping on cots and on the floor at O'Hare. Logan International is no better."

"I didn't get a hotel room." When he called to tell his mother he would lay over in Chicago until he could get a flight, she had assumed he had checked into a hotel.

"Where are you?"

"I'm staying with friends," he admitted. At least he now considered the Nelsons friends, since they'd put him up.

"You never said anything to me about knowing folks in Chicago. But then, you really don't tell me much about who you know, or where you go. The only time you call is when you come back from wherever it is you disappear to."

Noah closed his eyes, slowly counting to ten. "Mother, please don't start with me. You know what I do, and you also know what I can't talk about."

Sylvia's sigh came through the earpiece. "You can't fault me for worrying. As a mother am I not entitled to worry about my children?"

He smiled. "Yes, you are. How much snow did you guys get?" Noah asked, segueing to a safer topic of conversation.

"They've estimated about twenty-eight inches, with four-foot drifts. Folks who were talking about a white Christmas will get their wish."

Noah ran a hand over his head. "It's the same here."

"When do you think you'll be able to get a flight out?"

"I don't know. The carrier will text me once my flight is rescheduled."

Sylvia sighed again. "I was really looking forward to celebrating Christmas with you."

"So was I."

"By the time you arrive, I'll have to go back to work."

It was Noah's turn to exhale an audible sigh. He'd agonized whether to tell his mother that he was a Navy SEAL, because it gave her reason to heap on the guilt, and he didn't do well with guilt. The first time he revealed his military status, she cried for days. Even when he had attempted to reassure her that as a member of the military every time he put on his uniform he did not become a target either for the enemy in a combat mission or a psycho with a grudge against the military.

"I promise to get up early and make breakfast for you, and take you to all your favorite restaurants for dinner."

"What if I cook for you and take you out to dinner?"

A bright smile flittered over his features. "That will work."

"Is this friend you're staying with a man or a woman?"

Again, he was faced with whether to lie or tell the truth, and decided on the latter. "My friend is a woman."

There came a pause on the other end of the connection. "Are you serious about her?"

"No, Mother. She's just a friend. I'm staying with her extended family."

"I'm not going to bring up you not wanting to get married because—"

"Please don't," he said, cutting her off.

There were times when his mother was like a dog with a bone. Once she latched on, she refused to let go. Once he turned thirty, Sylvia began a campaign to set him up with women she felt he would like.

Every time he came back to Boston, Sylvia would accidently on purpose invite a young woman over to the house, hoping they would hit it off. Even after admonishing Sylvia for her attempts to play matchmaker, she continued to do it, until his homecomings grew more infrequent. When she questioned him about it, Noah was forthcoming when he demanded she stop setting him up with women or he would limit his visits to no more than one or two a year. Sylvia, knowing he was serious, abandoned her crusade to find him a wife.

He chatted with his mother for another two minutes, and then rang off. He heard voices in the hallway through the bedroom door and knew people were up. Noah got out of bed and went into the en suite bath to shower. He emerged twenty minutes later in jeans, a sweatshirt, and thick cotton socks.

Sierra was still at the stove when Noah walked into the kitchen. He hadn't shaved and the stubble on his lean jaw enhanced his blatant masculinity. "How do you like your eggs?"

"Over easy, please."

He kissed her cheek, the minty scent of mouthwash wafting to her nostrils. "How did you sleep?"

"Like a baby. Why didn't you wake me up?"

"I figured you needed your sleep." There was a slight puffiness under his eyes. "Do you feel okay?"

"Yeah. Why?"

She scrunched up her nose. "You look a little tired."

"I'm good. By the way, have you eaten?"

Sierra oiled the grill, and then gently cracked two eggs onto the heated surface. "Yes. I managed to eat before everyone came down. You'll find meat, breads, fruit, and juice on the porch."

"You're pretty good at this," Noah said when she deftly turned the eggs over without breaking the yolks.

"I must admit that I don't cook enough."

"Don't you cook for yourself?"

Picking up a plate, she ladled the eggs onto it. "Not too often. It's no fun cooking for one person."

"I know what you mean. Has everyone else eaten?"

She nodded. "Yes. You're my last customer, so I'll grab a cup of coffee and sit with you."

Noah waited for her to fill a cup from the coffee urn and they walked into the porch amid raised voices and angry shouts. Daniel was reading his sons the riot act for throwing food at each other.

"But, he started it first!" Caleb shouted.

"I did not!" Isaiah countered.

Daniel wagged a finger at both boys. "I don't care who started it, but it's going to end now! Understand?" The boys nodded. "I can't hear nods."

Caleb dropped his eyes. "I understand, Dad."

"Me too," Isaiah whispered.

"Is it *me too* or *I understand*?" Daniel was relentless.

Isaiah's lower lip quivered as he struggled not to break down. "I understand, Dad."

"That's better. Now empty your plates and go sit in the living room and think about what you've done."

"Can we go downstairs?" Caleb asked.

"No."

Waiting until her sons left the room, Naomi rested a hand on her husband's arm. "Danny, don't—"

Daniel rounded on his wife. "Stay out of this, Nay. Aren't you the one who complains they don't listen to you when you tell them to do something?"

A flush suffused Naomi's pale complexion, the color nearly matching her red hair. "Only sometimes."

"It should be no time, Naomi. They're getting older and in a few years they'll be teenagers, and I'll be damned if I'll have my sons disrespect an adult." Naomi glared at Daniel, and then got up from the table and stalked out.

"I'm sorry you had to witness that," Sierra whispered to Noah.

"There's no need to apologize. I don't want to take sides, but your brother is right. If parents aren't on the same page and establish boundaries for their children, then once they become adolescents it will be too late. As a teacher I'm sure you hear this all the time."

Sierra took a sip of coffee. "I do. I cringe whenever I hear kids curse at their parents as if they're talking to their peers."

"I wasn't willing to test Sylvia, because I wasn't certain whether I'd have to pick up my teeth with a rake."

Throwing back her head, Sierra laughed until tears filled her eyes. "I don't think it would've been my mother, but Nana would've taken a wooden spoon to my behind. She used to say in her day grown folks didn't tolerate nonsense from kids. She claims her father would take her brothers out to the woodshed and light them up."

Noah nodded. "I remember a boy who lived on the farm next to my grandfather's who practically lived in the woodshed. It appeared that whippings didn't do him any good because he was mandated to a juvenile detention facility before taking up permanent residence in a state prison."

"Hitting a child doesn't always work. Abusing a child turns them into abusers."

Noah pushed several blueberries around a dish with his fork. "I've always wondered what type of father I'd be like if I had kids."

Sierra stared at his profile. "Probably a badass like my brothers."

"I don't think so."

"Yeah, right," she drawled. "Instead of hitting your kids you'd put them in a headlock until they cried uncle."

He smiled, the dimple in his left cheek deepening. "I'd never touch my girls."

"You'd rough up your sons, but not your daughters?"

"You're pregnant?"

Sierra looked up to find her father standing behind Noah. "No!"

"Who else is pregnant?" Evelyn asked.

Within seconds the word was repeated by those sitting at the table. Sierra had had enough. "Good people, I'd like everyone to know that I am *not* pregnant."

"I don't know what you're waiting for," Evelyn announced.

Philip shook his head. "Let it go, Evie. The more pressure you put on Sierra to get married and have a baby, the more she balks."

"What's the harm in wanting to see my only daughter married and a mother?"

In the past Sierra would get up and walk out whenever her mother would go on and on about her unmarried daughter being too picky, that no man would ever be good enough for her, but not this morning. "Don't you have enough grandbabies, Mama?"

Evelyn gave her a haughty look. "A grandmother can never have too many grandbabies. I'm certain Noah's mother would agree with me."

"I'm afraid she would."

Sierra elbowed him in the ribs. "You're not supposed to agree with her," she said sotto voce.

Noah, resting an arm over her shoulders, pressed his mouth to her ear. "Humor her, babe. I go through the same thing with my mother. There were times when I came home on leave, she would have a woman waiting for me to meet. She finally got the message once I didn't come to see her as often."

Turning her head, Sierra met his eyes. His moist breath feathered over her mouth. "If you're my boyfriend, then I expect you to take my side."

"And if you're my girlfriend, then you should be a little more tolerant."

Her eyes lowered to his mouth. "You like tolerant women?"

His firm lips parted. "I love easygoing, open-minded women."

Sierra felt heat in her cheeks under his gaze. "In other words, you want a submissive, dutiful, obedient woman who will not challenge you even if she's not in agreement."

"That's where you're wrong, babe. A submissive woman is a boring woman."

"Why don't you two get a room!" shouted Luke from the other end of the table.

"We have one," Sierra countered, smiling from ear to ear. She stood up, Noah also coming to his feet. "Excuse me, but I have to get a head start on my dishes for tonight's dinner." She had volunteered to make macaroni and cheese and collard greens.

Noah caught her arm, stopping her retreat before she could reach the kitchen. "You should stop fighting with your mother."

"What makes you think I'm fighting with her?"

He pulled her against his body, and laid his chin on her head. "Your mother is no different from millions, maybe even billions, of women who want the best for their daughters. And the best is seeing them married to a man willing to love and protect them."

"You're a fine one to talk, Noah. Didn't you just tell me about your mother playing matchmaker?"

"It's not the same."

"Why isn't it the same? Are you saying women aren't equal to men? Or that we need you more than you need us?"

"That's not what I'm saying, but there are times when women do need men for more than procreation. Case in point: your crazy-ass ex who disrupted your life so that you had to change your phone numbers and get a restraining order. But even the threat of being arrested and going to jail didn't stop him, until your brother got involved. Are you aware of how many women lose their lives because of spurned husbands or boyfriends? Too many," he added, answering his own question. "Mark did what I would've done if some man was harassing my sisters, and thankfully my brothers-in-law haven't demonstrated any signs of stupidity that would make me get in their faces."

Sierra digested what Noah said. He was right about a woman needing a man's physical and emotional protection when she found herself unable to handle certain situations. "Okay," she conceded. "I promise to ignore my mother when she goes off about me not being married."

Noah tightened his hold on her body. "That's my girl."

She eased out of his embrace, fearful that if he continued to hold her she would beg him to kiss her, reminding her what she had been missing since she ended her relationship with Derrick. And it wasn't that she hadn't attracted several men who'd expressed an interest in taking her out, but once bitten twice shy.

Why, she thought, as she walked into the kitchen, couldn't she have met Noah before Derrick? Even if they were to remain friends, at least she wouldn't have to concern herself with trying to fend off a stalker.

Naomi joined her, rinsing and stacking dishes in the dishwasher. "I'm going to recruit Mark, Noah, and Pilar to help me and Danny decorate the tree. I'm also going to get the kids to help me trim the lower half, to give them something to do before they start binge-watching holiday-themed movies."

"That's a good idea."

Sierra knew it would take hours to put all the ornaments on the eight-foot spruce. Store-bought and handmade figurines, trinkets, and baubles dated back more than a century. Her grandmother had saved the tree ornaments from her childhood, wrapping them in tissue paper and storing them in airtight containers. What had begun with several dozen now numbered more than five hundred one-of-a-kind and contemporary collectibles. Every Christmas, a family member would purchase a new ornament and add it to the ever-increasing collection. The highlight of the evening came when the younger Nelsons recognized an ornament they'd made from prior years.

Despite her nieces and nephews viewing the same movies every year, they never tired of seeing them again. Once the tree was decorated, gaily wrapped presents were piled on the velvet skirt, embroidered with the names of the children. Sierra had mailed her gifts to Chicago over several months, eliminating the need to put them in her checked luggage. However, she did bring a number of gift cards with her for her parents and the older children.

She opened the refrigerator and removed large plastic bags filled with collard greens. She had admitted to Noah that she didn't like cooking for herself, yet she enjoyed preparing for a crowd, and planned to use the downstairs kitchen for her dishes.

Chapter 6

Noah balanced several plastic containers of Christmas ornaments against his body as he climbed the staircase leading from the basement to the great room, where heat from burning logs in the fireplace added to the festive scene.

When Sierra mentioned that her parents had renovated the lower level, he could not have imagined the spaciousness and the furnishings conducive to entertaining and total relaxation.

Two bedrooms were set up dormitory style for the Nelson boys and girls. A kitchen with a fully stocked bar, several wall-mounted televisions, leather seat groupings, and a gaming area with pool, Ping-Pong, and air-hockey tables beckoned him to linger there for hours. After seeing the basement, he knew why the Nelson children loved hanging out at their grandparents' home.

Every area of the basement was functional, including the storeroom. Floor-to-ceiling shelves were packed with board games, bedding in clear protective bags, children's toys, and boxes containing small household appliances. The Nelsons had an area for luggage and two locked metal file cabinets with labels indicating financial and tax records.

Mark also carried several containers with ornaments, while Daniel and Pilar hoisted large black garbage-type bags filled with Christmas presents over their shoulders.

Naomi confided that every year the kids tried to break into the storeroom because they knew Christmas and birthday presents were placed there, but couldn't come up with the combination on the door's lock. She had discovered their subtle subterfuge when she found several sheets of paper with various number combinations in the wastebasket. Noah told her she had to at least give them credit for attempting to work out the mathematical sequence in order to gain entry.

Trimming the tree became a group project as the children sat on the floor and gently removed the tissue paper protecting the fragile ornaments. Noah was amazed by the ritual where each child stood in line, selected a branch, and carefully placed the trinket on the tree. It was done quickly and precisely because they wanted to finish the task and retreat to the basement to watch movies.

"That was the fastest I've ever seen them accomplish that," Naomi remarked when the children raced out of the room to the staircase.

Noah picked up a fragile glass ball that resembled a snow globe. "I thought they would be more excited to see some of their personal artwork hung on the tree."

Pilar laughed softly. "Usually they are, but this year we told them they couldn't watch their movies until they helped decorate the tree. Every year we have to fight with them to turn off movies they've seen so many times they can recite the dialogue verbatim, and come put their ornaments on the tree. This time we decided to reverse the tradition."

Noah smiled and shook his head. He found it amazing that parents had to concoct their own schemes to best their children without resorting to hostile threats. His sisters had complained to their husbands about the number of hours their sons spent on their electronic devices, but to no avail, until their grades began slipping. It was only after a parent-teacher conference that his firefighter and DEA agent brothers-in-law lowered the hammer: No devices were allowed whenever they sat down to eat as a family. And that included when they dined out. They placed time limits on their computers in addition to the already installed parental controls, and they had to leave their cell phones on their parents' dresser before retiring for bed.

It appeared to him that every generation of parents was beset with dangers facing their children. Whether binge drinking, cyberspace bullying, illegal or prescription drugs, drag racing, or women being raped on college campuses, Noah knew being a parent was the most challenging job in the world.

He hadn't felt the pressure to become a father for two reasons: his role in the military, and he hadn't met a woman with whom he wanted to share his life and future. Noah also knew time was winding down on his career as a SEAL, and if he was to remain in the navy he would have to apply for another position within the branch. He'd earned a degree in civil engineering, which would make him eligible to apply to the Civil Engineer Corps. He would become part of a team constructing city-size bases, airfields, and harbor facilities around the globe.

Noah shook his head as if to erase his musings. He knew the time he had spent with Sierra and her family had something to do with his looking at the world differently. Interacting with her family, watching antics of her nieces and nephews, and bonding with her male relatives when they spent hours talking about all things military made him aware of what he had been missing: becoming a part of a tight, extended family unit. There were similarities because both his sisters, like Sierra, were elementary school teachers and their sons were in the same age range as Daniel and Naomi's Caleb and Isaiah. The most obvious difference was he hadn't grown up with his father, and both sets of his grandparents were deceased.

Noah loved his mother and sisters, doted on his nephews, but the traditions established by his Southern grandparents died when they did. His mother refused to keep the old traditions because she felt them trivial. Every year, his grandmothers had celebrated the New Year with Hoppin' John—a rice dish made with black-eyed peas simmered with spicy sausages, ham hocks, or fatback. There was always a large bowl of collard greens, which signified money, and cornbread, which signified gold. He remembered the saying: *Eat poor that day, eat rich the rest of the year.* The rice represented riches and the peas symbolized peace.

When Sierra mentioned she did not like to cook for one person, Noah wanted to ask her if she would be willing to cook for him, but he hadn't wanted to put her on the spot. Although he was beginning to like her a lot and wanted Sierra to be more than a mere acquaintance, he didn't know if she would want more. It was obvious her ex had turned her off when it came to men, so much so that she had been reluctant to even date again. Noah knew he had one or maybe even two more days to let her know that he was willing to take the risk to turn their charade into a reality.

He picked up a dazzling laminated angel with a gold cord and hung it on one of the upper branches. Each of the handmade ornaments was signed and dated by its designer. He found a number of them Sierra had made as a child. Naomi and Pilar called it quits once they were unable to reach the branches without standing on a ladder.

Sierra walked into the room, carrying a tray with mugs of cocoa topped with whipped cream and shaved chocolate. She had covered her short hair with a blue bandana. "The tree looks wonderful. I thought it was time you take a break and enjoy some refreshments."

"You are an angel," Pilar crooned, taking a mug off the tray.

Naomi took her mug, then Mark, and finally Noah. "Thank you, darling."

Sierra flashed a demure smile as she lowered her eyes. "You're welcome, sweetheart."

Mark, waiting for Sierra to leave, turned to Noah. "You've really got it bad for my sister, don't you?"

He exchanged a long, penetrating stare with Sierra's younger brother. "I do."

Mark smiled as attractive lines fanned out around eyes that had spent too much time squinting in the desert sun. "I'm glad."

"What my gorgeous husband isn't saying is that he would gladly welcome you into the family if you married his sister," Pilar stated proudly, as if she had just solved the mystery concerning the disappearance of Jimmy Hoffa.

"Who's marrying who?" Luke asked as he walked in holding Delia's hand.

Naomi rolled her eyes upward. "My dear sister Pilar is talking about wedding plans for Noah and Sierra."

Luke pulled over a folding chair and helped Delia as she slowly sat down. "When are you two tying the knot?"

Noah believed he could feel the heat of five pairs of eyes burning into him like a laser. "We're not. We haven't talked about marriage." It was the first time since the charade he hadn't had to lie about his relationship with Sierra.

Delia, rubbing her extended belly, glared at him. "Can you see yourself married to her?"

Noah smiled. "Yes, I could."

Again, he hadn't lied. He knew if he fell in love with his pretend girlfriend there was no doubt he would want to marry her. Of all of the women he had known, Sierra topped the list when it came to compatibility, and what shocked him more than anything was that he'd met her just twenty-four hours ago. He had several members on his team who admitted they'd fallen in love with their wives within minutes of meeting them, and after facing imminent death each time they embarked on a mission, they did not want to waste time contemplating if she was the *one*.

His mother had related stories of girls in her neighborhood who'd married their boyfriends just before they were shipped out to Vietnam. The same had been true when men were drafted during the Second World War and Korean War.

Delia gasped softly and then went completely still. "I really felt that."

Luke hunkered down in front of his wife. "Was it a contraction?"

"No. It wasn't strong enough to be a contraction."

Pilar came over and rubbed her cousin's back. "Why don't you go and put your feet up, *mi'ja.*"

Delia grimaced. "I'm all right. I promised Evie that I would make the *arroz con gandules.*"

"You're not the only Puerto Rican in this family who can make rice and pigeon peas. And thanks to you I now know how to make your *sofrito.*"

Noah was relieved the two women were talking about food rather than about him and Sierra. He sipped his cocoa. The slight bitterness of the chocolate was offset by the sweet, frothy cream topping. Luke, taking Pilar's advice, helped his wife stand and then led her up the staircase to their bedroom.

Naomi slowly shook her head. "I don't think she's going to make it past the New Year."

"When is the baby due?" Noah asked.

"She says January tenth."

Pilar smiled. "My girls want the baby to be born December twenty-eighth, so they can share the same birthday as their cousin."

"What if she's also having twins?" Naomi threw out. "She is a lot bigger with this baby than she was with David."

Noah met Mark's eyes, both shaking their heads at the same time. It wasn't often he was privy to conversations between women, yet it was apparent Sierra's relatives felt comfortable discussing any- and everything with one another.

Their cocoa break ended and they went back to completing decorating the tree with yards of tiny white lights that appeared like stars in a nighttime sky once the overhead lights were extinguished. The falling snow had changed over to sleet, and the frozen particles pelting the windows competed with the crackling and hissing of dying embers on the grate behind the decorative fireplace screen. Pilar and Naomi emptied the large garbage bags, placing the gifts around the tree skirt, and then stepped back to survey their handiwork.

Pilar came over to stand next to Noah and looped her arm through his. "How does it look?"

He smiled. "It's perfect. It reminds me of the cover of a children's book I bought for one of my nephews."

"How many nephews do you have?"

"Four. Both my sisters have two boys. They both professed that they wanted a girl, but it didn't happen."

"Are they older or younger than you?"

"Older, and because they're over forty they don't plan to have any more children."

"I guess that leaves you, bro," Daniel drawled, "to give your mother a granddaughter."

"I suppose it does," he said in agreement. If he truly believed in the power of suggestion, then Noah knew he would be married to Sierra and the father of several children if he went along with the Nelsons' wishes.

Mark rested an arm on Pilar's shoulder. "You did good, baby. This is when we all try to get some sleep before the real festivities begin later tonight. Noah, I don't know if Sierra told you, but we eat around eight and open presents at the stroke of midnight. Then get ready to throw down in the kitchen with the dudes for a Christmas Day brunch."

"Are you game, Brother Crawford?" Daniel asked.

"Hell yeah!" The two women gave him admiring

glances. He still had to decide whether to make an omelet, frittata, or chicken and red velvet waffles. He'd taken an inventory of the freezer in the basement and found it stocked with chicken, steaks, pork chops, and bagged shrimp. "I'll see you guys later."

Turning on his heel, he went in search of Sierra and found her in the formal dining room setting the table, with seating for twelve, with china, silver, and crystal glassware. The ornate fabric runner down the center of the exquisite mahogany and cherrywood table, silver candelabras, wreaths cradling votive candles, and crystal bowls filled with bouquets of pine, cranberries, and strands of colored beads turned the table into a visual still-life masterpiece. She had already set a smaller table for the children with place settings for five. The fireplace mantel was decorated with wreaths of lilies, pine, and silver bells.

He applauded and her head popped up. "It looks exquisite."

Sierra crossed her arms under her breasts. "Thank you."

"We finished the tree."

She closed the distance between them and wrapped her arms around his waist. "And I'm finished in the kitchen. Are you ready to take a nap?" Bending slightly, Noah swept her up into his arms, and Sierra held on to his neck to keep her balance. "Put me down, Noah. I can walk."

He kissed her nose. "You couldn't walk last night when you fell asleep in my bed."

"I don't even remember falling asleep until I woke up this morning."

Taking long strides, Noah quickly covered the distance from the dining room to the staircase. "That's because you were probably jet-lagged and exhausted."

Tilting her head, she looked up at him. "Weren't you also jet-lagged?"

Noah nodded. "That and a little hungover from drinking more beer than I'm accustomed to."

"How many did you have?"

He smiled. "I stopped counting after three."

"I should've warned you that my brothers prefer beer to hard liquor. However, tonight will be different because we're serving wine plus Grandpa's special Christmas punch, which has anyone who drinks it believing they can see into the future."

"Damn!"

"No, Noah. Double damn. Just be prepared when everyone watches as you take your first sip. It may taste like Kool-Aid or Hi-C, but once it goes down it explodes like napalm."

"Are you certain it isn't moonshine?"

"I don't know because I've never tasted moonshine. It could be, because Grandpa grew up in Tennessee before he came to Chicago, so it could be he learned to make it from his father and uncles."

Noah shouldered open the door to their bedroom, and placed Sierra on the bed. He sat on the side of the mattress and removed his socks. "I've sampled moonshine and it truly lived up to its name as white lightning, because after a few sips I was lit up like an exploding M-80."

Sierra swept the bandana off her head and fluffed up her short hair. "Wine happens to be my cocktail of choice. I'll occasionally have a margarita or a cosmo, but nothing stronger." She adjusted the pillow under her head. "I didn't expect you to make the beds."

Noah lay down next to Sierra and pulled her close. "I like everything neat."

She met his eyes. "Are you OCD?"

He smiled. "I'm not that bad. I'm probably more anal than obsessive compulsive."

"We should get along well, because I'm also a little anal."

Noah's smile faded. "Should, Sierra? We're already getting along. So well that everyone believes we've known each other for a while."

"It is weird." She let out a sigh. "I feel as if I know you as well as I know my brothers."

He rested his arm over her waist. "The only thing I have in common with your brothers is the military."

"Maybe that's it." Sierra yawned against his sweatshirt.

"Go to sleep, babe. What time do you want me to wake you up?"

She yawned again. "Six."

Noah shifted and reached for his cell phone on the bedside table, and set the alarm for six. The distinctive sound of sleet tapping against the windows faded as the frozen precipitation turned to rain. He knew it was just a matter of time when the airport would reopen, resuming flights in and out of O'Hare. He would miss the Nelsons, the large house filled with laughter, heated conversations, the tantalizing aromas of food, and the live Christmas tree.

He stared at Sierra's delicate features, her head resting on her folded arm as she slept. There was no need for him to photograph her, because he had committed her image to memory like a permanent tattoo. Noah understood her annoyance with her mother's badgering her to find a husband with whom to settle down and have children, but he also recognized Sierra's need for independence, something she'd probably had to struggle to achieve when growing up as the only girl in a family with three boys.

Noah might not understand everything about his personality, but there was one thing he did know: He was a pragmatist. If it wasn't real to him, then it was nothing more than fantasy. However, Sierra was real, yet she was also a fantasy—his version of the perfect woman with whom he could live happily ever after, much like the princes and princesses in fairy tales. He wasn't a prince but a SEAL sniper who was able to eliminate his target with one fatal shot.

Pressing his head to the pillow under his shoulders, Noah closed his eyes and willed his mind blank. He did not want to think about returning to his base, training for the next mission, or boarding a military transport to take him to a part of the world where his life and very survival would become the responsibility of the members of his team. They all were dependent on one another to complete the mission and return home without leaving anyone behind.

His chest rose and fell, his breathing slow and even, and after a while everything around him disappeared when Morpheus claimed him.

Chapter 7

Noah pulled out a chair at the dining room table, seating Sierra before he sat beside her. Music flowed from hidden speakers as four generations of Nelsons sat down to enjoy another Christmas dinner. The gathering was a little more formal than the night before. The men wore slacks, shirts sans ties, while their female counterparts had selected skirts or tailored slacks, blouses, and a few opted for pumps. Sierra's grandmother and grandfather were seated opposite each other at the head of the table. Evelyn had prepared plates for her grandchildren, serving them before the adults.

Philip seated Evelyn, and then took his own chair. He nodded to his father. "Pop, you can bless the table."

Stephen bowed his head, everyone following suit. "I forget who said this, but I've always liked it. To my family. While our clan may be strange in many ways, it is nice to know I have a loving family whenever I am in need. And that is the strangest thing of all. I thank the Lord for our differences, for what we search for, and for what we have found. I thank Him for what brings us together and for what sets us apart. Most of all I thank Him for our special family that shares one heart. Amen."

Noah smiled and said amen along with the others. *For what we search for, and for what we have found.* The phrase bombarded him like missiles. Was the woman sitting by his side what he'd been searching for and now found? He knew he didn't have much more time to figure that out, because the news had reported that O'Hare would reopen sometime after midnight, and once the planes were de-iced and the runways plowed, flights would resume. That meant if he was lucky he would spend Christmas Day with the Nelsons and Christmas night with his family.

Philip picked up a platter with carved turkey, holding it while Evelyn selected a few slices. A merry-go-round of platters and bowls filled with prime rib, fresh ham, collard greens, rice and pigeon peas, macaroni and cheese, sweet potato casserole, green beans with white potatoes, cornbread, and roasted Brussels sprouts with bacon were passed around the table.

Sierra tapped Noah's cordial glass containing a clear liquid. "That's Grandpa's special brew."

Noah picked up the glass, put it to his mouth, and tossed it back in one swallow. It began icy before exploding in a fireball in his chest. Tears filled his eyes and he blinked them back before they fell. "Holy . . ." He managed to swallow the curse before it slipped past his lips.

"How do you like it, sonny?" Stephen asked.

Noah's shoulders shook as he tried not to laugh. "It tastes like my grandpop's hooch."

Stephen nodded. "That's because it is hooch. I've tried to get my boys to drink it, but they claim it's too strong for their candy asses."

"Pop! The kids can hear you," Evelyn admonished softly.

Stephen glared at his daughter-in-law. "I'm willing to bet they've heard a lot worse from their own parents."

"Nana, please tell Pop that the children don't need to hear that type of language from their great-grandfather."

Sandra slowly shook her head. "My telling Stephen what to and what not to say will go in one ear and out the other. I've been married to him for sixty-eight years, and he never listens to me until I threaten him with divorce."

Heads turned in Sandra's direction as if they'd been choreographed in advance. "You talked about divorcing my father?" Philip questioned.

Sandra's expression reminded Noah of someone hiding a secret. "More times than I can count," she admitted, "Contrary to what you want to believe about your so-called perfect father, he's not that perfect."

Sierra leaned forward. "Are you saying, Nana, that Grandpop fooled around?"

"Oh! Stephen would never cheat on me. When we were first married we lived in an apartment, and Stephen used to hang out on the weekends with some guys in the neighborhood who were into shady stuff."

Philip swallowed a mouthful of mac and cheese, and then touched the napkin to his mouth. "What do you mean, Mama, by shady stuff?"

"I think they used to boost clothes and meat and then sell them to folks on the block. A few of them were also running numbers. I told Stephen if he didn't stop going down to that basement to drink hooch and play cards, then I was going to leave him.

Apparently he thought I was bluffing, but when he came back from work and found me gone, it finally hit home for him."

"Where did you go, Nana?" Mark asked.

"Next door to my neighbor. I knew Stephen wouldn't ask my parents about my whereabouts, because he didn't want to have to explain to my father that he couldn't find his wife. Daddy and Stephen never got along too well. Daddy wanted me to marry his best friend's son, but I ran away and eloped with Stephen."

Totally engrossed in his grandmother's revelation, Luke rested his elbows on the table. "What happened after that, Nana?"

"I was pregnant with your father at the time, so I didn't want to go back to my parents, and I also didn't want to lose my baby's father. I'd peek through the curtains of the neighbor's living room to watch Stephen coming and going. After a few days he looked like what you young folks call a hot mess. When I thought he'd suffered enough, I waited for him to leave for work before I went back to our apartment. When he came home and found me in bed, he swore on the Bible that he would never go back to that basement again."

"Did you ever go back, Grandpa?" Daniel asked.

"Hell no. Not when your grandmother told me she had gone to stay with her old boyfriend, who said he would pay for her divorce, marry her, and then raise my boy as his own. It wasn't until years later that she confessed to being next door."

Everyone laughed until tears rolled down their faces, and Noah saw the love in Stephen's eyes as he gazed down the length of the table at the woman who truly was the love of his life. Dinner had become a leisurely affair, as no one seemed anxious to leave the table. It was after ten when the Nelson men and Noah volunteered to clear the table and put away leftovers, while the women and the children retreated to the great room.

Philip patted Noah's back. "Are you certain you want to get involved with this crazy family?"

"I'm already involved—with your daughter."

"I don't want to get into your personal business, but you intend to take your involvement with my daughter to another level?"

"Are you asking me if I plan to marry your daughter?"

Philip nodded. "Yes."

Noah angled his head. "Maybe one of these days."

"What's stopping you?"

"My career. It's . . . it's what I do."

A beat passed. "I have an idea of what you do," Philip said in a quiet tone. "The first time I saw you walk in with my daughter, the first thing that ran through my mind was that cocky SOB has to be Special Ops." He leaned in close. "SEALs?" Noah's impassive expression did not change. There was a barely perceptible nod of his head. "And you believe that's a deterrent to planning a future with Sierra?"

"It's part of it." Noah didn't want to tell Philip that the other part was he had to be in love with Sierra in order for him to propose marriage. And that would only come with time.

"What's the other part?"

"Sierra's not in love with me. We like each other, but we haven't reached the stage where we can honestly say that we're in love. I suppose with time that will come."

"But you're sleeping together."

"Yes, Philip, we do share a bed, but even the best sex in the world can't save a marriage when two people fall out of love. For me, it has to be more than that. And I know it's the same with Sierra."

"My daughter's lucky to have you. No pressure. Okay?"

Noah gave Philip a bro hug. "Okay."

"Let's get this kitchen cleaned up so we can join the others."

Noah heard laughter and music coming from the direction of the great room. There was still a half hour before midnight, the time to open presents, and he could feel the energy even before walking in. The rug had been rolled up and Sierra was dancing with one of her nephews.

Crossing his arms over his chest, he smiled as she executed the steps to the latest dance craze.

The playlist segued into a slower dance number and he strolled across the floor and extended his hand. "May I have this dance, Miss Nelson?"

Sierra inclined her head. "Of course, Mr. Crawford." She buried her face against the column of his strong neck. "You dance well."

"I only slow dance."

She breathed in his ear, and Noah was helpless to control his growing erection. He'd shared a bed with Sierra not once but twice, and each time he had been able to control himself. It was on a very rare occasion that he would sleep with a woman and not make love to her. Thankfully the next tune was also slow and it allowed time for his erection to go down. A cheer went up from the assembly, and he turned to find

Philip and Evelyn kissing under a sprig of mistletoe someone had hung from the large crystal chandelier.

"It's your turn, Dad," Caleb shouted.

Daniel pulled Naomi to her feet and over to the chandelier. Wrapping his arms around her waist, he bent her back and kissed her until she struggled to free herself. Their children were cheering as if their team had won a sporting event.

Naomi was blushing when her husband finally released her. "You're next, Delia."

Luke eased Delia from her chair, his hand going to the small of her back. "Kissing is what got her into this condition," he teased. Cradling her face in his hands, Luke gave her a tender kiss, before leading her back to the love seat.

Luke slapped Mark's back. "You're up next, little brother."

Mark and Pilar danced salsa and locked lips as everyone counted to eighteen before they finally came up for air. They alternated bowing to applause and whistling. Mark gestured to Noah. "You're up next."

Noah saw indecision in Sierra's eyes as he reached for her hand. "We can do this," he whispered in her ear.

He waited until they were under the mistletoe, and then swept her up in his arms and brushed a light kiss over her mouth, slowly deepening it when her lips parted. His curiosity as to how her lips tasted was assuaged as he made love to her mouth. He ended it, both staring at each other in shock. Bending slightly, Noah set Sierra on her feet to thunderous applause.

"You're next, Nana and Grandpa," Mark said to his grandparents. Stephen and Sandra, sitting together, held hands and kissed each other, which thrilled their great-grandchildren.

Noah knew he could easily get used to the tradition of couples kissing under the mistletoe, because it was an open and unashamed display that reaffirmed their love for each other. The music and dancing continued until the clock on the mantel chimed the hour. It was midnight, and a minute later it was Christmas.

Noah volunteered to become Santa as he sat on the floor and handed out gifts. The younger Nelsons screamed and cheered when they received many of the items on their Christmas list. Pilar's twin daughters were almost hysterical when they were given the latest version of the iPhone.

Delia dissolved into tears when she peeled back the tissue paper in a box to find a christening set Sierra had crocheted for her new baby. Delicate scalloping and silk ribbons on the dress, coat, and the hat made the handmade garment a treasured heirloom Delia could pass down through future generations.

Sierra had knitted and crocheted for family members scarves, hats, and sweaters, whose prices would be prohibitive if sold in stores. He opened a box with a tag bearing his name, and he stared at her in amazement. Noah opened the box to find a charcoal-gray knitted cashmere scarf. He mouthed a thank-you and she nodded in acknowledgment. It was after one, and presents and gift cards were scattered about the floor as everyone decided it was time to retire to bed.

Sierra came out of the bathroom in a nightgown to find Noah sitting up in bed. He patted the mattress. "Come to bed with me."

Her bare feet were silent on the rug as she

walked around the bed, got in, and pulled the sheet and blankets up to her neck. She shivered slightly when Noah's bare leg rubbed against hers. "Merry Christmas."

His mouth covered hers. "Merry Christmas." He pulled her into his arms. "I hadn't expected you to get me anything."

"I must confess I made the scarf for my grand-father, but Nana told me he's developed an allergy to wool, so you got it by default."

He kissed her forehead. "Lucky me. Your needle-work is exquisite. Who taught you to knit and crochet?"

"I volunteer at a senior center on the weekends, and I bonded with a woman who had a shop where she carried some of the most expensive yarns on the West Coast. At one time she made knitted garments for several celebrities. Nana taught me to knit and crochet, but it was Mrs. Wells who introduced me to imported yarns. She said if you're going to wear a handmade garment, you should use materials of the finest quality."

"If you ever retire from teaching, you can always have a second career as a knitting instructor."

She rubbed her toes up and down his hairy legs. "Once I retire from teaching, I doubt if I'd want to teach again—not even if it's needlework."

"What would you do?"

"I don't know yet. I have at least another twenty-five years to make up my mind."

"Do you believe in destiny?" Noah asked after a lengthy silence.

"I don't know. Why?"

"Originally I wasn't scheduled to be on the same flight as you. I'd agreed to give up my seat on an earlier flight, to a wheelchair-bound college student who'd broken both legs in an automobile accident. If I'd never made that decision, we never would've met."

"I think it worked out well for both of us. You've made this Christmas one I'll remember for a long time."

Noah closed his eyes as he buried his face in her hair. "I've known my share of women, but you are the first one I feel so at ease with. I will never forget you."

"Nor I you."

It was the last thing they said as they fell asleep in each other's arms.

Chapter 8

Noah woke with a start. He had a hard-on. He tried not to panic, hoping Sierra wasn't aware that his body had betrayed him.

Rising on an elbow, he peered over her shoulder to find her still asleep. He managed to slip out of bed without waking her, picking up his cell phone as he walked into the bathroom. It wasn't quite seven, and he knew he could not get back into bed until his erection went down. He waited, suffering through the pleasurable throbbing that refused to give him ease. Then he did what he hadn't had to do in years. Stepping into the shower stall, he turned on the water and the cold spray took its effect.

Realization came at Noah like someone hitting him in the nose. He wanted Sierra in his life, both in and out of bed. She was the whole of all of the little things he liked in other women, tied up in a big red bow. It had taken only days for him to fall in love with her and her family. She was open, unpretentious, generous, spirited, and loyal to those she loved. He went through the motions of washing his hair and body. After his shower, he wrapped a towel around his waist and stood at the vanity, staring into the mirror. He looked the same, even though he knew he wasn't the same man who'd boarded the jet to fly across the country to spend the Christmas holiday with his family.

Noah had just finished brushing his teeth when his cell phone chimed, indicating he had a text. The message he'd been waiting for finally came through. His cancelled flight was rescheduled to take off at 11:48. It was 7:22, and he had to pack and get to O'Hare by nine-thirty. He walked into the bedroom and opened the armoire to get a set of underwear.

"Why are you up so early?"

He held his hands in front of his groin as he half turned to see Sierra sitting up in bed. "I just got a text from the airline that I have an eleven o'clock flight."

She scrambled off the bed. "I'll drive you to the airport."

Noah shook his head. "No, babe. I'll call a taxi."

"That's okay. I don't mind driving you. As soon as I shower and get dressed we'll be on our way."

He knew it was pointless to argue with her. "Okay."

Sierra maneuvered into the long line leading to departures. She wanted to cry but knew Noah would probably believe she was being melodramatic, and that wasn't the lasting impression she wanted to leave him with. "It looks as if everybody is trying to get out of town."

"Yep."

She gave him a sidelong glance under the sunglasses perched on the bridge of her nose. The weather had cleared, the skies were blue, and the temperatures were predicted to top out in the low forties. Noah was dressed as he'd been the first time he walked down the aisle of the aircraft to sit beside her. He was now Captain Crawford.

"Maybe I should give you my number so if you're ever in my neck of the woods, we can get together over dinner and drinks."

"You don't have to give me your number, because I can get it on my own."

She blinked once. "How?"

He smiled. "Remember I'm assigned to intelligence."

She returned his smile. "I suppose that makes you a spy."

"I guess you can say that. Tell your brothers that I'm sorry I wasn't able to compete in the Christmas Day cook-off, but maybe one of these days when I'm in the neighborhood I'll take them up on their challenge."

"They're going to miss you."

Noah placed a hand on her knee. "What about you? Will you also miss me?"

"I'm missing you now. I must confess you're the best pretend boyfriend I've ever had."

"How many have you had?"

"Only one."

Noah's fingers tightened on the skinny jeans covering her knee. "Same here. I must admit it was fun. But not so much fun that I'd want to do it again, because once you tell one lie then you have to tell another to cover that one. After a while you just run out of lies, or you can't keep them straight."

"I think we did all right. Not quite an award-winning performance, but close."

"I happen to think we were spectacular. The *sweethearts* and *darlings* rolled off your tongue like silk."

Sierra stared out the windshield. "Maybe it was because that's what I felt at the time I said it."

Noah went completely still. "Are you saying it wasn't all an act?"

Her eyelids fluttered wildly. "Do you want a lie or the truth?"

"The truth, of course!"

"I didn't want you to be my pretend boyfriend. I wanted what we had to be for real."

"Why didn't you say something?"

She frowned. "And have you believe that I was a horny, desperate woman willing to sleep with a man she'd known a couple of days? You don't know how many times I wanted to beg you to kiss me, and when you did last night, under the mistletoe, I knew I wanted more than a kiss. I wanted you to make love to me, but when we got into bed together and nothing happened and I thought you hadn't found me physically—"

"Stop it, Sierra! Did you feel how my body reacted to you when we were dancing? And when I woke up this morning I was so hard that I was forced to take a cold shower. That's something I have not done in almost twenty years. And I wanted to curse the hell out of you because you turned me on and there was nothing I could do about it."

"You can curse me later because you're here." She leaned over and pulled the lever to open the hatch to the SUV.

Sierra looked up into the rearview mirror, watching Noah as he got out of the car and removed the duffel from the cargo area. It had been her intention to drop him off and drive back to the house, but she just couldn't sit there and watch him walk into the terminal and disappear out of her life. Unbuckling her seat belt, she got out and came around to the sidewalk as Noah waited to check his bag at curbside check-in.

Tears filled her eyes and overflowed as she tried smiling. First she was standing alone there, and then she found herself in his arms, his mouth capturing hers in a marauding kiss that sucked the air from her lungs.

"I love you," she whispered when she finally broke the kiss.

Noah stared at her as if she had taken leave of her senses. "I love you, too." He winked at her. "I'll be in touch."

Sierra nodded, then turned and went back to the vehicle she had left idling at the curb. She shifted into gear and pulled out into traffic leading to the airport exit. An emotion she had never experienced filled her as she struggled not to cry. It wasn't sadness or disappointment, but a soaring happiness that made her feel as if she could walk on air.

She drove back to the house where she had grown up and experienced so many happy memories. This Christmas was one she would remember for a very long time. She had met a stranger on the plane, invited him to share the holiday with her family, unaware he would change her forever. Sierra hadn't lied when she told Noah she loved him, because she did. It wasn't an all-encompassing love where she couldn't live without him, but a love that was easygoing and without the angst she'd had in past relationships.

Her mother was in the kitchen sipping coffee when she walked in. "I had to take Noah to the airport," she explained when Evelyn gave her a questioning look. "I really like him."

"I do, too."

"Like him enough to marry him if he asked you?"

A smile parted Sierra's lips. "Yes."

Evelyn ran her fingers through her short silver curls. "Good." She held out her arms. "Come and give your mama a kiss."

Sierra did not hesitate when she walked into her mother's embrace, as she had as a little girl. Then her mother didn't have to ask for a kiss, because Sierra loved hugging her. She loved her mother's protective embrace, the smell of her perfume, and knew nothing could hurt her as long as her mother held her. She was still in her mother's arms when her father entered the kitchen.

"He's gone, isn't he?" Philip asked perceptively.

She turned and smiled at her father. "Yes. He finally got a flight out."

Philip nodded. "I really like that young man. I hope we'll get to see him again."

"I'm certain you will, Daddy."

Sierra sat back and studied her face in the vanity mirror. She hadn't lost her skill when it came to applying makeup. She was going to a New Year's Eve party for the first time in years. One of the teachers at her school had decided to host a small gathering at her house because no one wanted to go to a club or restaurant.

Her return flight to San Diego was without incident, and when she deplaned, the heat had hit her like someone had opened the door to a blast furnace, because she was wearing too many clothes. She hadn't bothered to unpack as she fell into bed and went to sleep.

She had just slipped into her dress for the party

when the intercom rang. Walking on bare feet to the door, she picked up the receiver. "Yes?"

"I have a delivery for an S. Nelson."

Her brow furrowed. She wasn't expecting a delivery. "Who's it from?"

"Captain America."

She clapped a hand over her mouth. Noah had disguised his voice. "I'm buzzing you in."

Sierra waited until she saw his face through the security eye before she unlocked and opened the door. She barely had time to catch her breath when she found herself in his arms, his mouth on hers. He lifted her effortlessly off her feet and carried her through the entryway and into her living/dining area.

Her hands cradled his clean-shaven jaw as she held him as if he was her lifeline. "Noah," she moaned between kisses. He finally set her on her feet, but continued to hold her. A tailored, dark blue suit, crisp white shirt, and gray silk tie had replaced the fatigues, and there was something about him that made him even more attractive than she remembered.

"How did you find me?"

"A good spy can always find his target." His eyes moved slowly over her face. "You look incredible. Are you going somewhere?"

"Yes. I'm invited to a friend's house for a small celebration. I was told I could bring a plus-one."

Noah angled his head. "I was hoping to take my girlfriend out to a little bistro not far from here, and then come back and bring in the year that will start a new tradition for us." He reached into the breast pocket of his jacket. "I have a belated Christmas present I'd like to give you."

Sierra took the silver-wrapped square box from

him and sat down on the pale suede-covered love seat. "You really didn't have to give me anything."

Noah dropped down next to her, stretched out his legs and crossed his feet at the ankles. "It's a little token of my appreciation for you putting me up during the layover."

She removed the tape and paper to reveal a velvet box. Sierra knew without removing the top it contained a piece of jewelry. A slight gasp escaped her when she saw a delicate gold bracelet with a diamond heart clasp. It wasn't the bracelet that shocked her but the SEAL Trident.

"You're a SEAL."

Noah nodded. He took the bracelet and fastened it around her left wrist. "You're the first woman I've told that I'm a SEAL, and hopefully you'll be the last, because I want you to give me a chance to prove I'm worthy enough to celebrate next Christmas and all the Christmases to come with our blended families."

Sierra knew Noah was offering her an indirect proposal of marriage. "You'll have that chance."

"And to be fair, I'll allow you an out. You'll have a year to come to terms with whether you're willing to become the wife of a Special Operations soldier. I may be away for extended periods of time, and when I have to leave for a mission, I can't tell you where I'm going or what I'm ordered to do."

Leaning into him, Sierra rested her head on his shoulder. "Do I have to remind you that every Nelson woman, beginning with Nana, has been a military wife? I'm certain I can pass the test."

He closed his eyes, smiling. "You have a lot of wonderful women as role models."

"I'm ready to go out with you and start our own New Year's Eve tradition."

"What about your friend?"

"I'll tell her something came up and I couldn't make it."

Noah had risked everything—including his pride—to return to California to a woman he hadn't known a week, to share next Christmas and all the Christmases of their lives together as husband and wife, parents and grandparents, and hopefully great-grandparents.

The Christmas Lesson

✢

CHERIS HODGES

Prologue

Prom Night—Ten Years Ago

Kayla Matthews wasn't going to let being stood up for the prom stop her from showing off the black and gold dress she and her mother spent three weeks finding.

And, Kayla wasn't looking forward to spending Saturday night at home listening to her little sister whining about why she couldn't go to the prom. Like, duh, she was only in the eighth grade. Autumn always wanted to do everything that Kayla did, despite their age difference. Their sibling rivalry was starting to get on Kayla's nerves and her mother's as well. For the most part, she just let Autumn have her way because when Kayla walked across the stage at West Charlotte High School, she was out of there.

Though she would miss DeShawn Carter, her best friend, more than anything—including The Chicken Coop, a staple in Charlotte dining. Thinking of DeShawn made her happy and sad at the same time. She wished that he'd seen her as more than just one of the guys. Maybe that had been why she'd decided to come to the prom, so that she and DeShawn could spend some time together. Who was she kidding? Tonight DeShawn was going to be focused on finally getting Daphne Marshall to give him some booty. She rolled her eyes as she thought about Daphne the sex fiend.

The rumor was that there wasn't an athlete that she wouldn't bed and DeShawn was on her list, and he had the nerve to go to the prom with her. Sighing, Kayla decided to have fun in spite of everything.

Walking into the ballroom at the Omni Hotel in uptown Charlotte, Kayla put a smile on her face as she heard her favorite song blaring from the speakers. Davida Martin waved her over to the table where she was sitting.

"Glad you made it," she said.

"I started to stay home, but look at this dress." Kayla twirled and showed off her form-fitting dress with the flared skirt.

"It's about time you started dressing like a girl," Davida said. "I saw your boy dancing with—"

"Don't tell me," Kayla said as she rolled her eyes and sat down.

"She looks like one of those BET dancers, but I'll give it up to DeShawn. In that tux, he looks like a black James Bond." Davida nodded to her left and Kayla saw DeShawn coming their way.

"Hey, Kayla," he said, then sat down beside her. "I have to say, you're looking good."

"Thanks, and who knew you owned something other than basketball shorts and T-shirts."

"Mmm, and you have legs—pretty nice ones, I might add." He gave her a lascivious glance and

Kayla shivered. Was he really looking at her like that? Maybe tonight would be the night that she . . . Davida kicked her underneath the table.

Kayla turned to her and furrowed her brows.

"I thought he was sick?"

Kayla locked eyes with her should've-been prom date, Ramon Clarkston. He had his arms wrapped around Pia Marvin, the only person in the world that Kayla actually hated. And there she was with Kayla's prom date. Bitch. Pia glanced in her direction and smirked, as she held on tighter to Ramon's arm.

"Don't even worry about her," Davida whispered. "And she looks like a tramp."

"And obviously, that's what he wants. I never liked that guy," DeShawn said, focusing his gaze on Kayla.

She turned her back to the door and focused on DeShawn. What was that look he was giving her? "Shawn, where is your date?"

He shrugged. "Last time I saw her, she was heading outside to smoke,"

"Or suck a—"

"Davida!" Kayla exclaimed. "Don't do that."

DeShawn laughed. "I knew what I was getting into when I decided to come here with her. She tried to grab my junk and I turned her down. She called me a few names and I realized that I should've come here alone."

Or asked me, Kayla thought as she smiled at DeShawn.

"What?" he asked, noting his friend's stare.

Kayla rose to her feet. "Let's dance." He took her hand and they headed for the dance floor. Davida smiled.

"That's what y'all should've done from the start," she muttered.

* * *

As soon as DeShawn and Kayla made it to the dance floor, a slow jam started playing. "We can sit down if you want," he said, though he wanted to wrap his arms around her.

"No, it's cool."

DeShawn opened his arms to her. As they danced, he buried his nose in her hair. She smelled good, as usual. Strawberries and roses.

His hand slipped from her back to her booty. He tensed for a second to see if she was going to flinch. She didn't. Good Lord, she felt good.

DeShawn had been feeling different about Kayla for months, but they had been best friends since freshman year. Kayla was the girl who knew about football and basketball, she was the girl who didn't do drama, and the one who should've been his girl-friend.

"If you don't move your hand, my knee will meet your family jewels," she whispered.

"Sorry." He rested his hands on the small of her back.

"That's all right, this time." She leaned her head on his shoulder and DeShawn felt his body tense.

The song ended and DeShawn didn't want to let her go. Instead, they stood in the middle of the dance floor. So many things ran through his mind, but DeShawn didn't say a word. This was his best friend, the girl he could talk to about anything. The girl who was driving him crazy in this black and gold dress.

"Shawn, what's wrong with you?" Her voice broke into his thoughts as he stared at her.

"Nothing, I just . . . Damn, you look amazing."

She smiled. "I'm starting to feel like you think I look like crap every other day of the week."

"Not at all," he said. "You always look good, but tonight . . ."

"Look at this shit," Ramon snapped as he approached DeShawn and Kayla.

DeShawn narrowed his eyes at Ramon. He'd never liked this dude, who thought he was going to be the next Kanye West, and when Kayla told him that he was going to be her prom date, he was pissed. And then he stood her up. Now, he was standing here with an attitude.

"I thought you were sick," Kayla snapped.

"And you said this nigga was just your friend. I knew you were a lying bitch."

DeShawn saw red and clocked Ramon in the jaw. Screams and shouts of "Fight, fight, fight!" filled the room. DeShawn kicked Ramon in the shin, causing him to fall to the floor. Kayla tried to grab DeShawn, and when he turned to look at her, Ramon gained the upper hand, pushing Shawn in his chest, forcing him backward. As the crowd gathered and security rushed toward the fight, Davida grabbed Kayla. "Let's get out of here."

Kayla looked back at DeShawn as a security guard slapped handcuffs on him.

Once Davida and Kayla got outside of the ballroom, Kayla paced back and forth.

"Calm down," Davida said as she reached into her purse and pulled out a stick of gum. "DeShawn should've knocked him out."

"This is all my fault." Kayla ran her hand across her face. "I should . . ."

"Tell DeShawn that you're in love with him. That you came to the prom to be with him and ride off into the sunset."

She grabbed Davida's arm. "You weren't supposed to let those words leave your mouth, ever!"

"This is our senior year, and I've watched you be his friend for the last four years. You gave him advice on dating girls who you knew were no good for him and . . ."

"DeShawn!" Kayla said, praying he hadn't heard anything Davida said. "Are you all right?"

He crossed over to Kayla, rubbing his jaw. "I'm good. I just have to get out of here or I'll be subject to arrest. How did you get here?"

"I rode the bus."

Davida looked at her watch. "You know what, I'm not ready to go, and since he has to leave, then you can go with him."

Kayla rolled her eyes. "All right," she said, then turned to DeShawn. "You're ready?"

"I don't want to ruin your night," he said. "If you want to stay and hang out with . . ."

"I'm ready to go," Kayla said, then smiled at him. DeShawn draped his arm across her shoulder.

"You're my best friend, Kayla. You never let me down."

Davida gave her girl a thumbs-up signal before she returned to the ballroom. DeShawn and Kayla walked to his car in silence. She looked at his jaw and saw the beginning of a nasty bruise.

"Well, your modeling career is going to have to be put on hold," she said as she stroked his cheek.

DeShawn grabbed her hand and they stood nose to nose. "I told you not to go out with Ramon. You deserve so much better."

"I know, but I didn't want to come to the prom alone. It was just one night."

"Kayla, you know you're too good for him. You deserve the best, and that's all I want for you."

She nodded as her knees trembled. Kayla wanted to tell him that what she wanted was him. But she didn't want to lose her friend. DeShawn took her hand. "Just think, we're going to be out of here in a few more weeks," he said with a smile.

"Yeah. I'm just waiting for the right acceptance letter, and I'll be so excited."

He nodded. "UCLA. Ever thought about Chapel Hill?"

"Not at all. I've been wanting to leave North Carolina for years." She smiled. "And I didn't get a full ride to UNC."

DeShawn shrugged. "You also can't run the ball like I do."

"Please, had I not helped you with algebra, running the ball would've been the least of your worries, because your mama said she was not raising a dumb jock."

DeShawn laughed as he unlocked the door of his 1996 Ford Mustang and opened the door for Kayla. She gave him a curtsy before she got into the car. When she looked back at him and saw his smile, her heart melted.

DeShawn hopped in the car and turned to his friend. "Want to get something to eat? I'm starving."

She glanced at her watch. "As long as I'm home by my twelve-thirty curfew. I don't want to hear my mama's mouth or spend the rest of my senior year on punishment."

"Come on, as long as she knows you're with me, she'll be fine." He winked at her.

"All right fine, as long as we go to IHOP," she said. "I want some pancakes."

DeShawn wanted something. Kayla. He didn't know when she stopped just being his friend Kayla, and became the star of his dreams Kayla. The girl had always been fine, and every time one of his football friends asked him to hook him up with her, they nearly got into a fight. Going to the prom with Daphne the sex fiend, he'd only done it to get Kayla's attention. But it hadn't seemed to work when she happily announced that she was going to the prom with punk-ass Ramon.

"Why did you want to go to the prom with Ramon?" he asked after they'd ridden for a few miles in silence.

"Seriously? Why did you take Daphne the sex fiend?"

"Well, why do most people go out with her?" He chuckled.

"So disgusting! That girl probably has a petri dish of STDs."

"Some people might call you a hater."

Kayla rolled her eyes. "Might say the same thing about you, if that jerk hadn't stood me up. I'm sorry you got kicked out of the prom for fighting him."

"You know I would never let anyone disrespect you." He placed his hand on her knee. "You're my people."

She turned toward the window. "DeShawn. I lo . . . I'm going to miss you next year."

"Me too."

He stopped at a red light and they faced each other. He leaned in to her and just as their lips were about to touch, a horn blared.

"What are we doing?" Kayla eased back into her seat. "I think you should just take me home. I'm not hungry."

He nodded as the car behind them pressed on the horn. Speeding off, DeShawn took Kayla home, and she bolted out of the car as if she was on fire. He didn't have a chance to walk her to the door and apologize for the almost kiss in the car. She glanced over her shoulder and then rushed inside.

"Damn it," he muttered. "I messed everything up."

Chapter 1

Kayla Matthews was not looking forward to Christmas, especially not this year. Sighing, she looked at her boarding pass. *Charlotte, North Carolina, here I come.*

Kayla hadn't been home in more than a decade. It wasn't that she hated going home, it was just that being in Los Angeles gave her the excuse she needed to stay away.

For a while, she'd been happy on the West Coast—working as an education consultant for Long Beach Community College. Five years ago, the grant had run out and she took a pay cut to keep the job she loved.

Things had been fine for a while, then her ex-husband, Raul, took care of the household bills. All of a sudden, overdue notices began coming in daily. Kayla was beyond pissed off. Even with her pay cut, their bills should've been paid on time.

Kayla closed her eyes and went back to six months ago when everything went to hell.

"Babe," Raul said as he burst through the door. "We're going to be rich."

Kayla looked up from her laptop and raised her right eyebrow. "What are you talking about?"

"The next Hamilton. I just made an investment with Julia Potter, the creator of The Obama Years. The music is great, the settings are going to be realistic, and . . ."

"Raul, really?"

He nodded excitedly. "It was only ten thousand dollars."

"Where in the hell did we get ten thousand dollars?"

"Borrowed it from your savings and mine."

Kayla stood still and took a deep breath. "Raul, that was all of our money!" she shrieked. "Have you lost your mind?"

Raul folded his arms across his chest. "That is that bull-shit I've been talking about."

"We're about to get evicted. I just negotiated with the power company to keep our lights on for one more week." Kayla picked up her plastic cup and tossed it at Raul's head. "An investment means stocks—not some crazy-ass musical."

Raul shook his head as he wiped the water from his face. "You're a dream killer."

"And you're an idiot."

"I'm so sick of this shit."

"Really? You know what I'm sick of? Not knowing what utility is going to get cut off this week. I'm sick of not knowing when my husband is going to get a job and try to help me keep this family afloat."

Raul scoffed. "Family? Really?"

She narrowed her eyes at him. "You're such a bastard sometimes."

Raul stomped out of the living room. Kayla closed her eyes and counted to ten. They were about to be homeless because she had been going to use some of their savings to pay the rent. Though jail would keep a roof over her head, she couldn't kill her husband and drop his body in the middle of the Pacific Ocean. However, she could sell everything that he *held dear, especially that 1965 Mustang that he'd sunk more money into than they had available.*

Kayla opened her eyes and slowly rose to her feet. When she walked into the bedroom, she was happy to see Raul packing.

"Are you at least going to leave your half of the rent?" Leaning against the door, she decided that she was done fighting for this marriage, and with a man who obviously wanted to be someplace else.

"All I'm leaving is you." Raul zipped his suitcase and shook his head.

Kayla folded her arms across her chest. "You've been planning this for a while, huh? Had you told me sooner, I would've gladly helped you pack."

"Platinum, World, and Emerald passengers are welcome to board at this time."

Kayla snapped to attention. She'd used the couple's travel credit card, since it was still in both of their names, and upgraded her seat. If she had to leave Los Angeles, at least she'd do it in comfort. Besides, after what she'd seen in the *LA Weekly*, she'd end up paying off the credit card anyway. Raul's great investment was a complete mess. She'd never see that money that Raul sank into that pile of steaming crap. Kayla deserved this luxury flight.

Chapter 2

DeShawn Carter was about to shut his computer down when the door to his office swung open.

"Mr. Carter, there's a fight in the gym!" a frantic student exclaimed. DeShawn leapt to his feet and darted downstairs to the gym. It was too close to Christmas break to have to deal with this foolishness. Especially when he had to find at least one hundred thousand dollars to cover the school's budget short-fall. When he arrived at the gym, DeShawn didn't find a fight but rather balloons, streamers, and the band playing "Happy Birthday."

He dropped his head and laughed. "Y'all got me out of breath. There better be some chocolate cake."

Taylor Parker, DeShawn's girlfriend, walked out to the center of the court holding a chocolate sheet cake with a sparkling candle in the center. "Happy birthday, darling."

DeShawn smiled for the crowd, but kept his comments to himself. He and Taylor hadn't called each other sweet names in months. As a matter of fact, she hadn't spoken to him all week. Not that he'd minded. His relationship with Taylor, who was one of the board members of the school, was starting to feel like it was a business transaction. Over the past three months, they were no longer talking about their future together as a couple but about how his job was in jeopardy because of the school's finances. And when he'd let her know that it was the board's fault for their inaction on finding new donors and applying for new grants, Taylor would accuse him of being against her. Or when she was feeling especially petty, she'd tell him that their relationship made it hard for her to fight for his ideas if she wanted to be taken seriously. All he really wanted to know some days was why were they still together?

DeShawn crossed over to her and kissed her cheek, then blew out the candle. "Thank you."

The band started playing again and DeShawn turned to his students, accepting the hugs and cards. He glanced over at Taylor, who was deep in conversation with the chairman of the board. The way she touched his arm and smiled at him, DeShawn knew she was flirting. He didn't even care.

"Mr. Carter, is it true you turned down the NFL to be our principal?" Harris James, a sophomore football player, asked.

DeShawn nodded at the school's star running back. "First, I gave up the NFL to be a teacher."

"Why?" The boy held up his smartphone, showing a photo of DeShawn catching a pass during his rookie season with the Dallas Cowboys. "You were awesome, man! You could've been better than Mo Goings."

"Then who would've been here to keep you knuckleheads in line?"

Harris shook his head. "You gave up the NFL for us?"

DeShawn shrugged. "Why not? Somebody had to give up something for me in order for me to be successful. How could I not pay it forward?" It also didn't hurt that DeShawn suffered a shoulder injury in his second year in the league, which he didn't recover fully from. So, instead of risking his health further, DeShawn took the money and ran. Since he had a degree in education, he'd gone back to UNC–Chapel Hill to get his master's degree, and decided to teach in his hometown. After three years of working in some of Charlotte's underperforming schools, DeShawn was tapped to lead Millwood Academy.

"But what about the money?" Robert Martin, the quarterback, asked. "You could've made millions."

"Sometimes, there are more important things in life than money. For me, it's you guys and this school."

"Man, Mr. Carter, you're something else." Harris smiled at DeShawn.

"Crazy is what he is. I want that NFL money."

"Get those grades first, then I will introduce the team to Mo Goings."

The football players gasped. "For real?"

DeShawn nodded. "Whole team average needs to be at least a three-point-two."

"Aww, man!" they cried.

"How are we going to do that?" Harris asked as he slapped his hands against his thighs.

"Back in my day, the kicker was always the smartest man on the team. Start a study group."

"We ain't never going to meet Mo," Harris said.

"Never say never. What's the motto?" DeShawn folded his arms across his chest.

"I can. I will. I can and I will achieve," the boys

barked. DeShawn gave them all a fist bump before moving over to another group of students. By the time he made it around the gym and shook hands with all the kids, DeShawn actually felt good about his birthday and the upcoming holiday break. But what he was most thankful for was it being the end of the day!

Being that his birthday was so close to Christmas, DeShawn never made a big deal about it. As a kid, he received combo gifts. However, having so many people around always made him feel good. He loved Christmas, normally. But this year, he was stressing more than celebrating because the school he loved was in trouble.

He was about to head out the door when Taylor stopped him. "You're not going to have any cake?"

"I have a few reports to finish up. Why don't you take my cake to Lucas?"

She folded her arms across her chest and cocked her head to the side. "What's that supposed to mean?"

"I have eyes, Tae."

"Then you should get them checked. He's the chairman of the board, and though you keep acting otherwise, the school is in trouble. I'm trying to intercede on your behalf. I can stop if you'd like. But wouldn't you like to ring in the New Year employed?"

DeShawn knew she was right, but he wasn't ready to admit that. As a private charter school, they depended on donations and a small amount of state funding. Donations had been down 20 percent this year.

"And what did you and Lucas come up with? You know, since you're working so hard for me over there feeding him cake and shit."

She rolled her eyes. "I'm going shopping, because you're acting like a child."

DeShawn watched her walk away and shook his head. *Why do I even put myself through this bullshit?* Heading back to his office, DeShawn decided that he wasn't going to worry about Taylor and Lucas. All he needed to do was focus on getting more money for his students.

As he read through his emails, DeShawn smiled when he saw an email about the West Charlotte Christmas social. It had been ten years since he'd graduated from high school. He wondered how some of his friends and former teammates were doing these days, and what they looked like. Chasing after students and having access to the school's gym allowed him to stay in good shape. Not as tight as he was when he was in the league, but he still had his six-pack and strong arms. Thinking of his high school days when he ran track, his best friend, Kayla Matthews, popped into his mind.

He'd always regretted that they lost contact when she'd gone to Los Angeles. More than anything else, he regretted never telling Kayla the truth about his feelings for her. How could he have asked her to stay in North Carolina when she'd been happy about getting a full ride to UCLA? And he'd known that her family couldn't afford to send her to Chapel Hill without a full scholarship.

DeShawn remembered that day. They'd just grabbed lunch from their favorite sandwich shop and were trading chips when Kayla hit him with her killer smile.

Lately her dimples had been popping—just like her smooth, caramel skin.

"What's up?"

"*This girl is going to Cali!*"

"*Really?*"

She reached into her backpack and pulled out her letter from UCLA. "*I got accepted! Can you believe it? I thought I was going to be stuck at Chapel Hill working in the cafeteria trying to pay for the other half of my tuition.*"

DeShawn took the letter and read over it. He wanted to be as happy as she was, but LA was so far away. "*Wow, you're going to be in Hollywood.*"

"*I know.*" She popped a chip in her mouth and DeShawn couldn't take his eyes off her sexy lips. Cherry red looked so good on them.

"*What?*" she asked, locking eyes with him.

"*I'm so proud of you. And I'm going to miss you.*"

"*Maybe when Carolina plays the Bruins we can hang out.*"

"*Don't think they're on the schedule this year, but there's no bad reason not to come to LA.*"

She smiled again and his heart melted. He started to open his mouth and tell her to stay and go with him to Chapel Hill. But he knew Los Angeles was her dream. Of course she wanted to get away from North Carolina, and as much as he wanted her to stay, he couldn't ask her to give up her dream.

"*What's wrong? You look like you want to say something.*"

Their eyes locked and DeShawn smiled. "*I'm just so proud of you.*"

"*Thank you.*" She reached over the table and gave him a tight hug. "*I'm going to miss you.*"

"*I'm going to miss you even more.*" They pulled apart and looked at each other. He wanted to kiss her, and as her bottom lip quivered, DeShawn wondered if she wanted to kiss him, too.

Rising from his desk, DeShawn hoped that Kayla would come home for the holidays. Then again, he wasn't sure if he was ready to see the married Kayla. Eight years ago, when he'd taken his last road trip with the Cowboys to Oakland, he'd reached out to Kayla and found out that she had gotten married.

His heart shattered like a plate glass window being hit by a rock. Married? Of course he'd played it off as if he'd been happy for her, and even offered her two tickets to the game.

"Aww, that is nice," she'd said. "But Raul and I won't be able to make it. That's a five-hour drive, and we're going to see a performance at the school tonight."

"I didn't realize Oakland was so far away from LA," he'd said, trying to hide his disappointment that he wouldn't get a chance to see her.

"Umm, someone needs a map," she quipped. "Maybe we can get together after the game? I'd love for you to meet my husband."

The words *my husband* coming out of Kayla's mouth jabbed the knife deeper into his already broken heart. DeShawn always felt that Kayla would end up in his arms, wearing his ring—just like one of those crazy chick flicks.

Now, he wondered if Kayla and her husband had children, and if so, how many. And were those dimples still as sexy as they were in high school?

DeShawn couldn't help but think about all the times they'd missed each other over the years. She couldn't come to his college graduation because she'd been doing an internship in LA. And when she'd given him a call to congratulate him after he'd been drafted, he'd missed the call because he was at a huge party.

And then there was the husband. He could've met the man, had he wanted to, but he didn't.

Life moved on, and DeShawn focused on the promise he'd made to his mother. Luwan made him promise to get his degree and be more than just a jock. While he'd kept his word to her, DeShawn had also listened to his father, Stewart, who told him to get that NFL money and keep that degree for plan B.

Teaching had never been his goal, but knowing that so many black students didn't see male teachers who looked like them, when he took his first teaching job DeShawn finally understood why his injury had been a good thing. Though this hadn't been the future he'd planned, it was a good life.

Returning to his desk, DeShawn replied to the email confirming that he would attend the holiday party. He wasn't going to take Taylor with him, because he wanted to have a good time.

"Welcome to Charlotte, North Carolina. Thank you for flying American Airlines and enjoy your stay."

Kayla yawned and lifted her hands above her head. She was happy to be on the ground, but being in Charlotte was bittersweet. Autumn was supposed to pick her up, and Kayla knew she wasn't going to have a warm reunion with her sister.

Their relationship had gone from bad to worse. Things had gotten so bad between them that her mother had had to make the call to Autumn to get her to pick Kayla up.

"You girls need to get it together and stop acting as if you're strangers."

"Well, technically we are."

Nora sighed. "Your sister is coming to pick you up. Try to be nice."

"I will if she does," Kayla muttered.

As she meandered slowly through the airport, not thinking about what time her sister was going to arrive, Kayla thought about her life in Los Angeles. She and Raul met during her sophomore year at UCLA. He'd been a theatre major at USC, and was stunning. Tall, caramel-brown skin, and a ponytail. Sitting in a coffee shop, she'd watched him walk into the building, and their eyes met. When he smiled at her, Kayla's knees went weak and she was glad to be sitting down.

He'd ordered his latte and crossed over to her. "Good afternoon, do you mind if I join you?"

"Not at all." She'd cleared a space for him at the table, then extended her hand. "I'm Kayla."

"Raul. Nice to meet you. Did I interrupt you finishing your screenplay?"

"No. Besides, I'm not a writer."

"I thought only beautiful writers sat in the front table at coffee shops."

Kayla laughed. "No, I just wanted to get away from campus for a while."

"USC?"

"Umm, no! UCLA."

"Well, I won't hold that against you."

They had fallen into an easy conversation that reminded her of DeShawn, who she missed immensely.

They had spent more time together, and over time Raul became more and more like her best friend. By senior year they'd become lovers. She'd wanted to share her new relationship with DeShawn over the years, but he was always busy. And when she saw how much of a star he was on the football field, she understood why.

She wondered if DeShawn was still in Charlotte and if she'd get a chance to see him while she was in town. Grabbing her bags from the claim area, Kayla headed to Starbucks.

After picking up her chai latte, Kayla took a slow sip and walked to the exit. A blaring horn caused her to look up. Locking eyes with her sister, Kayla offered her a half smile.

Autumn lowered the passenger-side window. "Can you hurry up?"

"Hello to you, too, Autumn," Kayla said, remembering that her mother had asked her to be nice.

Autumn rolled her eyes. "Welcome home, Kayla."

She dropped her bags in the back seat and got into the car. "Thanks for letting Mom talk you into picking me up."

"Well, I figured things must be pretty bad in Los Angeles if you're coming home after all these years. So, did he hit you or cheat on you?"

"What?"

"Your husband. What did you do to make him leave you?"

"All you need to know is that we're not together anymore."

Autumn flung her hair back. "Oh. Right. The divorce is final and everything. Rodney and I were going to come to LA for our anniversary, but we ended up in San Diego. It was so romantic."

Kayla rolled her eyes. "I bet it was." One thing she knew about her brother-in-law was that if there were a picture in the dictionary for henpecked, his smiling face would be right there.

"Oh, sorry. Don't want to rub it in that you don't have a man."

"You can't give us five minutes."

"What are you talking about? I'm just trying to be sensitive to your feelings."

Bullshit, Kayla thought with an eye roll.

"Anyway," Autumn continued, "what are you getting Mom for Christmas?"

"Haven't thought about it yet. I'm moving back here and I have a lot more on my mind than Christmas."

Autumn sucked her teeth. "Well, Christmas is less than a week away, so you might want to get something more on your mind than your move. She's expecting a big family Christmas this year."

Kayla closed her eyes and began rethinking her decision to return home.

By the time they arrived at their mother's house, Kayla was sick of Autumn's bragging. It was as if her sister was scratching at her pain. Typical Autumn.

"Kayla!" Nora exclaimed when she walked in the door. Kayla rushed over to her mother and gave her a tight hug.

"Hey, Ma."

Autumn sucked her teeth. "I'm here, too."

"Girl, I see you every day. This one is just a picture on my phone."

Folding her arms across her chest, Autumn rolled her eyes. "Well, I guess it's like that when you can't afford to come home."

"You know what! I'm sick of your damned mouth." Kayla stopped herself from getting in her sister's face and shaking her by her shoulders.

"Girls!" Nora exclaimed. "It is almost Christmas, and this is the first time that we've all been together in a long time. Can we have some peace?"

"Sure, Mom," Autumn said. "I have to go meet my husband." She turned to her sister. "See y'all later."

Kayla plopped down on the sofa and looked around the living room. It looked as if time had stood still, and she felt such a sense of comfort. She glanced at the picture of her father hanging over the fireplace. Kayla missed him immensely. He'd passed away when she was six years old and Autumn was three. That year, Kayla had lost her love for Christmas and the holiday season. While she mostly held her feelings in, Autumn acted out, which meant that Nora spent most of her time making sure Autumn was all right. Kayla always felt as if she had to make sure her mother didn't have two problem children. That's why Kayla could not wait to graduate and move to Los Angeles. No more dealing with Autumn's tantrums.

"How are you doing over there?" Nora asked when she returned to the living room with a tray of deviled eggs.

"Oh, Mom! I haven't had these in years." Kayla took one and nearly swallowed it whole.

"They don't have real food in LA?"

Kayla laughed as she wiped her mouth. "They really don't have Duke's Mayonnaise."

"You didn't answer my question, though. How are you doing?"

"Mom, I'm fine."

Nora raised her right eyebrow. "I don't believe you. With everything that happened, I know it was hard to come back home."

Kayla nodded and took another deviled egg from the tray. "But here I am, ready to start over." She forced a smile and ate the egg.

"I wish I could get my hands on that sucker Raul. How dare he put you in this position?"

Kayla rolled her eyes and released a sigh. "Because he's an asshole."

"Watch your mouth."

"Sorry. But it's the truth. Anyway, what are you planning for Christmas dinner?"

"Autumn and Robert wanted to do some catered thing. But I'm not eating generic mac and cheese. And we're going to put the tree up on Christmas Eve. It will be nice to have both of you here this year."

Kayla rose to her feet and stretched. "Sounds fun."

"Don't act like that. You and your sister need to stop this crap between y'all." Nora folded her arms across her chest. "Why do you two act like oil and water all the time?"

"Because Autumn thinks I owe her something and I don't understand, nor do I care to."

"Listen, your sister loves you, and both of you act as if you can't stand to be around each other. And I get pulled in the middle all the time. I'm sick and tired of it. You two are not little children anymore."

"Why don't you tell her that? I've been gone for ten years and she's still holding on to a grudge that I don't even know what it's all about."

"All I want is some peace between you two. That's all."

"It's hard, but for Christmas, I'm going to try." Kayla smiled at her mother.

"Guess who I saw at the grocery store yesterday?"

"Who?"

"DeShawn Carter."

Kayla's breath caught in her chest. "How is he?"

"Still fine and single. He told me that West Charlotte is having a Christmas social in a few days. You should go."

"I don't know, I haven't seen those people in years and . . ."

"So what! Have some fun and get out of this funk. I want you to have some fun."

"Mom, I have to find a job, find a place to live and . . ."

"You know Rome wasn't built in a day. You have a place to stay, and the job will come."

Kayla smiled. "Well, let me take a shower and unpack. Maybe I will go to the social and check out some old friends."

Nora smiled. "And by old friends I know you mean DeShawn. I've always liked him and wondered why you two never dated."

"DeShawn was my friend. It was like I was one of the boys," she said. But her mind went back to prom night, when things nearly crossed the line from friendship to that kiss.

Sighing, she thought about the biggest regret in her life. Letting DeShawn go. But once he made it to the NFL, she thought that he would move on with his life and become a millionaire. She knew that she wasn't going to be able to compete with all of the groupies and other women that he'd be around. And he was all the way in Dallas.

Besides, she'd been happy with Raul, for a while anyway. But when his acting and writing career didn't take off, he retreated into a world of fantasy that Kayla ignored until it became impossible to do so.

"You want some dinner?" Nora asked, breaking into Kayla's thoughts.

"No, I think I'm going to take a shower and go to bed. This time change is taking hold of me."

Nora gave her daughter a tight hug. "You rest, and we'll go shopping later if you feel like it."

"Sounds good, but I'm broke, remember."

"Did I ask you for money? I said we're going shopping."

"All right, Mom." Kayla kissed her mother on the forehead, then headed for her bedroom.

She wasn't surprised to see that her room hadn't changed much. The pale pink walls were still there, and the full-size bed that she'd slept in all of those years still had the daisy comforter on it. Kayla fell back on the bed and sniffed the familiar smell of home. She closed her eyes and drifted off to the most comfortable sleep she'd had in months.

DeShawn wiped the sweat from his brow as he stopped in the middle of the greenway. It was unseasonably warm for a December morning. He'd been jogging for an hour to try and get rid of the stress he'd been feeling. One of the school's biggest donors had cut their annual donation by 40 percent, which put the school even more in the red. Taylor had been emailing the board about the need for an emergency meeting. DeShawn was sure that his future hung in the balance.

"Can't worry about that now," he mumbled as he started running again. He stopped short when he saw a woman who looked like Kayla stretching on a bench. He crossed over to her.

"Kayla?"

Her head popped up, and when she smiled, his knees went weak.

Those dimples. That smooth skin.

"DeShawn!" She threw herself into his arms. His body returned to the ballroom where they'd danced ten years ago. She felt good and looked even better.

DeShawn stepped back before she could feel his desire growing. "It's good to see you."

"You too."

"When did you get into town?"

"Yesterday. My mama told me she saw you."

"She didn't tell me that you were blessing the Queen City with your presence, Hollywood." DeShawn drank in her image, clad in yoga pants and a cropped UCLA tank top. He wanted to touch her sculpted abs, but that would've been too forward.

"How have you been?" they asked in concert, then started laughing.

"I'm just out here trying to raise these kids," DeShawn said.

"Oh, you have children?" A crestfallen shadow clouded her face momentarily. "I know we haven't talked in a while, but you could've told me about the babies. I would've sent a gift or something."

"Oh, yeah? For about one hundred and fifty of them. I'm the principal at Millwood Academy." DeShawn started laughing.

"Wow, I had no idea. You look like you're still playing football. Obviously, I haven't been watching it lately." A slight blush spread across her cheeks.

DeShawn grinned and rocked back on his heels. "I had to retire a little earlier than expected. But it was worth it. I love working with these kids. But enough about me. What have you been up to?" He glanced down at her left hand and noticed there was no wedding ring there. He wasn't disappointed at all. Still, he wondered if she was upset about it and when her marriage ended. What if the man died?

She sighed and ran her hand across her face. "Well, I was working at Long Beach Community College, but budget cuts led to me being cut. So, I'm back."

"What are you going to be doing while you're here?"

"That's a good question. I have no idea at this point. Right now, I'm just going to celebrate the holidays with my family."

"Sounds like a good plan to me."

"Oh, happy belated birthday." She smiled again and those dimples drove his heart into overdrive.

"Thanks for remembering. So, are you going to the Christmas social?"

"I was thinking about it."

"Stop thinking and just go. We will have a great time. That is, if your husband doesn't mind."

"Got rid of that problem." She rolled her eyes. "And it was the best decision I've ever made."

"Ouch. I thought you and Raheim were in it for the long haul," he said, not attempting to hide his smile.

"His name is Raul, though I've been calling him everything but that lately." She sighed. "But anyway. Are you going to the social?"

DeShawn smiled and thought about seeing Kayla in a strappy gown holding a glass of champagne. She snapped her fingers in his face. "Hello?"

"My bad, I was just thinking about something."

"Your wife?" Kayla asked.

"Oh, hell no, I'm not married."

Kayla threw her hands up. "Whoa. You sound like you're the one who went through a nasty divorce."

"Marriage isn't for me, unless I meet the absolute right woman." *And she could be standing here in front of me right now.*

"Trust me, you don't want to marry the wrong person. Been there, done that. But now I'm happily divorced." She shook her head. "I never want to do that mess again. Hey, race you!" Kayla took off like a bullet. Her form from their track days was amazing.

And as much as he wanted to give her a challenge in the race, DeShawn couldn't take his eyes off her shapely ass. "Damn," he muttered as he started running to catch up with her.

Kayla ran away from DeShawn, not because she wanted to race, but because she couldn't stand there looking into his dark brown eyes and pretending that she wasn't still affected by that man. And what a man he'd grown into. Tall, dark, and handsome was definitely an understatement when it came to DeShawn. If he was fine in high school, now he was a sex symbol. She could only imagine how many girls acted out in school just to be sent to the principal's office. His glistening dark brown skin was almost her undoing. She remembered how she would watch him from the corner of her eye at track practice and how excited she'd get when he'd take his shirt off at the end of practice and strut around showing off those abs.

She released a cleansing breath as she reached the entrance of the greenway. When DeShawn touched her elbow, Kayla almost screamed.

"Damn, girl! You still got that speed."

"I did give myself a head start, and you know I was always faster than you." She winked at him. "But I couldn't carry a football, so it didn't matter."

"Want to grab a smoothie? There's a shop across the street that has a mean mango and banana drink."

Kayla glanced down at her watch, then realized that there was no need to pretend she had something to do. "Sure."

DeShawn smacked her backside like he used to do when they ran on the relay team together. "We got a lot of catching up to do."

Kayla's cheeks reddened as she smiled. How could this much time have passed, yet she was still so deeply attracted to this man?

They walked to the smoothie shop in a comfortable silence. When he put his arm around her while they crossed the street, Kayla closed her eyes and let her mind wonder what could've been if they had been more than friends.

"So," DeShawn said, breaking the silence. "You and Autumn aren't still beefing, are you?"

"Autumn is Autumn."

"Your sister has been one of the school's benefactors, though."

"Nice," Kayla said with an eye roll. "I'm surprised that she didn't try to date you."

DeShawn laughed. "She did."

Kayla shook her head. "Really?"

"I knew what it was all about. She missed you and wanted to get you back home by pissing you off with her happiness with me."

Kayla thumped him on his shoulder. Damn, his body was rock hard. "I would've killed you both. But you would've went first, since you know better."

"Aww," he said. "I had no idea that you cared." He leaned in and kissed her on the cheek, and Kayla wanted to melt.

They walked into the smoothie shop, ordered their drinks, and grabbed a table in the corner.

"When did you and Raul get divorced?" He jabbed at his drink with his straw.

"It was finalized last month. But we probably should've ended things last year." Kayla took a sip of her drink, then looked at him. "And you never took that trip down the aisle or came close to it?"

He shook his head. "Nope. I thought I was going to, but I can't find what I'm looking for."

"Please, I figured after you made it to the NFL you'd have a harem."

"Really, Hollywood?"

"Stop calling me that. I never got into the whole Hollywood scene. As a matter of fact, that's why I'm not married now."

"You married an actor?"

Kayla rolled her eyes. "No, worse, a wannabe producer. But I don't even want to think about that idiot."

"No love lost, huh?"

"Just a lot of money." Kayla sighed and rolled her eyes. "That fool took all of our money and invested it in a play about Obama that flopped like a dozen pancakes."

"Wow. I think I heard about that. Damn."

Kayla nodded. "Imagine how I felt when he strolled into our place and said he just put all of our money in this lame duck. Not to mention we'd been struggling to pay our bills. If I wasn't afraid of jail, he would've died that day."

"I'm sorry you had to deal with that, Kayla." DeShawn placed his hand on top of hers and she felt electric jolts.

"It's all right."

"Actually, it isn't. You should be treated like the queen you are, and never worry about some knucklehead making you feel insecure about your finances."

Kayla got lost in his eyes and his words hugged her heart.

"What?" he asked as he noted her silence.

"Nothing. It's just . . . Well, you always had a way with words. Thanks for that."

"Kayla, I hate that we . . . um . . . lost contact all those years ago."

She nodded. "Me too. But we can catch up now."

"I say we start tonight with a movie."

"*Remember the Titans?*"

DeShawn nodded. "You know it. I'll pick you up from your mom's place around eight."

"All right. Well, I'd better get back to the house. I slept through a shopping trip last night, and I told my mama that I'd join her and Autumn for a trip to the mall today."

"Good luck with that. How did we do it back in the day when we'd spend hours at the mall?"

"Doing nothing, broke as hell," Kayla said with a laugh.

"But you always had money for Cinnabon!" He slapped his hand on the table. "And were selfish! Never wanted to share the extra icing."

"That was the best part of it all. And I was only thinking about you. All that sugar would've slowed you down on the field."

DeShawn's face softened. "This feels so good."

"I know. But I'd better get out of here if I don't want to face the wrath of Autumn. She lives for shopping."

"Before you go, give me your number so I can call you and make sure you haven't forgotten about our movie date later." DeShawn pulled his phone out of his armband and Kayla rattled off her number.

"Got you locked in." Then he snapped a picture of her.

"Come on, man, I look a mess."

"You're never a mess. You've always been beautiful."

Kayla smiled, and those dimples were back. As

she rose to her feet, DeShawn drank in her image and was filled with want and desire. How was he going to keep his hands to himself when they watched the movie? It was tough to do in high school; now it was going to be virtually impossible.

Chapter 3

Kayla walked into her mother's house and was surprised to see Autumn sitting at the kitchen table munching on bacon and eggs.

"Oh, you've been out running, huh?"

"Yeah." Kayla struggled not to roll her eyes. It was too soon for another sister battle.

"Guess that's the Cali thing to do, huh?"

"I like running, it clears my mind. And I ran track in high school, remember?"

Autumn rolled her eyes. "Oh, how could anyone forget the amazing Kayla running in circles for all the applause."

Sighing, Kayla took a seat at the breakfast bar and glanced around the kitchen. It seemed to be the only room her mother had changed. Stainless steel replaced the familiar white appliances that had been a part of the past. "Where's Mom?"

"In the shower. You want something to eat? I think there are some eggs left."

"I'm good. I had a smoothie and I ran into DeShawn on the greenway."

Autumn rolled her eyes. "That guy."

Kayla scoffed. "Guess you're still salty because he wouldn't date you?"

"That's what he said? Didn't nobody want his broke-down ass. I was just being friendly."

"Sure."

Autumn dropped her fork. "What are you, jealous?"

"Hardly."

"Why are you acting like you and DeShawn dated or something? According to you, he was just your friend."

"He is my friend."

"Tell the truth and shame the devil, you let him hit that, didn't you?"

"You're so crass."

"And maybe if you didn't have a stick up your ass, you'd still have your husband."

"I'm not doing this with you. Have your temper tantrum alone." Kayla hopped off the barstool and headed to her room. Autumn followed her out of the kitchen.

"You always thought you were better than everybody. Now, look at you—broke and divorced. Don't come waltzing in here like you're the shit when it's obvious that you're a failure."

Kayla wanted to slap the taste out of Autumn's mouth, because her words hurt with the sting of the truth.

"I can't control what you think. But know this, Autumn—I also don't give a damn what you think. As a matter of fact, you can kiss my black . . ."

"Girls!" Nora exclaimed. "I'm not having this!"

They whirled around and looked at their mother. "It's Christmas and this is the first time in years we've been together. And we're going to celebrate without all of this bickering. Do you hear me? If I have to get a switch, don't think I won't!"

"Yes, ma'am," they mumbled.

Nora turned to Kayla. "Now, you get ready so we can get to the mall before it gets too crowded." Then she focused on Autumn. "And there'd better not be a dirty dish in the sink. When I get dressed, we're leaving and no one is going to be arguing today!"

Kayla took off for the shower. When her mother threatened them with a switch, they always took notice, no matter how grown they were.

About an hour later, the Matthews women were on their way to the mall. Despite Autumn volunteering to drive her Benz, Nora loaded her girls into her old minivan like they used to do back in the day. Kayla climbed in the back seat and smiled. When they were younger, she'd grab her favorite book and read while her mother drove and Autumn talked about herself.

That hadn't changed, because her sister was going a mile a minute about how she was going to decorate her house and what Rodney had better buy her for Christmas.

"You're going to drive that man into the poorhouse," Nora said as she turned into the mall parking lot.

"He can be roomies with Kayla," Autumn snipped.

Kayla cleared her throat. "He'd probably be happier than sharing a house he can't afford with you."

"Stop this right now!" Nora said. "You two need to grow up."

"I was just joking," Autumn said. "She's the one who took it personal."

"Whatever," Kayla said.

"I will get a switch. I'm not playing."

"Yes, ma'am," Kayla said.

Autumn nodded. "Let's just get this over with. I hate the mall. I prefer using Closet Cloud."

"You act like you're the Queen of Sheba sometimes," Nora said. "You need to humble yourself."

Amen, Kayla thought as they crossed the parking lot.

"Do you just save these lectures for me, or did you tell Kayla these things before she took off to California?"

"I don't have anything to do with the fact that you're an ass," Kayla snapped.

Nora stopped walking and turned to her daughters. "You know what, I'm not putting up with this from you two. Figure out how to get home on your own. And when you come back to the house, you'd better have some Christmas spirit in you."

Kayla and Autumn looked at each other as their mother stalked away. "Autumn, we can't keep doing this."

"What's the problem? You can't handle not being the center of attention?"

Kayla rolled her eyes. "That's always been your petty job. And I'm sick and tired of fighting with you for no reason. What's your problem with me?"

"You're the problem. You left town and didn't look back at all. Mom was worried about you and you didn't give two shits. You were out there living the life until everything fell apart. Now you're back and I'm supposed to be happy and bow down because the queen is back."

"Forget you, Autumn. You don't know what I've been through, and I've never pretended I was better than you. I was simply older than you and I wanted to make sure my little sister didn't make some of the mistakes that I made or saw other girls make."

"You wanted to run my life."

"Whatever. You wanted to grow up too fast, and the last thing Mama needed was your bullshit. Things were hard enough without Daddy, and you—"

"Stop it!" Autumn yelled as she pushed her sister. "Don't act like you were perfect. And don't tell me I caused problems that weren't there."

"You made everything that didn't go your way a problem, with your whining and bitching."

"Don't act like you were the only one who saw her pain. Most of it was worrying about sending you to college because you wanted to get away, like home was so bad."

"You ever consider your role in that?" Kayla rolled her eyes and folded her arms across her chest. "Why do you hate me so much?"

"Kayla, I've been jealous of you all my life."

"Why?"

She sighed and ran her hand across her face. "You remember Dad. You know what his voice sounded like. All I know about him is the pictures in photo albums." Tears welled up in Autumn's eyes. "You and Mom always had that. Y'all had those memories and I had nothing. Then you two would pull out the photo albums at night and talk about him. It was like I was on the outside looking in. I resented you for that."

"Why did you let it fester?"

Autumn folded her arms across her chest. "You're not easy to talk to, Kayla. You're always looking for an argument from me."

"I don't have to look far, Autumn. I say good morning and you start with an attack. If you wanted to talk about how you were feeling, you could've done that a long time ago."

"How? Whenever you had free time you were running track or hanging out with DeShawn."

Kayla couldn't say that her sister was wrong. Back in the day, she did spend more time with DeShawn than she did with her sister. Being with him had been easy and simple. And it took her mind off missing her father, not being able to share track stories with him and stare into his eyes.

"We both could've done things differently, then and now. The best gift we can give Mom this year is not arguing."

"Fine." Autumn sighed. "And I'm sorry that your life in California came crashing down because your husband was a stupid asshole. If you want to, we can go kick his ass."

"Raul isn't worth it, but thanks for the offer." Kayla opened her arms to her sister and they hugged tightly.

"I still say you and DeShawn did it."

Kayla pinched Autumn on the shoulder. "We did not!" *At least not yet.*

"Well, if you get a second chance, I hope you plan on taking it. Broke down or not, he's still fine." Autumn winked at her sister, then pulled out her phone. "I'm going to call an Uber."

"Wait." Kayla pointed at their mother's van. "Mom never left."

"She is so shady."

"I guess that's where you get it from," Kayla quipped.

"Where *we* get it from." She wrapped her arm around Kayla's shoulder and they waved at their mother. Nora opened the door, got out of the car, and walked over to her daughters.

"Can we finally shop now?" Nora asked.

"Yes, we can," Kayla said.

* * *

DeShawn sat down on the sofa and picked up his laptop. He really didn't want to check the emails that had stacked up in his inbox since his run. But he couldn't keep hiding from reality—even if he was supposed to be on vacation. He clicked the email icon and there was the message he'd been dreading. The board had called an emergency meeting for tomorrow.

"Shit," he muttered as he read over the email. "This is going to be good." Slamming his laptop shut, DeShawn padded into the kitchen and grabbed a beer from the fridge. At least he still had Kayla to look forward to.

"DeShawn!" Taylor walked in the front door of his house, reminding him that he needed to get his key back.

"In the kitchen," he called back. She walked in, dressed in a black pantsuit and holding her iPad.

"We have a situation and we're going to need to put our heads together so that we can convince the board that we're going to save the school."

DeShawn sipped his beer and eyed her nonchalantly. "Umm, no."

"Why are you drinking this early in the day? Do you realize how much trouble you and the school are in? I didn't . . . What's going on with you these days?"

DeShawn leaned against the sink and downed the rest of his craft beer. "I have a better question for you: What's going on with you? Taylor, once upon a time you gave a damn about educating the kids at Millwood. You and I were on the same page. Something changed, and I don't understand where and when that happened."

"This isn't about me. This—"

"It is about you. And don't stand there and act as if you and Lucas aren't—"

"So, this is about your imagination running wild. There is nothing going on with me and Lucas. If you think that there is something going on with us, then you must be doing something on the side yourself."

"What are we doing, other than arguing? That was a nice little show that you put on at the school on my birthday, but you and I know this isn't working."

"How did a discussion about the school turn into this?"

"Because I don't want to waste any more time, Tae. This isn't working."

She slammed her iPad on the breakfast bar. "Who is she?"

DeShawn sighed and shook his head. "She's you. Taylor, you're not the woman I see spending the rest of my life with, and I'm tired of wasting your time and mine."

She released a sigh and shook her head. "What was this relationship about? Job security?"

"Never that. You're the one who changed, and I don't like who you've become."

She snatched her key off her key ring and tossed it in his direction. "I'm out. And for the record, Lucas wants you out. So, if I were you, I'd watch my back." Taylor stormed out of the house and slammed the front door so hard that it vibrated throughout the house.

"Tell me something I don't know," he muttered as he grabbed another beer.

Chapter 4

It was after four when the Matthews women finally left the mall. Kayla was happy that she and her sister had called a truce and were able to have a good time with their mother.

"What are we doing tonight?" Autumn asked as they got into the car. "Are we going to get the tree?"

"Not yet," Nora said. "I haven't decided if I want a live tree or not."

"And I have plans this evening. DeShawn and I are going to watch a movie."

Nora glanced at Kayla and smiled. "So, you've seen him."

"They went running together this morning, still being lame." Autumn yawned. "I don't know why y'all don't . . ."

"DeShawn and I are just friends and we haven't seen each other in ten years. We're just catching up and rebuilding our friendship."

"Umm, yeah, okay."

"Leave her alone," Nora said. "But I do have to say, I've always liked DeShawn. And for him to come back to Charlotte and take over that school because he wanted young black men to see a teacher who cared about them and looked just like them. He could've been coaching in the NFL, from what I heard."

"Oh, you just heard that?" Kayla laughed.

"Well, I did keep an eye on what was going on with DeShawn, hoping that he would be around when or if you came back. You know he's never been married."

"Ma!" Kayla said as Autumn chuckled.

"Just putting it out there. I always thought you two should've gotten together anyway," she said. "Let's stop and get something to eat."

"Sushi?" Autumn suggested.

"The only fish I want is breaded and fried. We're going to Hometown Delights."

Kayla looked at her watch. "Maybe I should call DeShawn and let him know I might be late for the movie."

"We'll have you out of the restaurant in time to watch your movie. I'll even buy you some popcorn," Autumn said. "And I'm not trying to be a jerk about your current situation."

"Thanks." Kayla rolled her eyes. "But I'm sure DeShawn will have popcorn at his place."

"Oh. You're watching the movie at his house. With no parental supervision, huh," Autumn said.

"Hush."

Nora laughed. "I'm still going to have to get a switch for y'all."

Arriving at the restaurant, Kayla felt excited to be with her sister and mother for the first time in years. The Christmas music blaring from the speakers belied the heat outside. Autumn shimmied her shoulders to Donny Hathaway's soulful voice.

"I love this song. But it never snows here for

Christmas. Rodney and I were going to head to Denver this year, but we have a reason to sweat for the season now." She nudged Kayla in the side.

"Where is Rodney?" Kayla asked.

"He's going to be back tonight. He's been in New York for the last week, doing some IT work at the company's headquarters. I thought he was coming in last night. I drove all the way to the airport only to get a text saying that he wouldn't be here until tonight." Autumn shook her head and sighed. "That man can be infuriating sometimes."

Kayla nodded but noticed the look on her mother's face. She couldn't help but wonder if her sister was hiding something. Since things were going so well between them, she decided to keep her questions to herself.

DeShawn finished vacuuming the living room and then started the search for his *Remember the Titans* DVD. When he found it on the back of the shelf, he smiled. How many times had he and Kayla watched this movie? She loved Denzel, like most women, but he watched the movie with her because it made her smile and he loved those dimples. Loved so much about her that he'd never been able to say so. Kayla had to be one of the strongest women he'd ever known.

She ran track to honor her father's memory, and she'd wanted to go to UCLA because that had been his dream as well. Unlike a lot of the girls in their high school, Kayla knew what she wanted. Over the years, he'd say that her strength had grown. He wished they'd been able to stay closer, especially after what she said about her husband. Seeing her today made him realize that she was the one who got away. As much as he wanted to tell her that tonight, he knew it was too soon.

He was going to make some snacks and open a nice bottle of wine. Tonight, he wasn't even going to talk about the school, because he wanted to have a good time, not think about the target painted on his back.

Pulling out his phone, he texted Kayla to make sure they were still getting together at eight. He really just wanted to hear from her.

Yes, I'm having a late lunch with my mom and Autumn right now. But I'll be ready at eight. Please tell me you have kettle corn.

I'll get some. I forgot you like that nasty stuff.

Shut your mouth. Kettle corn is the best!

I'll take your word for it. I can't wait to see you tonight.

I'm looking forward to it as well.

DeShawn shoved his phone in his pocket and grabbed his keys. He needed to go find kettle corn.

He headed to the farmer's market, hoping to catch it before it closed. He remembered how he and Kayla used to go there and buy cranberries and popcorn to make garlands for the winter athletic banquet. He'd always thought it was a tedious undertaking, but being with Kayla always made it fun. He'd never told her about his fantasy of wrapping her up in that garland and then freeing her with his lips, tongue, and teeth.

Back then, he probably would've gotten something

wrong—bit when he should've licked, or licked where she needed to be bitten. But today, he'd lavish that amazing body with so much pleasure that she'd go hoarse screaming his name.

Or maybe she'd make him scream. Kayla had lips that launched wet dreams and fantasies. He wondered how her lips would feel against his, how those lips would feel wrapped around the throbbing erection pressing against his zipper. He shook those erotic thoughts from his mind as he walked into the market. He was happy to see a display of kettle corn, cheddar cheese popcorn, and his favorite caramel popcorn. He grabbed a bag of each flavor and headed for the cashier. When he saw the cranberries, he grabbed a package for old times' sake. Maybe they could decorate his tree and he could possibly get that taste of her he'd been fantasizing about for a decade.

Kayla knew she was excited to see DeShawn when she turned down her favorite dessert at Hometown Delights. Her mother must have known it, too, when she told the waiter that she and Autumn would take their cake to go.

"Guess somebody has to get ready for her date," Autumn said as she downed the last of her Duplin wine.

"It's not a date. We're just watching a movie."

"At least wear some pretty panties, just in case."

"Autumn!" Nora said through her chuckle. "You can put a little lipstick on, though."

"Mom!" Kayla exclaimed.

"And do something with your hair. It's been a long time since you've seen this man, and I know for a fact that friends make the best lovers. Your dad and I were best friends before we started dating. Best thing that ever happened to him was the day I told him that I didn't want to be his friend anymore."

"This is not the same thing," Kayla said. "Besides, DeShawn—"

"Has probably been in love with you as long as you've loved him." Nora shook her head. "But both of you are pretty clueless."

"Amen," Autumn said. "I knew he was in love with her when he turned me down."

"Autumn," Nora said. "You're a mess. Come on, let's go so Kayla can change her clothes for her date."

"It's not a date," she said as they rose to their feet. "It's just a movie."

"Whatever you say, Kayla," Autumn said.

The ride back to Nora's was light and fun as her mother and sister teased Kayla. She wondered if DeShawn was as aware of her feelings as her mother and sister seemed to be. One of the reasons she'd lost touch with him had nothing to do with the distance between them, but more to do with the unrequited love she felt in her heart.

Kayla had always believed that DeShawn saw her as one of the guys, and she couldn't take that. Being across the country gave her the distance that she needed to forget about him. She thought that when she and Raul had married she would've gotten over DeShawn. But the end of her marriage and seeing DeShawn again awakened a desire in her that she'd thought was dead.

When they arrived home, Kayla thought she'd be able to dress herself for her movie with DeShawn. But when she walked in her room and Autumn followed her, Kayla knew her sister was going to offer her fashion advice.

"I can dress myself," Kayla said as she watched her sister plop down on the bed.

"Sure you can, but you and this man haven't been alone in ten years. Show him what he's been missing. As much as I hate to admit it, you have an amazing body."

"It runs in the family." Kayla smiled at her curvy sister. Autumn shimmied her shoulders.

"And you need to use what you got to get what you want. You can stop denying it, but you want DeShawn." Autumn nodded. "Go for it."

"While you're sitting here giving me advice on what to do about DeShawn, can I ask you a question?"

"What?"

Kayla inhaled sharply. She knew the peace between them was temporary, but she was concerned about her sister. Focusing on Autumn, Kayla just asked the question.

"Is everything all right between you and Rodney?"

Autumn's smile faded. "What do you mean?"

"Never mind."

"No, why do you think there is a problem in my marriage?"

Kayla leaned against the dresser and sighed. "You and Rodney are normally joined at the hip, and all I've seen so far is you doing a lot of talking about him."

"He's on a business trip. You know what, I know misery loves company, but don't try to make me a member of your party."

"I'm not. Even though Raul and I were at each other's throat before the divorce, I wouldn't wish this on anyone."

"Don't worry, my marriage is fine."

Kayla didn't like the look in her sister's eyes, but she was going to take her at her word.

"Can I be honest?" Autumn said. "I never liked Raul."

"Well, we don't have to worry about seeing him ever again, thank the Lord."

"And Rodney and I are working through some issues. Mainly, he wants a baby and I don't."

Kayla sat beside her sister and wrapped her arm around her shoulders. "Why don't you want a baby? You'd be a great mother."

"No, I wouldn't. I'm not selfless like Mom. I like being a housewife without the mother part."

Kayla dropped her hand to her abdomen and closed her eyes. The day she'd miscarried her baby had also marked the end of her marriage. She'd been in her office and a student had found her collapsed on the floor. After she'd been rushed to the hospital, no one could find Raul.

Kayla had never felt more alone in her life. She'd called her mother after the doctor told her about the miscarriage. She'd been eight weeks pregnant, and had wanted to go to North Carolina and tell her mother in person that she'd be a grandmother soon.

That call had forced her to take stock of her life and her marriage. Kayla had been hiding in California, living a life filled with regrets rather than the life she'd dreamed about when she'd been a student at UCLA. When she'd tried to tell Raul about wanting to shake things up, he seemed to tune her out. He'd wanted a Hollywood lifestyle, and put them in the poorhouse to get it.

He hadn't comforted her after they lost the baby; in fact, Raul acted as if it didn't even happen.

"What's wrong?" Autumn asked, breaking into her sister's dark thoughts.

"Nothing." Glancing at her watch, Kayla rose to her feet. "I'd better get ready."

"You shower and I'll pick out your outfit." Autumn rubbed her hands together.

"Why am I scared all of a sudden?" Kayla walked into the bathroom and took a quick shower. Autumn knocked on the door as Kayla shut the water off.

"The outfit is on the bed. Just put it on and you don't even have to worry about wearing panties."

"Autumn!" When Kayla opened the door, her sister was gone. She walked into her room and looked at the red maxi dress laid out on her bed. *Festive, but it's just a movie.* Kayla was about to grab a pair of jeans and T-shirt when her door opened.

"Put on the dress!" Nora said.

"Ma!"

"Autumn told me to make sure you didn't come out of this room looking like you're going to a football game. Put on the dress."

"Fine," Kayla said as her mother shut the door. She picked up the dress and held it against her damp skin. It would work. She'd wear the damn dress.

Chapter 5

DeShawn looked at the white rose he'd gotten for Kayla. Part of him wanted to toss it out the window. Maybe it was too much. After all, they were just going to watch a movie that they had seen a thousand times. And she was his friend. But he wanted more, and wanted to make his intentions clear. He was going to give her the rose.

Ten years was a long time to keep silent. That was going to end right now. He cranked up his car, headed in the familiar direction of Kayla's childhood home. When he'd moved back to Charlotte after his career in the NFL ended, Nora's house had been the second stop he'd made. Of course, he'd been hoping to run into Kayla. But her mom informed him that she was still in California.

They'd talked for an hour that day, and DeShawn had even offered to take care of her lawn work, but Nora said she'd had it handled and told him that she'd love to have him over for dinner.

Before the problems started at the school, he'd have dinner with her once a month. But he hadn't been brave enough to ask for Kayla's phone number, since the last number he'd had for her was disconnected. How could he tell Kayla's mother that he wanted to make love to her daughter? Her married daughter, at that.

Now he would have the chance to put all his cards on the table with Kayla and teach her a Christmas lesson they'd both enjoy.

He was about twenty minutes early when he arrived at Kayla's, but he'd waited long enough, and being early wasn't going to hurt anything.

"Hello, DeShawn," Autumn said when she opened the door. "Nice to see you. Come on in."

He smiled at Autumn, with her flamboyant self. Sometimes it was hard to believe that she and Kayla were sisters. They were like night and day. "How are you doing, Ms. Lady?"

"I'm great. Have a seat. Ma, DeShawn is here."

Nora walked into the living room with a smile on her face. "Hey there, DeShawn. How are you?"

"I'm good, Miss Nora." He crossed over to her and gave her a hug.

"I didn't get a hug. I'm feeling some kind of way," Autumn quipped. Then she walked into the kitchen.

"That girl is something else," DeShawn said with a laugh.

Nora nodded. "She gets it from her father. Come on and sit down."

Autumn returned to the living room with a pitcher of eggnog and three glasses. "Kayla should be down in a minute."

"Thanks," he said as she poured the eggnog.

* * *

Kayla wasn't sure why she let Autumn and her mother talk her into wearing a dress. She looked at her reflection in the mirror and thought the red maxi dress was too much, but it did give a boost to her C-cup cleavage. She started to adjust her girls, then dropped her hands.

"It's just a movie." Still, Kayla toyed with her hair until she was satisfied with her bushy curls. She headed into the living room and was surprised to see DeShawn sitting on the sofa, sipping eggnog with Autumn and Nora.

"Wow," he said when their eyes locked. "Kayla, you look amazing."

"Thanks," she said as she crossed over to him and gave him a tight hug.

Autumn nudged her mother. "That's an extra friendly hug."

DeShawn and Kayla broke their embrace.

"Whatever," Kayla said. Her cheeks heated with embarrassment.

"Ladies, it was good to see you again," DeShawn said as he and Kayla headed for the door.

"Sorry about that," she said once they were outside.

"Everything is cool. Your family still cracks me up." He chuckled. "I think your sister was trying to get me drunk with the eggnog."

"Maybe we should've taken some of that with us." Kayla laughed, though she knew drinking alcohol would be a bad idea. She gave DeShawn a sidelong glance. He made those black slacks and white oxford shirt look so good. You couldn't tell her that he wasn't a *GQ* model.

"Do you want to go out? I mean, you look so great in that outfit, I'd hate to waste it sitting on my sofa."

"No, the sofa is fine. Because we're not going to

find *Remember the Titans* on the big screen. And you got my kettle corn, right?"

"And a few more surprises." He opened the door for her. Kayla shivered as she thought about the surprises he had in store.

DeShawn got into the car and handed Kayla the rose from his dashboard. "This is for you."

"Thanks. It's beautiful."

"Just like you," he said as he started the car.

Kayla blushed and turned to the window. "You're being extra sweet right now."

"Well, I've missed you, and I just wanted to share that with you."

"Thanks, DeShawn."

"You sure you want to spend the evening on my sofa?" He gave her a slow once-over, then pulled off from the curb.

"Just like old times. Only we can officially have adult beverages without looking over our shoulder for your mom."

DeShawn laughed, thinking about the days when they snuck rum and cola into their cups as they watched movies or studied. "You know I would've never made it out of calculus if it wasn't for you."

"And look at you now, running a school. I'm so proud of you."

He sighed. "Don't be. If things don't turn around with the fund-raising, I'm not going to be running anything."

"What's going on?"

"I don't want to bore you with that."

"That's what I did in California, so it's not boring. If I can help, I'd love to."

"Kayla, I'm going to take you up on that offer. I hope you don't regret it."

She smiled. "I won't."

When they arrived at DeShawn's ranch-style house in South Charlotte, Kayla marveled at the manicured lawn and the sparkling Christmas lights decorating the porch and the shrubs. Then there was the inflatable snow globe in the middle of the yard.

"Someone is in the holiday spirit," she said as they climbed out of the car.

"It's the most wonderful time of the year." He pulled Kayla into his arms and spun her around as if music was playing. She went along with it, laughing the entire time.

"All that's missing is snow," Kayla said. He spun her around one more time.

"When's the last time it snowed in Charlotte at Christmas?"

"That's a good question."

"Let's go inside before Mrs. Grant comes out here with her fruitcake."

"What's wrong with a good piece of fruitcake?"

"It's not good."

"Then let's go," she said.

As soon as they walked up the steps, the door next to DeShawn's house opened. "Mr. Carter, have you forgotten about your fruitcake?"

"Hey, Mrs. Grant. I've been busy. Just haven't had time to stop by."

"Umm-huh. So, who's this lovely lady? She doesn't look like that uppity one who was here earlier."

Kayla raised her right eyebrow but didn't say a word. She couldn't be jealous that he had someone else at his house. *The man is single and fine. Besides, we're just friends.*

"This is Kayla Matthews. We went to high school

together, then she disappeared on me and went to Hollywood."

"Oh, you're an actress? I thought you were a model."

"That's really nice, but I'm not an actress."

"You sure look like one. Baby, you want some fruitcake?"

"Say no," DeShawn whispered. "Tell her you're on a diet."

"I'd love some." Kayla nudged DeShawn in the stomach. Mrs. Carter's face lit up.

"Hold on right there."

DeShawn shook his head. "You don't know what you just did."

"She seems so sweet. Stop being mean."

"You'll see."

A few minutes later, Mrs. Grant, dressed in a flower-print housedress, hobbled across the yard with a covered dish in her hand, "I bake about three of these every week until Christmas. Everyone loves them." She smiled and handed Kayla the dish. "Go on, open it. This one has nuts in it."

DeShawn covered his mouth to hide his laugh as Kayla opened the dish. The little cake was shaped like a brick, and when she touched it, it felt like one as well.

"This looks great, I'm sure we're going to enjoy it."

"Go ahead and break a piece off now."

DeShawn shook his head. *Don't do it,* he mouthed. Kayla winked at him and attempted to break off a piece of the cake.

"You know what," Kayla said with a smile, "I want to enjoy this with a cup of coffee." She licked her finger.

Mrs. Grant nodded. "That's going to be good. And

you know you can stand to put a little meat on your bones, so have a big piece for breakfast."

"Will do."

DeShawn couldn't take his eyes off Kayla's lips as she licked her finger. Did she realize how sexy she was? His body was filled with want, and at that moment, he wanted to be that finger.

"DeShawn, are you going to open the door?"

"Huh? Yes." He turned to Mrs. Grant. "Thanks for the cake."

"Oh, that's for her. I'll bring you yours tomorrow." The older woman smiled at him. "You know, I will never be able to thank you for all that you did for my grandson. He's going to be playing in one of those bowl games on TV. And that's all because of you."

"You don't have to thank me for doing my job. Let Marquis know that I'm going to be rooting for him."

The older woman waved at the duo as she crossed over into her yard. When Mrs. Grant was out of earshot, Kayla turned to DeShawn. "That was the nastiest thing I've ever tasted."

"I tried to tell you, but you didn't want to listen. Come on, let me get you a brandy to wash that taste out of your mouth." What he wanted to do was lavish her sexy mouth with kisses until she didn't think about fruitcake ever again.

"Brandy? Aren't you fancy and old now?"

DeShawn opened the door and held it for Kayla. "You're going to be just as old as I am in a few months."

"Ooh, you remembered."

"Your birthday is Valentine's Day, it's kind of hard to forget. Grab a seat on the sofa and I'll be right back with the popcorn and drinks." Before leaving the room, he flipped a switch and turned the Christmas tree lights on. The twinkling white lights cast a glow over the room that made Kayla shine. He thought about making love to her underneath the tree and what a great gift that would be.

She walked over to the tree and stood there looking as if she was right at home. As if she belonged in that spot.

"DeShawn, you know what's missing from your tree?"

"Let me guess— popcorn and cranberries?"

She turned back and looked at him. "Yep."

He held up a finger. "Be right back."

DeShawn grabbed the tray with the kettle corn, caramel corn, the plain popcorn, and dried cranberries. Then he slipped a bottle of wine underneath his arm.

"Look what I got," he said as he set the tray on the table. "Kettle corn and popcorn to string."

Kayla clasped her hands together and crossed over to the sofa. "You remembered."

"How could I forget? We did this for three years because you wanted to make the banquets look better."

"And it worked. You got pretty good at stringing popcorn. Let's see if you still got it." Kayla grabbed a handful of kettle corn. DeShawn laughed as she stuffed a few kernels in her mouth.

"They don't have kettle corn in Hollywood?"

She tossed a few kernels at him. "Shut up. You know it's just something about Carolina corn that's sweeter."

"There's something I've always wondered," he said as he closed the space between them.

"What's that?"

"How sweet are you?" DeShawn captured her mouth, slipping his tongue between her lips. It seemed as if she melted in his arms like butter on hot grits. He couldn't believe Kayla was in his arms and he'd finally gotten his kiss. When their lips parted and he looked into her eyes, one thing was certain: This was not going to be enough.

"DeShawn," she murmured as she ran her fingers up and down his neck. The waves of desire that she sent through his body felt like a forest fire.

"Kayla, I—" She cut him off when she leaned in for another kiss. Her lips were like sugar, her tongue was like nectar, and he was ready to taste every inch of her delectable body.

She pulled back from him, pressing her hand against his chest. "We're going to watch this movie, right?"

"We can do anything you want. But I've been waiting ten years for that."

"Was it worth it?"

DeShawn nodded. "And I tell you something else, I'm not going to wait another ten years for another kiss, Hollywood."

"Is that so?"

DeShawn nodded and brushed his lips across hers again. "But right now, we got popcorn to string." As hard as it was for DeShawn to let her go, he was encouraged to know that it wouldn't take another decade for him to have his chance with Kayla.

Chapter 6

The movie credits were rolling by the time Kayla and DeShawn had strung the last of their garlands.

"Now, let's put them on the tree," she said.

DeShawn looked at the ten strings of garland and his six-foot tree. "I think we have more than enough for the tree. You might need to take some to your mother."

"Good idea. We're getting our tree on Christmas Eve. You should come over and join us."

"Are you sure?"

Kayla nodded as she picked up a string of garland. "It's food and a lot of fun, especially since Autumn and I have called a truce."

"That's good. I know your mother is happy."

"Well, as long as we can make it last. This might be the only Christmas present I can afford to give them." Kayla pulled a kernel of popcorn off the end of the garland.

"I'm sure they understand your situation."

"I'm glad someone does, because I don't. If I could get my hands on Raul. This isn't where I thought I'd be in my life right now."

DeShawn pulled her into his arms and gave her a hug. "It's going to work out just fine. You're smart and there are some great jobs in education around here."

Kayla pulled out of his arms. "Speaking of that, where are those reports that you wanted me to look over?"

"Do you still want to do that?"

She nodded. "It will give us a reason to polish off this wine."

"All right," he said, then kissed her on the cheek. "Be right back."

Kayla exhaled slowly as she took a seat on the sofa. That kiss. She couldn't forget that kiss. Even when she and DeShawn were stringing the garland, she was thinking about that kiss, his lips, and those hot hands.

Ten years had been a long time for her to fantasize about what could've been. She was happy that the reality lived up to everything she'd built up in her head. He was tender, gentle, and delicious. Now she wanted more, but how was she going to bring that up?

Kayla always had a problem telling DeShawn what she wanted. Her reasoning had been that she wanted to always have him in her life as a friend. Now she knew the friendship wasn't going to be enough. Not when he had her thighs quivering every time he smiled at her.

DeShawn returned to the living room with two binders, his laptop, and an iPad. "Just remember, you volunteered for this." He handed Kayla the iPad. "Click on the Numbers app and there's a list of donors and their contributions this year and what they contributed last year."

Kayla looked up at him. "Question: Do you guys hit up the same donors every year, and have you all set up an endowment?"

"Yes and no. Our board hasn't been the most creative in fund-raising. Too many of them are on the board to pad their résumés. They don't care about my kids, they just want to move forward with their political ambitions. Everyone believes exploiting kids will help more than taking care of them and making them the next generation of leaders. But let me get off my soapbox," he said.

"No, you should make that case with the board when you present this proposal. Shake things up and don't be afraid to call in the media."

"You're pretty hardcore," he said with a smile.

"I had to do something similar at Long Beach Community College when it became a political hotbed and the students suffered. The thing about people with political ambitions, they don't want the media to see their flaws."

"Why did you stay away so long?" DeShawn ran his finger across Kayla's cheek.

"I was trying to build a life in Hollywood. I thought that was my dream, but it turned into a nightmare."

"Maybe it's because everything you needed was right here all along?"

"Been watching *The Wiz*? You got a chance to do your thing, and I needed my chance as well."

"I know. And as selfish as this may sound, part of me wanted you to stay so that we could—"

She placed her finger to his lips. "We can't change the past and we have to finish this report."

"Now, that is a blast from the past." DeShawn chuckled. "I remember when I wanted to ask you to the prom and you stopped me so that we could finish a social studies project."

"DeShawn, I already knew that you'd asked Daphne the sex fiend."

He threw his head back and laughed. "That's mean, and I haven't heard that in a long time. You know she's a minister now and her son is a volunteer at Millwood with the basketball team."

"Wow. How old is her son?"

"Seven, and not mine, because I got kicked out of the prom before I could find out if the rumors were true."

Kayla slapped him on the back of his head. "And who told you to go all Rambo in the middle of the ballroom?"

"I wasn't going to let anyone, especially that dude, disrespect you. I was glad to see you waited for me, though."

Heat rushed to Kayla's cheeks and she turned away from him. That night would've been their first kiss, would've changed everything. What if she had stayed in North Carolina?

DeShawn took her face into his hands and stared into her eyes.

"Kayla, I should've told you this a long time ago. I love you."

"What?" Shivers of desire ran up her spine. "You can't be serious."

"I am, and what I thought was a simple high school crush is way more than that." He leaned forward and brushed his lips against hers.

"DeShawn," she breathed. "I always thought our friendship one of the most important relationships in my life, and when things started to change, I didn't want to lose you and what we had. But I feel like we still can't rush things."

"I don't want to rush anything, but I don't want to waste any more time either." He ran his thumbs across her cheeks. "The best Christmas gift I could ever get is a real chance to love you."

She wanted to say yes, wanted to tell him she could open up to him and fall in love. But she didn't trust herself after marrying a fool like Raul. Not that she believed DeShawn would be the train wreck that her ex-husband was. It wasn't as if DeShawn was a selfish prick like Raul.

"I-I . . ."

"You don't have to answer right now. I just wanted to let you know where I stand."

"And what about the uppity girl who was here earlier?" She wiggled her eyebrows.

"That was her last time being here. Taylor and I are officially over, and that was before you came back into my life. You know I've never been that guy with all the women. I just need one woman to love, and I want that woman to be you."

DeShawn captured her lips in a hot kiss, causing her to melt in his arms. Maybe it was the soulful voice of Donny Hathaway and the twinkling lights of the tree that made her believe in this gift. Kayla pressed her body against DeShawn's, wrapping her arms around his neck and pulling him closer.

As his fingers danced around her collarbone, Kayla knew if she didn't stop this kiss, things were going to go farther than she was ready to go. She pressed her hand against his chest and pulled away from him.

"Whew," she breathed. "DeShawn."

"I know. Slow down. And we will. I think we should go grab something to eat other than popcorn."

"IHOP," she said excitedly.

DeShawn laughed. "You still eat those silver-dollar pancakes with whipped cream and powdered sugar, don't you?"

"Do I hear judgment in your voice?" She laughed. "Those are the best pancakes ever. And you have a nerve, Mr. Chocolate Chip Pancakes."

"I've upped my game to banana-nut pancakes with chocolate chips, thank you very much."

Kayla slipped her shoes on. "Let's roll, darling."

"Yes, ma'am."

As they headed out the door, Kayla glanced over at Mrs. Grant's house. "I'd better send her a thank-you note for that cake."

DeShawn shook his head. "She will bake you three more before Christmas and another one for New Year's Day."

"Point taken. She is a sweet little lady, though."

DeShawn placed his hand on the small of her back. "Yes, but if you say her name three times, she will appear like Beetlejuice. Come on, let's go."

By the time DeShawn drove Kayla home, it was after two a.m. They'd spent the evening in IHOP reliving old times and eating each other's food. She'd threatened him with her fork when he'd reached for her last silver-dollar pancake.

"You're selfish," he'd said before swiping it anyway. Kayla had taken a piece of his banana-nut pancake, which he'd drizzled with chocolate sauce.

"Whatever. We're going to have to run five miles in the morning to burn this off."

Though DeShawn had several ways he could think of to burn off the massive amount of calories they'd taken in, he kept silent. "You want to hook up and run in the morning?"

"Yes. Eight too early for you?"

He looked at his watch. "Yes. How about ten, and then we can have brunch afterwards? And maybe a little Christmas shopping."

"You want to go shopping?" She raised her right eyebrow. "The man who believed the purpose of the mall was to meet girls and eat Cinnabons?"

"Yeah, and who said anything about the mall? But now that you mentioned Cinnabons . . ."

She pointed her index finger at him. "That would defeat the whole purpose of running."

"So you say. I think it's a reward."

When Kayla had started yawning, DeShawn knew it was time for him to take her home. While he'd wanted her to spend the night, he knew it was best to take her home. They were going to take things slow, but all he wanted to do was make slow love to her all night long.

Pulling up to her mother's house, DeShawn stopped the car and turned to Kayla. "Hope your mom doesn't think I kept you out too late."

"I'm sure she's asleep," Kayla replied as she looked at the dark house.

"I had a lot of fun with you tonight, and thank you for your help with the school."

"No problem."

DeShawn leaned in and kissed her gently. "See you in the morning," he said when they broke the kiss.

"Looking forward to it." She opened the door and climbed out of the car. Kayla wasn't surprised that DeShawn also exited the car and walked her to the front door.

"I'm sure I would've made it here safely," she quipped as she pulled her keys from her purse.

"Just wanted to be sure. Go ahead and unlock the door."

She shook her head. "Good night, DeShawn." Kayla opened the door and he headed back to his car. But he didn't drive away until the door closed behind her.

Kayla felt as if she was floating on air as she took her jacket off and headed for her room.

"I'm surprised you came home," Nora said as she appeared in the hallway with a cup of tea in her hand.

"Mom, what are you doing up?"

"Waiting for you, and I couldn't sleep. How was the movie?"

Kayla smiled. "It was good."

"And all you did was watch the movie?"

"Ma, come on."

"You and DeShawn have been dancing around your feelings for years. I'm just trying to figure out if y'all are finally going to get it right. I just want you to be happy."

"I get that. We talked about our feelings and we're going to take things slow."

"So, you're planning on sticking around?"

"Well, going back to LA is not an option. I still can't believe things ended like this."

"Are you sure you're over Raul?"

Kayla scoffed. "Totally. He never talked about the baby. Never. I needed him so much and he wasn't there."

Nora drew Kayla into her arms. "I should've come out there."

"No. I-I didn't want to be a burden to you. I thought that when you got married your husband took care of you. Like Dad always took care of you."

"Honey, he should've taken care of you, and if you needed me you should've told me. It's never a burden to take care of either of my girls. But that fool should've helped you through the loss of the baby. That's something that changes your whole life. Before Autumn was born, we lost a baby. Your Daddy was there for me through every painful moment. Kept you from seeing me crying all the time. That's why I despise your ex. Hope he falls in the San Andreas Fault."

Kayla laughed through her tears. "Ma, I love you."

"Love you more. Now, go to bed."

"Yes, ma'am," she said, then kissed her mom on the cheek.

"Oh, I invited DeShawn over for Christmas Eve."

"I'm not surprised. Autumn said you would."

Across town, DeShawn lay in bed staring at the ceiling, wishing Kayla was there with him. He imagined her naked body on top of his, straddling him as he sucked her caramel nipples. He could almost feel the grip of her thighs around him as she rode him like a prized steed. Ripples of desire made his body harden. DeShawn stroked his erection briefly, then bolted upward in the bed. He needed to get his hormones under control. He padded to the bathroom and took a cold shower. As the icy spray rained down on him, he couldn't help but think about Kayla standing underneath the water with him, her body soaking wet. Shutting the water off, he realized that a cold shower was a myth when it came to quelling desire. He was hotter than ever.

Drying off, he headed back to his bedroom and dressed in a pair of boxers and a cotton T-shirt. Sleep didn't come easy for him because every time he closed his eyes, Kayla's dimples haunted him.

After a restless night, DeShawn was up at seven, tweaking the report that he and Kayla had worked on the night before. By seven forty-five, he'd sent copies to all of the board members.

By the time he brewed his first cup of coffee, DeShawn's phone was buzzing out of control. A few board members had emailed him, talking about how impressed they were with his report.

Lucas Graham, the board chair, wanted a meeting and an explanation. Taylor even responded with a one-word text.

Impressed.

DeShawn sipped his coffee and grinned. "I'd like to see them fire me now."

Kayla woke up with DeShawn's name on her lips. Part of her expected to find him beside her in bed, but the crumpled pillow reminded her that last night had been a delicious dream.

"Mmm," she moaned as she thought about the way DeShawn had buried his face between her thighs and sucked her wetness until she screamed his name.

Kayla hoped that her mother hadn't heard her passionate cries. She hopped out of bed and headed for the bathroom to take a quick shower. She needed to cool off before she met DeShawn for their run.

She totally needed to remember that she was the one who said they needed to take it slow.

After her shower and dressing in her workout gear, Kayla headed to the kitchen and decided to surprise her mom with breakfast. Kayla was halfway through mixing the batter for blueberry pancakes when Nora walked into the kitchen.

"Umm, you're up loud and early."

"Mom, I didn't mean to wake you. Wanted to surprise you with breakfast in bed."

"Not with that noise," Nora quipped. "The coffee sure smells good."

Kayla crossed over to the coffeemaker and fixed her mother a cup of java. Nora took a seat at the breakfast bar as Kayla handed her the cup.

"Thanks, baby."

"Blueberry or cranberry?" Kayla asked.

"Both."

"Thought you'd say that."

"So, I was thinking, what are you going to do for work, since you plan on staying in Charlotte?"

"I don't know. I want to look into doing some consulting work until the New Year. But I'd really love to get back into education."

"Then why don't you talk to DeShawn and find out if he can point you in the right direction?"

"No," Kayla said as she dropped the batter on the griddle. "I don't want to look like some sort of leech. And I—"

"That man knows the scene around here, and he knows you. DeShawn wouldn't mind trying to help you get on your feet."

"I'm not trying to be a project for anyone. If I've learned anything lately, it's that I have to take care of myself and not depend on anyone to do it for me."

"That's no way to live, sweetie. The right people come into your life for the right reasons, and I think that you're back here to find those people again."

Kayla sighed as she flipped the pancakes. Her mother might be right, but she wasn't going to test that theory. She was smart enough to find a job on her own. After the West Charlotte social, she was going to look into hiring a headhunter to find her some opportunities, and go from there.

After the pancakes and bacon were done, Kayla made her mother a plate and then heated some maple syrup. "I should've called Autumn."

"You know that child doesn't get up before noon." Nora cut into her pancakes. "This is delicious."

"Thanks. Learned from the best."

Nora nodded. "Yes, your dad. He loved breakfast for dinner."

Kayla smiled at her mother, then poured herself a cup of coffee. "Ma, do you think you'll ever fall in love again?"

"I'm too old for that. But there was a time after your father was gone when I was open to it. But I was a lot younger. Like you. Kayla, don't let your ex put you on a path to be lonely."

"I'm not."

"Are you sure?"

"I'm going to wash these dishes and then DeShawn and I are going for a run."

"What you need to do is run into that man's arms," Nora muttered. Kayla pretended not to hear her mother as she started the dishwasher.

Chapter 7

DeShawn was about to head out when he saw Taylor walking up his driveway. "Shit," he muttered as he opened the door.

"DeShawn," she said with a bright smile. "I was really impressed with the email you sent to the board. Where has that been all year?"

"Is this something we can talk about later? I'm about to go for a run with a friend, and I can't be late."

She folded her arms across her chest. "I'm here about business, nothing else."

DeShawn smirked. "Here's the deal, Taylor. Our business can be handled through email, phone calls, and the occasional text message."

Before Taylor could reply, Mrs. Grant opened her door and waved at DeShawn. "Did y'all enjoy the cake? Oh," she said when she looked at Taylor. "You're not Kara."

Taylor raised her right eyebrow. "Is that why you're acting as if I broke some sort of rule by coming over here?"

"No. And, Mrs. Grant, her name is Kayla. She loved the cake."

Taylor scoffed. "And she has bad taste."

Mrs. Grant glared at Taylor. "She was such a pleasure to meet. Unlike your present company."

DeShawn held back his laughter as Mrs. Grant slammed into her house.

"So, you accused me of cheating because you've been doing that all along with this Kayla broad? Classy."

"Taylor, I never cheated on you, and what I do now is none of your concern."

"We'll see about that." She turned on her heels and stormed over to her car.

Glancing down at his watch, DeShawn was pissed because he was going to be late. He'd planned to walk to the greenway, but now he was going to need to drive and probably speed to meet Kayla.

Stretching on the park bench, Kayla glanced at her watch and was about to pull her phone from her fanny pack and call DeShawn. *Well, he never used to be late,* she thought. *But people do change.*

Kayla started jogging in place to warm up. She was going to give him another five minutes before she'd take her run alone. The most cynical part of her wanted to believe that was a sign showing her that she'd been right when she said she needed to depend on herself.

"Kayla," DeShawn said as he jogged over to her. "Sorry I'm late." He pulled her into his arms and spun her around.

"What's this all about?"

He kissed her cheek and smiled broadly at her. "I

put those suggestions and fund-raising ideas in a report and sent it to the board."

"And?"

"Now they want to work with me and get the ball rolling in the right direction. I can't thank you enough. Actually, I can. I need you to help me out with this presentation."

"I don't know about that."

"It's what you do, and I might have space in my budget to hire you to work with us."

"I can't work for you."

"Why not?"

"Because it's just not—"

"Kayla, you're beyond qualified for this, and it wouldn't hurt to have someone on my side at work."

"You make it sound like there is some kind of war going on at that school."

"Something like that. But, Kayla, you said you wanted to start over, and this is a prime opportunity for you to do that." He lowered his hands to her hips. "Think about it."

"I will. Now, let's go so that I can show you I've always been the fastest." Kayla took off down the path and DeShawn struggled to keep up with her. Not that she was that much faster than him, but he just couldn't take his eyes off her tantalizing backside as she ran. Hell, that was the only reason she'd ever been faster than him. He'd been watching her ass since high school, and, like a fine wine, it had gotten better and better.

"What's up, slowpoke?" Kayla looked over her shoulder and grinned at him.

"Whatever. You cheated."

She slowed down and jogged in place. "How did I cheat?"

DeShawn caught up to her and slapped her on her booty. "You put on those damn yoga pants." Then he took off. Kayla doubled her stride and caught up with him.

"Still the fastest," she said as she passed him. After four miles, they were sweaty and tired. Kayla and DeShawn collapsed on a bench, breathing hard and sweating as if it was the middle of July.

"You always did like to show off," he said.

"Everybody knew I was faster than you," she breathed. "But since you could catch a ball, you were the special one."

"Who told Coach she didn't give a damn about the Olympics because she had a brain?"

Kayla pinched his forearm. "I couldn't stand Coach Bean."

"I think that's one thing everybody at West Charlotte knew."

Kayla rolled her eyes. "Have you seen that ass?"

"Yeah, he's on the board of the school."

She brought her hand to her mouth. "Really? Hopefully he's not still trying to keep female athletes from living their dreams."

"He's not, and believe it or not, he has changed. People do that sometimes," he said with a wink.

Kayla placed her hand on her hip. "Have you?"

"Why would I change when I've always been perfect?"

She gave him a shot to his side. "Whatever. I see that ego is just as big as it ever was."

DeShawn wiggled his eyebrows. "That's not all that's big."

She shook her head. "Let's go. I want my smoothie." Kayla took off running, and once again, her behind mesmerized DeShawn.

When they reached the end of their run, DeShawn knew two things for sure: Kayla was faster than him and he wanted her more than he needed his next breath.

"What?" she asked when she locked eyes with him.

"Nothing."

She tilted her head to the side. "Shawn, I know you. What's going on in that head of yours?"

He closed the space between them and wrapped his arms around her waist. "I've been wanting to do this all day." DeShawn captured her lips in a hot kiss that made her knees weak. Pressing his body against hers, he wanted her to feel the effect that she had on his body.

Kayla broke the kiss and stared deep into his eyes. "DeShawn."

"I want you. I can't deny that."

"I-I want . . . We said we'd take it slow."

"I'm thinking we've gotten the slow thing down to a science. And waiting is overrated."

Before she could reply, he pressed his mouth against hers. Kayla's body melted against him as they kissed again. His hands roamed her sweaty back, and she remembered how she used to fantasize about moments like this after track practice.

Maybe he was right. They had taken things slow, waiting for ten years for something they both wanted. Pulling back from him, she smiled.

"Let's get out of here," she moaned.

"Are you sure?"

She nodded. "Very."

"Did you drive or walk here? My car is in the parking lot, and I can drive us right to my house."

Kayla nodded. "I walked. Let's go."

DeShawn had to stop himself from scooping her

into his arms and sprinting to his car. He had to be cool for the moment. But when he looked over at her and saw Kayla nibble her bottom lip, being cool went out the window. He did lift her into his arms and took off toward the parking lot.

"Really?" She laughed.

"Don't want to give you a chance to change your mind."

Once they reached his car, Kayla's heart was pounding like a bass drum. What if she didn't satisfy him? What if her dreams didn't live up to the reality of them being together?

The air between them sizzled with energy as he drove down the street about five miles over the speed limit to get home.

"Getting pulled over and getting a ticket isn't going to set the mood," she said when she glanced at his speedometer.

"Don't worry," he said, then put his turn signal on. "I got this. And we're less than a mile away."

That mile seemed like it was more than an hour away as the anticipation built. She shivered, thinking about his hands all over her body. Ten years ago, she never would have thought this was possible. Because he was her friend and every other girl at the school wanted him. So many people had believed that she and DeShawn were in a relationship that most of the girls at school didn't like her.

Maybe the hate had been worth it, because here she was in his car, about to change everything. Was this reward worth the risk?

DeShawn pulled into his driveway and placed the car in park. He hopped out of the car and crossed over to the passenger side to open the door for Kayla. He held her hand as he looked into her eyes.

"Should we really be doing this?" Kayla's lip quivered. The last thing she wanted was to lose another relationship. DeShawn's friendship was important to her, and crossing this line would change everything.

"Yes. Kayla, I know you said you want to take things slowly, and I'm all for that. But I'm not going to let you walk out of my life again without you knowing how I feel about you." He stroked her cheek. "It's not often that you get a second chance to make things right. I plan to make sure I get things right this time."

"DeShawn," she whispered.

He stroked her cheek again and captured her lips in a hot kiss. Kayla's body heated like a July afternoon, and her desire pooled between her thighs.

"We'd better go inside before Mrs. Grant comes out here."

Kayla nodded because she couldn't deal with that sweet old lady today when she wanted to strip her clothes off and make love to DeShawn. He opened the door and they crossed the threshold.

DeShawn pressed Kayla against the wall and slipped his hand between her thighs. She gasped as his thumb brushed against her clitoris. Her love-starved body ached with desire. Soft moans escaped her throat as he continued to stroke her.

"You feel so good." The heat from his breath sent tingles down her spine.

"DeShawn."

He lifted her sports bra above her head and palmed her breasts, tweaking her nipples as she cried out in desire. "Oh my God."

DeShawn took Kayla into his arms. "I need to be inside you."

He padded to the bedroom as Kayla held on to him tightly. Her lips brushed across his neck.

"Damn, girl," he groaned. "Those lips are magical."

"You think so?"

He laid her on the bed and pulled her pants off. DeShawn stared at her naked body. *Perfection* was too weak a word to describe this goddess. "You're so beautiful."

She reached for the waistband of his sweatpants. "My turn to see you."

DeShawn stepped back and stripped out of his clothes. She sat up and ran her hand down his six-pack. He shivered as she reached for his erection. Kayla slowly stroked him and he tossed his head back in delight.

"Damn, damn," he exclaimed.

"Need you."

"I'm here. I'm yours." DeShawn leaned into her and kissed her on the forehead. Then he eased on the bed beside her, caressing her cheek. She brought her mouth down on top of his. Sweet, tender, and delicious, Kayla knew she could get used to the taste of his kisses and the feel of his body against hers.

DeShawn wrapped her leg around his waist, and though he wanted to dive into her wetness, he knew he had to protect them.

"Need you inside," she moaned as she ground against him.

"Protection. Give me a second." As hard as it was to let her go, he did, and sprinted to the bathroom to grab a condom. After sliding the prophylactic in place, DeShawn returned to the room and licked his lips while staring at Kayla's naked body on his bed.

"Do you know how many times I've dreamed about this moment?"

"Then come over here and make all of our dreams come true."

DeShawn crossed over to her and spread her legs apart. Then he planted his face between her thighs, lapping her sweetness. She gripped the back of his neck, pushing him deeper into her wetness. DeShawn lashed her until she exploded, showering his face with her sweetness.

"DeShawn," she cried.

"You taste so good," he said as he pulled back from her. "Sweeter than my dreams."

"I need you."

He inched up her body. "You got me."

Plunging into her valley, DeShawn moaned. "You feel so good. So good."

"You're making me feel like this."

Their bodies rocked back and forth, their hearts heating with one rhythm. Kayla's body tensed as the waves of her orgasm kissed her senses. She'd waited for so long to feel this heat and passion. This was better than any dream—even the one she had last night. She opened her eyes and DeShawn was staring at her. He cupped her face and kissed her, slow and deep. She pressed her hand against his chest and pulled back from him.

"Wow," she whispered.

"Doesn't even begin to describe what just happened here." He kissed her forehead.

Nestling against his chest, Kayla released a satisfied sigh. "So, where do we go from here?"

"Nowhere. If I had my way, we'd stay in this bed to make up for all the time that we've missed."

She pinched his forearm. "That's not what I meant

and you know it. DeShawn, this is something we wanted, but do we want what comes next?"

"Us being together and having the future that we deserve. That's what happens next."

She turned her head away from him and blinked back tears. "Maybe we're moving a little too fast," she said.

"We're not moving too fast." He turned her face so that she was looking into his eyes. "I know you've been hurt, and you may be cautious about falling in love again . . ."

"That's not . . ."

"Kayla, I'm not going to hurt you. I've loved you too long to allow this chance to pass me by—again."

"What if I'm not ready?"

He dropped his head for a moment, then looked up at her with a smile on his face. "I'm ready to wait until you're comfortable. But you have to promise me that you're not going to run off back to California."

"There's nothing I want in California."

"Good. Then you can stay here and be the best Christmas gift that I've ever received."

"That's all you want for Christmas?"

"Well." He slipped his hand between her thighs. "I could use a lot more of this." DeShawn ran the pad of his thumb across her clit. Kayla shivered in anticipation.

"You can have as much as you want. From now until New Year's."

Chapter 8

It was after six p.m. when Kayla and DeShawn pulled themselves out of his bed.

"I'm pretty sure my mother is wondering where I am," Kayla said as she stretched her arms above her head. DeShawn licked his lips as he marveled at her naked body. A body he'd tasted every inch of. He especially enjoyed the sweetness between her thighs. He smiled as he thought about her nails digging into his shoulders while he sucked her wetness.

"What?" she asked when their eyes locked.

Smiling, he crossed over to her and pulled Kayla against his chest. "I'm sure your mom realizes that you're an adult and workouts take a lot of time."

She thrust her hips forward and DeShawn's body sprang to life. He'd wanted nothing more than to get right back into bed with his woman. He was claiming her as his and she would be his, real soon.

"I'm taking a shower," she said as she broke out of his embrace.

"Kayla, be my date for the Christmas social tomorrow night," he said with a wink. "Let's think of it as the prom we should've had."

"And why didn't we go to the prom together?"

He grabbed her bottom and grinned. "Because you didn't ask me."

She pushed his hand away. "Oh please! You had every chance to ask me. And it was the prom, not a Sadie Hawkins dance."

"Kayla Diane Matthews, will you go to the Christmas social with me? I'll even bring you roses and chocolate chip macadamia nut cookies, along with these lips."

"That's an offer I can't refuse." She stood on her tiptoes and kissed him on the cheek.

After the couple showered and ordered Chinese food from their favorite restaurant, they decided to meet later for a midnight showing of *It's a Wonderful Life.* Kayla had told him that she was willing to walk home, but DeShawn wasn't having it.

"You realize it's dark outside, right?"

"And? I'm a big girl, I can take care of myself."

"Just humor me. I don't want your mama asking why I didn't bring you home, and if something happened to you . . ."

"You can stop the guilt trip." She snatched his half-eaten spring roll off his plate.

"That was just cold. You know I love spring rolls."

She winked at him as she chewed. "Of course I do."

DeShawn shook his head, then leaned in to her and gave her a quick peck on the lips. "That was better than the spring roll."

"Umm, we'd better get out of here before we—" The doorbell rang and DeShawn frowned.

"I hope this isn't Mrs. Grant with another fruitcake," he said as he padded to the door.

Kayla scooped up some rice from DeShawn's plate

and added it to hers. She was about to scoop some in her mouth when she heard a female voice say, "DeShawn, we need to talk." Kayla dropped the fork and told herself to remain calm.

DeShawn wanted to slam the door in Taylor's face. But he was too much of a gentleman to do so. As she walked inside, DeShawn wished the floor would open up and swallow him.

"Now is not a good time, and you need to stop popping up at my house."

"Why? I'm trying to save your job and—" She stopped short in the hallway when she spotted Kayla sitting on the floor in the living room. "Oh," Taylor snapped. "I guess this is more important than the school you say you love so much."

Kayla rose to her feet and looked from DeShawn to Taylor. "You two need a moment?"

"Yes," Taylor began.

"No. Taylor is leaving."

"Who are you?" Taylor snapped.

Kayla scoffed and shook her head. "You guys can discuss this among yourselves." She speared DeShawn with an icy look, then crossed over into the bedroom.

DeShawn glared at Taylor. "You don't get to question who's at my house or what I do here. We work together, that's it."

"Did you ever love me? You replaced me without a beat or a second thought."

"Don't do that, Taylor. We weren't happy for a long time, and you know that."

"I know you're an asshole and you always put everything and everyone else above me. She's not going to stick around and take that. I was a fool for staying as long as I did."

"Get out, and for the last time, if you want to talk about work with me, use my email."

Taylor turned on her heels and stomped to the front door. When he heard the door slam, DeShawn dropped his head. How was he going to explain this? Heading for the bedroom, he expected Kayla to light into him about Taylor. But finding Kayla calmly sitting on the edge of his bed, tying her shoes, actually gave him pause.

"Kayla?"

She looked up at him. "I'm ready to go."

"Can we talk about what just happened?" He walked over to her and placed his hand on her shoulder.

"There's nothing to talk about. At least not on my end. You and Taylor obviously have something to work out, and I'm not going to get in the middle of this."

"You're not in the middle of anything. Taylor and I are over and—"

She threw her hand up and rose to her feet. "Women don't just show up at their ex's house without a reason."

"Negative. Kayla, you're the only woman I want in my house, in my heart, and in my bed."

She rolled her eyes. "Take me home."

"No. Not until I know that we're okay."

She folded her arms across her chest. "We're fine." Her face told a different story, with her eyebrow arched and a scowl on her lips.

Not wanting to press the issue, DeShawn pulled on a pair of gray sweatpants and his sneakers.

Kayla sighed and turned to DeShawn. "All right, we're not okay. Is everything done with you and Taylor? Because what I'm not going to let you do is blindside me because you changed your mind about who you want to be with."

"I know who I want to be with and who means everything to me. That's you. Taylor's on the board at the school, and we dated for nearly a year. But we were over before you came back to me."

"Wait a minute. She works at the school, and you want to bring me into that powder keg?" She laughed sardonically.

"Now you see why I need someone on my side."

She shook her head. "I'm pretty sure hiring me would lead to more drama, and that's the last thing I need in my life right now."

"No drama, but you know your stuff, and I need you."

"I'll think about it. But—"

"No buts, you'll think about it and that's enough for me." He kissed her on the forehead and stroked her cheek, "I'm sorry about that scene before."

"Umm-huh. I will say this, Mrs. Grant was right. She is uppity."

By the time Kayla made it home, she was happy and confused at the same time. Part of her had serious reservations about Taylor and DeShawn. The last thing she could take was another heartbreak. And then there was the way DeShawn made her feel. In his arms, she felt as if their love was a fairy tale that had come true. His kisses heated her like an oven. His touch filled her soul with desire and passion. Things that she had prepared herself to never feel again.

"Why are you so quiet over there?" DeShawn asked as he pulled up in front of Nora's house.

"Just thinking about how everything has changed and what this means going forward for us and . . ."

"Kayla, what are you not telling me? I see so much hurt in your eyes, and I don't want to think that I've put any of it there."

A single tear slid down her cheek. DeShawn leaned over and kissed it away.

"I'm not him. Whatever he did, I won't do it." He held her face in his hands. "I've waited too long to love you. I'm not going to mess this up."

Just as he was about to lean in and kiss her, a knock on the passenger-side window startled them. Kayla turned her head and saw Autumn standing there with a huge grin on her face.

"Get out of the car."

Kayla shook her head. "Only Autumn would pick this moment to come by and knock on the window."

"That's your sister. I believe she's the reason it's taken me this long to actually kiss you."

Kayla laughed as she remembered their first almost kiss in the basement while they'd been studying *Othello* for their English class. As they'd discussed Desdemona and Othello's relationship, DeShawn had inched closer to her, and Kayla had been ready to kiss him until Autumn burst through the door.

"Great timing as always," Kayla said as she opened the door to get out of the car.

"What are you talking about?" Autumn asked as she hip-checked her sister. Then Autumn turned to DeShawn. "What have you two been doing all day?"

"Chilling and catching up on old times," he said.

"With or without your clothes on?"

"Autumn!" Kayla exclaimed as she pinched her sister's arm.

"What?" she asked, pretending to be innocent. "I'm

just making sure he didn't take advantage of my big sister."

"Shut up," Kayla said and tried to hide her smile.

"Looks like somebody finally got it right," Autumn said, then dashed up the front steps.

DeShawn wrapped his arms around Kayla's waist. "I guess we are a little transparent." Then he pointed to a red hickey on her neck. "And there is this little love mark."

"You really did that?"

"I couldn't help it, you tasted so good and I got carried away."

"What are we, in high school?" Kayla laughed and DeShawn kissed her on the cheek.

"Put some toothpaste on it."

"And how do you know this?"

Winking at her, he said, "Years of practice."

Kayla rolled her eyes as they walked into the house. She was happy to see her brother-in-law sitting on the sofa talking to Nora.

"Rodney, nice to see you." Kayla crossed over to him and gave him a hug.

"Good to see you after all this time. I thought Autumn had run you back to Cali."

"Rod, stop. I told you we've made up and now that she's getting some, we might be best friends."

Kayla looked around for something soft to throw at her sister as embarrassment turned her cheeks crimson. Picking up a pillow, she tossed it at Autumn just as Nora stood up.

"Y'all better stop acting as if you don't have home training," she admonished as she crossed over to DeShawn. "Good to see you. Did you two have a good workout?"

Autumn started coughing, and Kayla turned her

head. "It was good," he said as he linked his finger with Kayla's pinky. "Ms. Nora, you know Kayla has always challenged me."

"Yeah, because she was always faster."

"Boom," Kayla said. "I told you, and now we have proof."

He let her finger go and pulled her into his arms. "I'll admit it, you were faster, and if Coach had listened, you might have won the gold in Sydney." DeShawn kissed her on the forehead.

"If I ever see that stupid coach again, I might punch him," Nora said. "Let me get you two some eggnog. Kayla, come in the kitchen and help me."

She nodded and followed her mother as they headed into the kitchen. When they were alone, Nora turned to her daughter.

"You look so happy," she said.

"I'm happy-ish," Kayla said as she crossed over to the cabinet.

"What is that supposed to mean?" Nora opened the refrigerator and pulled out the eggnog. "Hand me that bourbon. And by the way, you look more than happy-ish. Did you see the way that man was looking at you? Don't open your legs and close your heart." Nora pointed to the red love mark on Kayla's neck.

"Ma!"

"I'm not blind, and know that most people don't return from workouts smelling fresh like soap."

Kayla passed her mother the bottle of liquor and thought about telling her about the scene with Taylor at DeShawn's house, but she just pulled the glass mugs out of the cabinet.

"You care about him, don't you?"

Kayla nodded. "It's crazy, Mom. It's as if we were

meant to be and it took us this long to figure it out. But when we're together, it's like no time has passed at all."

"Let that be a lesson to you. Second chances don't come around often, and when they do, you have to take it." Nora stirred the eggnog. "Now, pour the eggnog and get back out there before Autumn scares that man away."

Kayla laughed and filled the mugs with her mother's potent mix. She took a sip of the nog, and she was thankful for her mother's heavy hand. Maybe she could drown out all of her second thoughts about DeShawn with the strong drink.

But why was she having second thoughts when she'd loved this man for so long? Had she really allowed Raul to harden her heart this much?

"What's taking so long with the eggnog?" Autumn called out.

"Coming," Kayla replied as she picked up the tray.

DeShawn rose to his feet and crossed over to Kayla. "You know your sister is crazy, right?"

"Known that for years." She grinned as he picked up a mug of eggnog.

"I can hear you both," Autumn said. "Kayla, stop keeping all the good stuff over there."

DeShawn took the tray from Kayla's hands and walked over to Autumn and Rodney. "Your Highness, here are your libations."

Kayla broke out laughing as DeShawn bowed to her sister.

Autumn took a mug from the tray and smiled. "I'm glad someone recognizes royalty."

Rodney shook his head. "Thanks for making my life harder, bro." Autumn shoved her elbow in Rodney's side.

"Remember that when *you* get hard later," she muttered, then took a sip of her drink.

"I'm going to back away now," DeShawn said as he set the tray on the coffee table.

"Good move," Kayla said as she sat on the love seat in the corner.

DeShawn crossed over to her and kissed her on the cheek. "This is fun."

She nodded and took a big gulp of the eggnog. He stroked her cheek and brought his lips to her ear. "But it doesn't compare to the fun we had earlier. I really want to taste you again."

Kayla nearly choked on her eggnog as she turned to face him. "You really need to stop talking like that."

"Why? Because you want it, too?" He held his mug up to hers. "Let's toast to the future. One with you and me being together."

She clinked her mug against his. "I'll drink to that."

DeShawn set his mug on the floor, then took Kayla's from her hand. "I'm serious. In the New Year, I want us to be a team in every way, at work and in life. I could kick myself for wasting all these years, away from the one woman I've ever truly loved."

"DeShawn, don't do this here. We—"

He took her face into his hands and kissed her, slow and deep. He didn't care who was watching and he ignored Autumn's cheering as he kissed his woman. All that he cared about was having her in his arms.

Kayla pushed back from him and they locked eyes, seeming to be at a loss for words. He brushed his lips across hers. "I love you. Always have and probably always will."

"DeShawn."

"Girl," Autumn said, "let that man finish!"

"Can we go somewhere and talk in private?" Kayla said as she shot a glance over her shoulder at her sister.

"Come on, let's go outside." DeShawn walked over to the front door and opened it. A cold breeze blew in and he quickly shut the door. "Better yet, let's go to your room."

"Leave the door open," Autumn quipped.

"Shut up," Kayla hissed as she and DeShawn headed down the hall. Once they walked into the bedroom, DeShawn closed the door and stopped himself from pressing her against the wall and kissing her senseless.

"What do you want to talk about?" he asked.

"What are we doing? I know that we care about each other and we feel as if we missed out on ten years of being together, but we can't pile all of that into these next five minutes and act as if we're ready to—"

He brought his finger to her lips. "I'm willing to wait, a little while. But Kayla, I need to know that you want this as much as I need to be with you."

She paused for a beat and DeShawn held his breath. What if he'd pushed too hard? He didn't know everything that had happened with her ex. If she wasn't ready, he didn't want to push her too hard. But he knew one thing was for sure: Kayla Matthews wasn't going to walk out of his life for a second time.

"DeShawn, I want to be with you. But I'm afraid."

"Don't be. Baby, I got you. And you don't ever have to live in fear." Closing the space between them, he pulled her into his arms. "Just let me love you."

"I will," she whispered. "I will."

He covered her mouth with his, kissing her slowly. Her body melted against him, and he loved it. Kayla's mouth was as sweet and potent as the eggnog they'd been drinking.

DeShawn pulled back from her and smiled. "As much as I want you, I can't do this at your mama's house."

Kayla laughed. "I guess that would be awkward."

He kissed her cheek. "So, have you had a chance to think about coming to work with me at the school?"

"That I don't know about. Your ex will probably try to block that, for sure," she said.

"I doubt it. Taylor is just like the rest of the board. Since I've dropped the nugget about the media, like you said, they're trying to make sure that we don't look bad in public. I'm meeting with them in the morning and I want you there by my side."

"Are you sure this is a good idea?"

"You see the reaction that your report got. I want you there by my side. And if it doesn't work out, I have a contact at the local community college who could use your expertise."

"You don't have to do that."

"I know what I don't have to do, but I want to make sure that you have every reason to stay here. I told you, no more running back to California or anywhere else. You're going to be here with me for the long haul."

Kayla smiled and wrapped her arms around him, hugging him tightly. "I'm yours, babe. And I'm not going anywhere."

"I'm holding you to that." He was about to bring his mouth down on top of hers when there was a knock on the door.

"What are y'all doing in there?" Autumn asked. "Mama said get out here and you better have your clothes on."

"Shut up, Autumn," Kayla said with a laugh.

"Told you we couldn't do anything at your mama's house," DeShawn whispered as he opened the door.

Chapter 9

The next morning, Kayla woke up around six a.m., much earlier than she would wake up on a normal day. Why had she agreed to go to this meeting with DeShawn?

She wiped her hand across her face and sighed as she thought about the night they'd spent together. After they'd drunk more eggnog and eaten some of Nora's brownies, DeShawn and Kayla had cleaned up the kitchen while Autumn and Rodney started to help Nora prepare the Christmas decorations.

"You look sexy covered in suds," he'd said as he flicked some dishwater in her direction. "Why don't you come home with me and let me run your bath water?"

She glanced over her shoulder. "Sounds like a good idea. They are going to start arguing in about five, four, three, two . . ."

"But, Mom, you should really consider the LED lights this year," they heard Autumn whine.

"I know what kind of lights I'm using, and I'm not changing them just because you say so."

Kayla turned to DeShawn as she dried the brownie pan. "Let's get out of here before they drag us into this fight."

"Kayla!" Autumn called out. "Please help me out here."

"Nope. My name is Paul and that's between y'all," she said. Turning to DeShawn she pointed to the door. "I'm going to pack a bag."

Autumn and Nora were so deep into their argument, going through the box of decorations that had been around for years, that they hadn't even known that DeShawn and Kayla had crept away.

When they'd arrived at his place, DeShawn noticed that he'd gotten an email from Lucas, the chairman of the board.

"Damn," he muttered as he read over the email. "The board is calling a meeting in the morning to discuss a change of direction with the leadership of the school."

"How is this different from your previous meeting that you had scheduled?" Kayla asked as she sat on the sofa beside him.

"Seems as if they're trying to pull the trigger on firing me," he said, not adding that he knew Taylor was behind it all. She'd told him that he'd pay for ending their relationship, and she knew what was important to him. The kids at that school.

Sighing, he'd risen to his feet and headed to the refrigerator and grabbed a beer. When he returned to the living room, Kayla took the beer from his hand.

"No drinking. What we're about to do is come up with a game plan to lay out why you're the only man who can lead this school." She set the beer on an end table and told him to get his tablet.

For the next three hours, Kayla and DeShawn had worked to put together a report showing the strides that the school had made under DeShawn's leadership and how, in spite of a shrinking budget, he'd managed to keep all of the main programs running at the school.

"You're still close with Maurice Goings, right?"

He nodded. "But I don't like leaning on my friends for—"

"Hush! I need you to have Maurice vouch for you. He's one of the most well-known and well-respected people in this city, and he's your friend. Based on what you told me about these people, a good word from Mo would have more impact than anything I can say or what this paper report will show."

DeShawn had glanced at the clock on the wall and decided that it was too late to call his friend. He knew Mo was a bona fide family man, and he didn't want to interrupt family time. So, he closed his laptop and took the tablet from Kayla's hands.

"I tell you what," he said. "We've done everything that we can do right now. Remember how I said you looked amazing in soapy suds?"

"Are you serious?"

He nodded and rose to his feet, then held his hand out to her. "Come on. It's bath time."

She took his hand and rose from the sofa. DeShawn had led her to the bathroom and slowly stripped her out of her tunic and leggings. He'd smiled when he saw that she wasn't wearing any undergarments.

"Just amazing," he said as he gave her a slow once-over. "Do you realize how beautiful you are?"

"You know I'm at a disadvantage here," she said as she folded her arms across her breasts.

DeShawn started running their bathwater, then

closed the space between them. He pulled her arms down and massaged her breasts until her nipples hardened like diamonds. Her soft moans filled the air like the notes of John Coltrane's sax. DeShawn's need for her made his body ache with desire. She tugged at his sweatshirt.

"I won't be naked alone," she quipped as she pulled the shirt over his head. DeShawn kicked out of his pants and Kayla pulled his boxers down to his ankles. With one hand she stroked his hardness until he tossed his head back in pleasure.

"Oh, that's not fair," he moaned. "Not fair."

"Neither was it fair for you to strip me naked and stare at me." She gave him one last long stroke. "I think we're even."

Shivers ran up and down his spine as he took a step back and added cocoa-scented body wash to the running water. "Turnabout is fair play," he said, then scooped her into his arms. DeShawn stepped into the tub and plopped Kayla down. Then he turned the water off and pushed the bubbles up onto her breasts. "Even more amazing than I thought you'd look." DeShawn slipped his hands between her thighs and stroked her most sensitive spot. Easing his finger inside, he made slow circles, causing Kayla to squirm underneath his touch.

"Umm," she moaned as she arched her body into his. Water splashed over the side of the tub. "DeShawn."

He brushed his lips against hers. "I love the way you say my name." He pushed his finger in deeper. "Say it again."

"DeShawn!"

Capturing her lips in a hot kiss, DeShawn sucked her tongue as if it were the sweetest candy he'd ever had the chance to taste. Breaking the kiss, they stared into each other's eyes, silently broadcasting how much they wanted each other.

Though he knew they needed to be protected, DeShawn couldn't wait to be inside his woman, and he drove into her wetness. The heat radiating from her body nearly drove him to the brink, and when she leaned forward, tightening her thighs around his waist, it was a struggle for him not to come.

Kayla rode him with zeal and zest, grinding against him until DeShawn exploded. She leaned against his chest, and as the bathwater covered her back, DeShawn kissed her chin.

"I'm sorry I was so reckless, but—"

"We're both responsible for what just happened. You don't have to worry about getting a disease or anything from me. It's been so long since I've done this without protection and—"

"What about a baby?"

Kayla eased off him and pressed her back against the tub. Tears welled up in her eyes and DeShawn drew her into his arms. "What's wrong?" he asked.

Kayla's tears turned to sobs as she leaned her head on his shoulder. "I-I had a miscarriage a few years ago. It started the breakdown of my marriage. I never told Raul what the doctor said. It might be impossible for me to have a child and . . ."

"Shh," he said. "It's all right."

"I've struggled with this for a long time. I don't kn-know how I can have a future with a man when I don't know if I can give him a family."

DeShawn had lifted her head from his shoulder and looked deep into her eyes. "Our future will be amazing. And here's the thing about life: No one can tell you what's going to happen. If we want children in our future, we have several options. Kayla, I meant what I said. We're going to be together for the rest of our lives, and I hope you don't think this changes anything or how I feel about you. I love you."

She wrapped her arms around his neck. "I love you, too."

DeShawn's hand on her shoulder brought Kayla back to the present. She turned and smiled at him. "You always wake up this early?" he asked.

She shook her head. "But we have a big day ahead of us, and I don't want our presentation to have any flaws."

"Lie down. We have time to worry about that later. Our meeting isn't for another four hours."

Kayla eased back into his arms. "Last night, I know I may have gotten a little intense, but I just wanted you to know exactly what you're getting into with me."

"I know what I'm getting into, and I'm looking forward to more of this."

"More of what?" She furrowed her eyebrows.

"You waking up in my arms, just not this early. I tell you what, if you go back to sleep, I'll cook us breakfast when we wake up in about two hours when my alarm goes off."

"Sounds like a plan."

DeShawn wrapped his arms around her and Kayla drifted right off to sleep.

Around eight fifteen, DeShawn slipped out of bed, leaving Kayla to sleep as he headed for the kitchen to cook them cheese omelets, grits, and bacon. Though he meant to wake her, he wanted a chance to call Maurice and see if he could get his friend to help him at the meeting.

"Yeah?" Maurice said when he answered the phone.

"I know the NFL's MVP isn't getting soft and sleeping in," DeShawn quipped.

"DC, brother, what's going on?"

"I'm just trying to keep my school open and these kids motivated. For some reason, they like you."

"Everybody loves me. What do you need? I think what you're doing at that school is amazing, and Kenya reminded me last week that we didn't make our donation yet."

"Not that I'm turning down your money, because we do need it. But I have a meeting today and I need a character witness."

"Say no more, let me check my calendar and make sure I can make it. What time and where?"

DeShawn gave him the directions and the time for the meeting. "Hey, I got a question for you," he said.

"No, I can't get you a walk-on tryout with the Panthers," Maurice joked.

"Please, I'm over playing football. I followed my dad's advice, took the money and ran."

"I still say you could've broken Smith's record. You were a hell of a back."

"My knee doesn't think so. But what I need to know is where you got Kenya's engagement ring. I need something special for my future wife."

"Whoa. You're ready to burn that player card, huh? Congratulations. I'm going to text you my jeweler's number. Let him know I recommended you."

DeShawn smiled as he watched Kayla walk into the kitchen. "Will do. I have to go. And, Mo, thanks."

She crossed over to him as he hung up the phone. "I thought I was dreaming when I smelled that bacon," Kayla said. "You need help with anything?"

He shook his head. "You've already done so much

for me, all I need you to do is sit down and let me serve you."

"Be careful, Mr. Carter. I could get used to this." Kayla sat on a stool in front of the breakfast bar and DeShawn leaned over and kissed her on the tip of her nose.

"I want you to, darling."

After breakfast, Kayla and DeShawn showered, went over their report, and then headed for the school. Though he hid his nervousness from her, DeShawn had more butterflies in his stomach than he'd had when he took his first carry in his rookie game with the Dallas Cowboys.

This wasn't a game, this was for his kids, for their future and for the school he considered his second home. Pulling into the parking lot, he took a deep breath.

"Are you all right?" she asked as she glanced over at him.

"I'm good. Let's get this over with." As they stepped out of the car, a classic red Corvette pulled up beside them.

DeShawn smiled as Maurice stepped out, dressed in a dark blue suit and a fedora. "Channeling your quarterback?" he asked as they shook hands.

"Whatever. Good to see you, dude." Maurice looked over DeShawn's shoulder at Kayla. "Is that her?"

"Sure is."

"Good job, bruh." Maurice crossed over to Kayla. "Hello. I'm—"

"Maurice Goings. It's nice to meet you," she said as she extended her hand. Maurice kissed the back of her hand and DeShawn gave him a shove.

"Calm down, player. I gave up being Mr. Steal Your

Girl a long time ago. You've met my wife. But you are
a beautiful woman. Are you sure this knucklehead is
good enough for you?"

Kayla laughed. "I'm sure. One hundred percent."

DeShawn glanced at his watch. "Let's do this."
Walking into the school, DeShawn felt as if he understood what his students meant when they always said
"squad goals."

His butterflies were gone, and he decided that no
matter what the board decided, he'd given his best to
the school and the students. One thing he wasn't
going to do was play politics with them.

"All right, what's the game plan?" Mo asked as they
stood outside of the conference room.

"We're going to lay out the facts and let the chips
fall where they may," DeShawn said. "If I didn't love
these kids and have a vested interest in their future,
I'd tell the board where they could go and how soon
they could get there."

"And I need you to tone it down a little bit," Kayla
said as she stroked his shoulder. "Calm, cool, and
collected."

"Kiss for luck?" he asked as he leaned in to her.
Kayla obliged his request, giving him a quick peck on
the lips.

"Aww, aren't you two sweet," Mo quipped.

DeShawn opened the door to the conference room
and all heads turned around and looked at him.

"What is she doing here?" Taylor snapped when
she locked eyes with Kayla. "This isn't a—"

"Kayla Matthews is an education consultant who's
been working with me to fix problems that all of
you have ignored," DeShawn began. "We've been
running this school on a shoestring budget for too

long because none of you really give a damn about what goes on here."

"You're out of line," Lucas said as he slammed his hand against the table.

DeShawn walked over to Lucas and shook his head. "I've hired a forensic accountant this morning, with my own money, to take a look at why the school is losing money. Three people have access to the accounts."

Dorothy Mays cleared her throat and raised her hand. "Mr. Carter, are you trying to say that there have been some improprieties with the school's money?"

"That would explain the budget shortfall when our donations and the money from the state have remained virtually stable."

Kayla reached into the briefcase she'd borrowed from DeShawn and passed out the reports that she and DeShawn had worked on the night before. When she got to Taylor, she dropped the report in front of her and smirked at the scowl on the woman's face.

"So, I understand that we're looking to make leadership changes here at the school, and if you all want to release me from my contract, that's fine. But you all know that this school means everything to me. These students and their future mean more to me than the politics of this board. Maybe that's why half of y'all don't like me. If we're not going to make this school successful and put these kids first, then I don't want to be here. And I'm sure many of the parents who enrolled their children here wouldn't want to be a part of a school that's just a breeding ground for board members with political aspirations at the expense of their children's future. When's the last time any of you made an effort to find out what's going on in the classrooms at Millwood? When the parents find out that the members of this board are here to make their lives better and not the lives of our students, I'm sure we're going to see a huge dip in enrollment. And trust me, I will let my kids' parents know exactly what's going on."

"Th-this sounds like blackmail!" Lucas exclaimed. "You can't come in here and accuse people of stealing money from the school, threaten to expose this farce and—"

"Shut up, Lucas," Brad McDuffie said. "What Mr. Carter is saying has merit. One of the reasons I came to this meeting was to ask if someone had been stealing money, because from the financial records that I've seen, we shouldn't be this deep in debt."

DeShawn liked Brad and he would love to see him replace Lucas as the board chair. He wished that he could make that motion.

Maurice stood up from his seat in the corner. "I'd like to add something, if I may."

"Please do," Brad said.

"No!" Lucas said as he rose to his feet. "This meeting is out of order. We didn't come here to listen to two stupid jocks talk!"

Taylor nodded in agreement. "We do have rules, and neither Maurice Goings nor this woman has a right to be here." She tossed her thumb in Kayla's direction.

"What is the real purpose of this meeting, then?" DeShawn asked as he pulled out his cell phone. "Because according to your email, Lucas, you wanted to see a change in leadership. Who did you think was going to be a better leader? Let me guess: You and

Taylor had some pillow talk and decided I needed to go."

"Don't you dare!" Taylor said as she rose to her feet. "You brought this on yourself and you don't deserve to be running this school! You're allowing the wrong head to make your decisions."

"I stopped doing that after you," DeShawn said. Mo cleared his throat.

"If I may, I came here today to bring you guys a check to start an endowment for the school." He reached into his jacket pocket and pulled out an envelope. "This money comes with strings attached."

Lucas groaned and Mo rolled his eyes at him. "If DeShawn won't be here to be a steward of this endowment, then I'm keeping my dumb-jock money. And in case you wanted to know, it's two hundred thousand dollars."

DeShawn turned and looked at his friend. That was totally unexpected.

"This is— Lucas began.

"Just what we need to ensure the longevity of our school," Brad said. "Thank you, Maurice."

"My pleasure. Now, I have to get to practice and do some dumb-jock things," he said, and speared Lucas with a cold look.

"And the board has to make some tough decisions right now," Brad said. "DeShawn, thank you for this report and for the information about the school's finances. It's time for us to take a vote."

DeShawn nodded toward Kayla. "We'll let you all work."

He took Kayla's hand and they followed Maurice out the door.

"So, what's next?" Kayla asked.

DeShawn shrugged. "I don't know, but if they're smart, the only changes that they're going to make will be with the board."

"If they cash that check, then that is just what they're going to do," Maurice said. "Kayla, it was nice to meet you. And, DeShawn, you better keep this one."

"That is the plan, bruh."

Epilogue

Christmas Eve

Kayla stood at the top of a small ladder and DeShawn held it in place. "Is the angel straight?" she asked.

"Not at all," Autumn said. "DeShawn, stop looking at her booty and help her get that thing straight."

"Autumn, stop being a brat," Nora said as she hung the garland around the fireplace. She looked up at the tree. "But that angel is crooked."

"I can get down and either one of you can do this," Kayla said with a laugh. Rodney walked into the den with a bowl of popcorn.

"Autumn, let's get this stuff strung," he said. "And the angel is crooked."

Kayla rolled her eyes and climbed down. "I'm done."

DeShawn took her into his arms. "You did a great job, baby," he said. "Don't listen to them." He kissed her slow and deep.

"Thank you," she said when they broke the kiss. Kayla stroked his chest. "Have I told you lately how proud of you I am?"

"Nope," he said as he spun her around. "I'm ready to hear it, though."

"I'm so proud of you and what you did at the school. You put those kids first and kept your job. That was huge."

"I couldn't have done it without you. This Christmas I got the ultimate gift."

"What's that?" she asked.

DeShawn stroked her cheek. "Baby, I got you. And I want to have you forever."

"You got me," she replied with a smile.

"But I want forever." DeShawn dropped down to one knee. "Kayla Matthews, will you make me the happiest man alive and say you will be my wife?"

She brought her hands to her mouth as happy tears ran down her cheeks. "DeShawn."

"As much as I love to hear you say my name, that's not the word I was looking for," he quipped.

"Say yes," Autumn said.

Nora pinched her little girl on the arm. "Let her say yes."

Kayla sighed and stroked DeShawn's cheek. "I would love nothing more than to be your wife," she said.

He reached into his pocket and pulled out a blue velvet box. When he opened it, Kayla gasped at the size of the solitaire diamond engagement ring. Even Rodney muttered *damn* when he saw the ring.

DeShawn slipped the ring on her finger and rose to his feet. "I love you, baby. Always have and I always will."

"Thank you," she said. "Thank you for teaching

me that I could love again. This was a Christmas lesson that I needed to learn."

"And you passed with flying colors, darling."

Kayla glanced out the window and pointed at the first flakes of snow falling from the sky. "This is perfect," she said. "A white Christmas."

"You're perfect," DeShawn said. "And I'm going to love you forever."

Kissing her fiancé, Kayla knew she was going to love him just as long.

Christmas with You

PAMELA YAYE

Chapter 1

"Marc, I need a favor."

Groaning inwardly, his cell phone pressed to his ear, thirty-year-old sports agent Marc Cunningham threw open the driver's-side door of his Infiniti Q50, and stepped onto the snow-covered pavement. His newest client, a defensive lineman aptly nicknamed "Bone Crusher," was on the line, and if Marc didn't have a soft spot for the NFL star he would have let the call go to voicemail. But, since he wanted to help the eight-year veteran, he said, "Anything for you, Javonte. What do you need?"

"Call Coach Schneider and tell him I'm sick."

Frowning, Marc stared down at the phone. "But I saw you last night at the club. You were laughing and cracking jokes, and you partied with your entourage until closing."

"That was then, and this is now. You have to help me out, man. I'm in bad shape."

Snow crunched under Marc's feet, sticking to the soles of his leather Tom Ford shoes as he slammed his door and strode around the hood of the car. The blustery November breeze blew open his camel-brown wool coat, chilling him to the bone.

"Good evening, sir. Welcome to the Peninsula Hotel."

Moving his cell phone away from his mouth, he addressed the tuxedo-clad valet with the salt-and-pepper hair. "Thanks, man. Stay warm. It's freezing out here!"

Marc tossed his keys to the valet, then nodded his head in greeting at the gentleman standing at attention in front of the sliding glass doors. Normally, he'd park his car himself, but he was running late, and every second counted. Shivering, he pulled up his jacket collar and marched inside to escape the bitter cold.

"Marc, hold on. I'll be right back. Someone's at the door . . ."

Pressed for time, Marc told Javonte he'd call him back, but the star athlete insisted he wait, and since he didn't want to upset him he said, "No problem. Take as long as you need."

Located in downtown Chicago, the landmark hotel was the epitome of class and sophistication, and as Marc entered the gleaming lobby, he noticed there were wreaths, poinsettias, and twinkling lights. Christmas was a month away, but a twenty-foot Douglas fir tree, decorated with red, gold, and silver ornaments, beautified the space. The fragrant scent, wafting through the air, tickling his nostrils.

Marc straightened his royal-blue tie. Having been to the hotel numerous times before, he knew it was popular among celebrities, trophy wives, and esteemed business men, and had dressed accordingly: freshly trimmed hair; tailored, black suit; personalized cufflinks; and on his wrist the gold Rolex watch that belonged to his late father, Eli Cunningham.

Pain stabbed his heart. His father was gone, and although Marc missed seeing him and hearing his voice, he chose to focus on the present, not the past. Confidence was everything in his field, what separated him from the other sports agents in the business, and he didn't want anyone to know he was still broken up over his father's death. He wanted the world to think he was at the top of his game. And he was. It didn't matter that he'd faced disappointments and hardships over the years; he was a Cunningham, and he could overcome anything—even grief, and an acrimonious divorce.

"I don't know what's wrong with me." Javonte coughed as if he was on his deathbed, gasping and wheezing uncontrollably on the phone. "I have the flu . . . no . . . it's worse than that. I have, um, pneumonia. Yeah, that's it. Call Coach and tell him I have pneumonia."

Marc could hear noise in the background, rap music and laughter, and suspected Javonte was partying with his friends. What else was new? When he wasn't living it up at the club, he was blowing money at the jewelry store, or test-driving sports cars that cost more than the White House. "I have to go," he said, anxious to end the call. "We'll talk tomorrow."

"No, we'll talk right now. You have to call Coach, ASAP, or I'll get suspended for skipping Sunday's game." He sounded frantic, on edge, and raised his voice. "You're my agent, the person who's supposed to look out for me. If I can't trust you, who can I trust?"

Raking a hand over his short, cropped hair, Marc blew out a deep breath. He loved working with professional athletes and derived great joy from helping them succeed, but he wasn't going to lie for Javonte. Not today, not ever. Well-liked in his field, Marcus didn't want to jeopardize his reputation by lying to a coach he respected.

Glancing at his watch, he sped through the corridor. Anxious to reach Avenues Ballroom, he marched past a pregnant mother pushing a stroller, an elderly couple kissing under the mistletoe, and tourists snapping pictures in front of a gold, star-shaped wreath.

"Now's not a good time." Hearing classical music, Marc stopped in front of the ballroom door and peeked inside. To his relief, the party wasn't over. Guests were socializing and mingling, and Marc slipped into the room unnoticed. "I'm at a charity event."

"Charity begins at home."

Marc grinned, couldn't help it. Javonte, the wise-cracking jokester, was always making him laugh, and although they'd only known each other for a few weeks, they'd developed a strong rapport. Tomorrow, he'd visit the football star and get to the bottom of things, but not now.

"I'm your biggest client. The ten-million-dollar kid," he bragged, a note of arrogance in his voice. "You *have* to listen to me. Boss's orders."

Annoyed, Marc pressed his lips together to trap a curse inside his mouth. He didn't have time to shoot the breeze with Javonte. His five o'clock meeting— with a golf protégée looking for representation—had lasted ninety minutes, and as a result he was an hour late for the charity dinner. The event was hosted by his mom, Dr. Bridgett Cunningham, and if she caught him on the phone there'd be hell to pay. It didn't matter that he had a law degree, money in the bank, and a lavish home in Barrington; she'd ream him out, and the last thing Marc wanted to do was upset his mom. Since his father died, she rarely smiled or laughed, and he wanted to make her happy. Hence, why he'd skipped the NBA game at the United Center with his buddies and drove straight to the hotel after his meeting ended. Now, if he could only get Javonte off the phone, life would be golden. "Javonte, I'm glad you signed with Titan Management last month, and I meant what I said about working diligently on your behalf, but—"

"But nothing! This is serious, Marc. Quit jerking me around," he interrupted. "It's your job to fix my problems. That's why I hired you."

"I'll come by your house on Monday."

"Be here first thing tomorrow morning, or I'm finding another agent."

Click.

His eyes wide, Marc stared down at his cell. Unsure whether or not Javonte was bluffing, he considered calling him back to smooth things over because he didn't want to lose him as a client. He had a larger-than-life personality, people loved him—especially Marc's boss, Leon Frederick—and he was a dynamic football player. Javonte could be stubborn at times, but he'd never disrespected Marc before. Marc wondered if his entourage was leading him astray. Two days earlier, his friends had convinced him to skip practice, and Marc feared his new client was headed down the wrong path. One that could cost him his career.

Needing a cold drink, he headed straight for the bar. Two inches shy of seven feet, Marc was used to strangers staring at him, and smiled at everyone he passed. It was an older, distinguished crowd, and he recognized many of his parents' friends and associates. Marc was starving, but he spent a few minutes speaking to his mother's colleagues from Bucktown Medical Clinic, and even posed for a picture with his father's old golf buddies. For three decades, his father had been president of Chicago State College—a historically black university founded in the eighteen hundreds—and seeing some of his dad's former colleagues and students touched him deeply. His father was admired and respected by everyone who knew him, and two years after his passing, his friends and family were still struggling with his unexpected death.

At the bar, Marc ordered a rum and Coke and discreetly checked his email. He had dozens of messages, but he couldn't concentrate. His conversation with Javonte had soured his good mood, and as he waited for the female bartender to prepare his drink, troubling thoughts overwhelmed his mind. Was Javonte going to complain to Mr. Frederick? Was he serious about finding another agent? Or just bluffing?

"Finally, you're here. It's about time!"

Breaking free from his thoughts, Marc glanced over his shoulder and saw his mother headed his way. It was hard to believe she was sixty-five years old. Slender, with delicate features and short, auburn curls, she carried herself in a regal, dignified manner, as if she'd been raised in Buckingham Palace rather than on a wheat farm in South Carolina. Her loose-fitting metallic gown was modest, and her diamond broach sparkled.

"Great party, Mom," Marc said, kissing her cheek. "The turnout's incredible, and everyone seems to be having a great time."

"How would you know? You got here five minutes ago."

"Mom, I had to work. You know that."

"Work?" she repeated, rolling her eyes, her curt tone of voice conveying her displeasure. "Is that what you call babysitting spoiled, overpaid athletes for eight hours a day?"

Don't start, he thought, searching the ballroom for the nearest emergency exit. He didn't have the energy to argue with his mom, didn't want to hear about what a disappointment he was to his family, and if she brought up his failed marriage, he was leaving. The holidays were hard enough without his mom reminding him about his past mistakes.

Needing an ally, he searched the room for his sister, Kingsley, and her fiancé, Zander.

"When are you going to quit working at that silly company, and finally put your law degree from Northwestern to good use? It's what your father would want—"

"No, Mom, it's what *you* want. All Dad ever wanted was for me to be happy."

Marc picked up his glass and tasted his beverage. The ice-cold drink hit the spot, quenching his thirst, but his empty stomach groaned and grumbled. He'd missed the five-course meal prepared by the celebrity chef, and scanned the room for a server in the hopes of scoring a plate. "Mom, I didn't come here to argue with you about my career. I came to show my support for a worthy, life-changing cause, and to spend some time with you."

Her face softened. "I'm glad you're here, honey. It's good to see you."

Hugging her with one arm, he swiped his cell off the bar with the other and punched in his password.

Marc touched the camera app, tightened his hold around his mother's waist, then raised his cell in the air. "Mom, we're taking a selfie. Smile!"

She didn't, and when the camera flashed she shielded her face with her hands.

"Marc, put that thing away. This is a classy, upscale event, not a backyard barbecue," she hissed, glancing nervously around the room. "And delete that hideous picture."

"Mom, it's a party. Relax." Chuckling, Marc slid his cell phone into his jacket pocket. "Are Kingsley and Zander here? I don't see them anywhere."

Sadness touched her features, and a frown twisted her thin lips. "No. I'd hoped Kingsley would be here, but I guess she's too busy playing house to support her family."

"Have you spoken to her since her birthday dinner?"

Bridgett shook her head, but beamed as guests walked past, waving and smiling.

"Mom, you need to apologize."

"For what?" she argued. "Having an opinion? Your sister is making a mistake shacking up with that man and his child, and I'm not talking to her until she comes to her senses."

"His name is Tyson, and he's a smart kid who hopes to be an airline pilot one day."

Her eyes narrowed. "I. Don't. Care. Kingsley has no business living with that man. It's wrong. I didn't raise her like that."

Marc knew better than to argue with his mom, and decided to try talking to his twenty-eight-year-old sister on Sunday when he went to her Wicker Park home to watch the football game with Zander. His sister's fiancé was a mechanic, and Marc thought the single dad was a positive influence on his sister. Since meeting Zander Daniels and his six-year-old son, Tyson, last year, Kingsley had become more thoughtful and compassionate, and now the siblings were closer than ever. A pharmacist, with a sharp mind and an effervescent personality, his sister was on the fast track to success, and he couldn't be more proud of her.

"Honey, I will be back shortly. The entertainment portion of the program is about to start, and I have to ensure everything runs smoothly." Straightening her shoulders, Mrs. Cunningham inspected her gown, then fluffed her hair. "Drink responsibly. I will see you later."

His mom left, rushing off to boss someone else around, and Marc sighed in relief.

Marc spotted a server holding a silver tray and stopped him mid-stride. "My man! Am I ever glad to see you," he said, licking his lips in hungry anticipation. "What do you have there?"

"A leftover appetizer tray from table nine," the server explained. "There are ham-and-cheese croquettes, blue crab beignets, and stuffed mushrooms, if you're interested . . ."

"I'm *very* interested." Marc clapped his back, then stuffed a twenty-dollar bill in the front of his shirt pocket. "Thanks, man. Keep them coming."

Marc was sitting at the bar, eating his second meal of the day, when he heard excitement ripple through the crowd, and glanced up from his plate to see what the commotion was.

That's when he saw her.

The svelte, statuesque beauty in the sequined minidress.

His eyes widened and his jaw dropped, hitting his chest with a thud.

Smitten, completely captivated, Marc admired her beauty. The flawless, almond-brown skin, the pronounced cheekbones, the button nose, and blinding-white teeth. Straight, shiny hair—that his hands were itching to touch—kissed her shoulders, and her curled eyelashes and dramatic makeup gave her a sultry, exotic vibe. Like a model in a fashion magazine. Stilettos elongated her long, silky legs, and her walk was mesmerizing—the sexiest thing he'd ever seen.

A hush fell over the room as the crowd parted for the curvy new arrival in the emerald-green dress. Swishing her shapely hips, she moved through the grand ballroom as if she was an international superstar and it was her own personal stage. She was an actress. Had to be. She had "it," the wow factor, that intangible quality that couldn't be defined or explained, and men and women alike gawked at her in open appreciation.

Marc suspected she was in her early twenties, and wondered if she was single. As she approached the bar, her floral perfume overwhelmed his senses. His mouth dried, and sweat drenched his palms. Like the sun, her smile was so dazzling and bright Marc had to look away.

Narrowing his eyes, Marc scanned her left hand for a diamond ring but didn't see one. Over the years, he'd met pop stars, elite female athletes, and even an Oscar-winning actress, but none of them had captured his attention the way the voluptuous beauty did. Drawn to her, he couldn't fight his feelings. Couldn't stop from trailing her around the room with his eyes. Determined to meet her, Marc stood, but before he could introduce himself, a short, stocky man with rimless glasses stepped forward, ruining his plan.

The stranger purposely bumped into her, and a confused expression marred her pretty features. "Excuse me," she said, stepping back.

"You're stunning," he praised, in an awestruck tone of voice, his eyes glued to her cleavage. "If you were a burger at McDonald's you'd be the McGorgeous."

"Ah, thank you, I think."

Amused, Marcus listened in on the conversation. Watching them through the mirrored wall behind the bar, he wondered how long it would take for the woman to give the stranger his walking papers. Marc wiped his mouth with a napkin, then tossed it down on his empty plate.

"I'm Warner, and you are?"

"Uninterested, and unavailable," she quipped, tucking her clutch purse under her arm. "Bye. Have a good night."

Wearing a toothy smile, Warner pointed at a barstool. "Sit. I'll buy you a drink."

"You seem like a nice guy, and I'm not trying to be mean, but I'm not interested."

The grin slid off his face, and he raised a thick, bushy eyebrow. "Why not?"

"Because I like my men the way I like my coffee— tall, strong, and black."

Marc cracked up, chuckled long and hard at her witty comeback, but when he noticed everyone at the bar staring at him—including the curvy knockout— his laughter dried up. Unlike his celebrity clients, Marc hated to draw attention to himself, and hoped he hadn't blown his chance with the brown-eyed beauty by eavesdropping on her conversation.

"I appreciate everyone coming out tonight to support the Sickle Cell Foundation. If my husband, Eli, was here, I know he'd be proud of our efforts, so thank you . . ."

Hearing his mother's voice, Marc stood to his feet and faced the raised, dimly lit stage.

"Our first performers of the night are a young, dynamic a capella group from right here in Chicago. Everyone, please give a warm welcome to Lyrical Soul!"

Cupping her hands around her mouth, the voluptuous beauty cheered, hollered, and whistled. The noise was deafening, and Marc knew he wouldn't be able to hear properly for a week, but he didn't move away from her. He moved toward her. Closed the gap between them.

Hearing his cell phone buzz, he checked the number on the screen. His least favorite client was calling. The hockey player had a monster-sized ego, and Marc didn't feel like hearing him bitch about his teammates. Last night, they'd talked for an hour, and although he prided himself on being available to his clients day and night, he couldn't take the call. Making a mental note to phone him in the morning, Marc pressed the Decline button and pocketed his cell. He returned his attention to the beauty with the spellbinding dance moves.

Intrigued, Marc studied her. She watched the performance with rapt attention, singing every word of every song. Everything about her was appealing. Her singing. Her enthusiasm. How she swiveled her hips and whipped her hair around as if she were the queen of rock and roll. And, when she signaled to the lead singer at the end of the group's ten-minute set, Marc suspected she was their manager.

In a stroke of good luck, the woman sat down on a stool at the bar and ordered a Mistletoe Martini. It was time to make his move. Filled with confidence, he stalked toward her, determined to sweep her off her feet—and into his bed.

Chapter 2

Maya Malone hated Christmas. Had since she was a little girl, growing up in a low-income-housing apartment with her mom and brother on Chicago's South Side. Raised by a single mother, who'd rather party than parent, Maya had never had a Christmas tree in her living room, or baked cookies for Santa, and the only presents she'd ever received during the holidays were from her foster parents. But, as Maya sat at the bar inside the Avenues Ballroom in the cocktail dress she'd designed, and sewed weeks earlier, listening to the ten-piece band play the instrumental version of "Silent Night," she felt an overwhelming sense of pride. She'd done it. Beaten the odds. Proved the naysayers wrong. Made a good life for herself. Working as a celebrity stylist for an up-and-coming a capella group had its pros and cons, but Maya was exactly where she wanted to be, and felt fortunate to be living the American dream.

"Is this seat taken?" a male voice asked.

Oh, no, he's back! Maya thought, rolling her eyes to the ceiling. All night, men had been chatting her up, asking her out, and offering their business cards.

Most of the men were old enough to be her father, but she'd been polite and respectful to all of them. It was flattering to receive male attention, especially after everything her ex-fiancé had put her through last year, but the stranger with the corny pickup lines who'd bumped into her earlier didn't light her fire.

Why won't he leave me alone? What do I have to do to get rid of him? Annoyed that he was bothering her again, Maya spun around, prepared to ask him to leave, but when her gaze fell across Mr. Eye Candy—the hottie her friends had spotted in the crowd earlier and shamelessly drooled over—she slammed her open mouth shut.

For a moment, she stared at the ridiculously tall stranger in the slim-fitted, designer suit. He reeked of confidence, his light brown eyes were weapons of mass seduction, and his crisp, refreshing cologne made her think of the beach. Her favorite place to be. Every time she travelled to LA she'd spend hours at Manhattan Beach, and just the thought of swimming in the ocean with the dark and handsome stranger made goose bumps prick her skin.

His lips were moving—oh, how she wished they were moving against her mouth!—but his unexpected arrival threw her for a loop, making it impossible for her to concentrate, and Maya didn't hear a word he'd said. To regain control, she picked up her Mistletoe Martini and took a sip. "Hi," she said brightly, finding her voice. "I'm Maya."

"I'm Marc. It's a pleasure to meet you."

No, sexy, the pleasure is all mine, she thought, giving her eyes permission to roam and lust. His deep, husky voice tickled her ears, making her feel dizzy. Maya wanted to invite him to join her, but when she remembered what happened last night at the show in

Newark, she had second thoughts. A middle-aged Spanish man had asked her to dance, and out of nowhere a petite redhead had showed up, slinging insults and causing a scene. If her girlfriends hadn't come to her rescue, Maya would probably still be at Fever Bar and Lounge, pleading her case. "Did you bring a date tonight, or are you flying solo, like me?"

"I'm as single as they come. No wife, no fiancée, no kids."

Surprised by his answer, Maya wondered what his story was. He was to-die-for, the most attractive man she'd ever seen in the flesh, and in her experience men who looked like him usually had girlfriends in every part of the city.

He sat down on the stool beside her, and when their arms accidently touched, electricity shot through her body. Their eyes met, and her thoughts scattered, jumping from one X-rated thought to the next. To break the spell, she tore her gaze away from his face and asked, "What's your story? Why aren't you married, with kids and a house in the suburbs?"

"I was married once, but it didn't work out."

Maya knew she was being nosy, getting all up in his business, but she couldn't resist asking about his failed marriage. "What happened?"

"Can I be honest?"

Intrigued, and wanting him to be forthcoming about his relationship status, Maya nodded her head. "Yes, absolutely. Feel free to speak your mind."

"Women don't want nice guys like me. They want thugs and bad boys, guys who'll lie and mistreat them, not honest, respectable men like me who love their moms, picnics in the park, a capella music, and *Sex and the City* marathons."

A giggle tickled the back of Maya's throat and fell out of her mouth.

"What's so funny?"

"You. I bet you've never even seen an episode of the show."

"Of course I have, and now I have an important question for you."

Enjoying their verbal banter, Maya shrugged. "Ask away. I have nothing to hide."

Marc wore a serious expression on his face, but the corners of his lips were curled in a half smile. "Which character do you most identify with on the show?"

"Is this a trick question?"

Marc chuckled, and Maya did, too. She liked his personality, how charming and personable he was, and she could easily spend the rest of the night talking to him. The Avenues Ballroom offered spectacular views of Water Tower Park and Michigan Avenue, and watching the sunset with a suave, debonair man who smelled like the great outdoors was a heady feeling.

The female bartender arrived and took their drink orders. The brunette winked at Marc, but he pretended not to notice, gave Maya his undivided attention instead. "I'm waiting . . ." he prompted, drumming his fingers on the granite countertop. "Do you have an answer?"

"I'm torn. I love Carrie, and Charlotte, and I see myself in both of them."

"So, you're a confident, fun-loving girl who dreams of having it all. A fabulous career, a loving family, a couple of cute kids, and a wardrobe that makes you the envy of all your girlfriends. Am I right?"

"Wow, how did you know that? I'm impressed. You hit it out of the park!"

"We want the same things out of life," he said smoothly, his eyes bright with desire and mischief. "We must be kindred souls."

Maya knew Marc was joking, but for some strange reason, his words aroused her. Maya imagined herself kissing him, right then and there at the bar, but wiped the thought from her mind. Despite her height, and her ballsy personality, she'd never made the first move with a guy, and she'd always been attracted to men who were strong and assertive.

"We have a lot in common, and our names even complement each other."

"You think so?"

"Heck yeah. 'Marc and Maya' sounds cool, like a Hollywood power couple."

Amused, she hid a smile. To cool her overheated body, she fanned her face and sipped her cocktail. Maya didn't know if she was sweating because of the temperature in the room, or because the dark-skinned hottie was staring at her, and when her body tingled and her nipples hardened under her dress, Maya was convinced it was the latter.

"I think you'd look great on my arm at the New Year's Eve black-tie party," he announced, a grin dimpling his cheek. "You should definitely be my date."

Yassssss! she thought, overcome with excitement. Maya told herself he was joking again, just teasing her, and changed the subject by asking Marc about his career. Convinced he was a professional basketball player, she was shocked to discover he was a lawyer who worked for a management company that represented dozens of celebrities, and high-profile people.

"Are you from Chicago, or just visiting?" Marc asked.

"Born and raised on the South Side and proud of it. You?"

"The North Side, but don't hold it against me." Chuckling, he unbuttoned his suit jacket, took it off, and put it on the stool beside him. "You work for Lyrical Soul, right?"

"Yeah, how did you know?"

"I put two and two together during their performance. You were rocking out pretty hard to 'Jingle Bells,' and you sang all of the songs, note for note, so I figured you worked for the group," he explained. "To be honest, I thought you were an actress."

"An actress?" Maya repeated, shocked by his confession. "Why?"

"Are you serious?" Raising an eyebrow, Marc pointed at the mirrored wall along the bar, and stared at her reflection. "Look at you. Not only are you physically beautiful, you glow from within. You have a spark about you, a light, and it's captivating."

Beautiful? Captivating? His words confused her. Was Marc for real? Had her girlfriends put him up to this? Expecting to see the members of Lyrical Soul hiding in plain sight, Maya glanced around the room, but she couldn't find her girlfriends anywhere.

"You look upset. Did I say something wrong?"

Never had Maya felt more wanted or desirable. Her gaze strayed from his eyes to his lips, and it took everything in her not to kiss him. To avoid acting on her impulses, Maya sipped her cocktail, drinking the sweet, fruity concoction until it was finished.

"Did I blow my chance with the prettiest woman in the room, or can I stick around for a few more minutes and enjoy the pleasure of your wonderful company?"

Sexual tension consumed the air, hovering above the bar like a fragrant mist. No one had ever said she had a "light" before, and his compliments wowed her. All her life, ever since she was a chubby third-grader, she'd been told she was too heavy, too dark, too tall, and being with a man who praised her appearance gave her a rush. Her ex-boyfriend had never looked at her the way Marc did. Desire lay naked in his eyes, and his broad smile gave her a brain freeze. His mouth looked inviting, tempting, and for the second time in minutes all Maya could think about was kissing him until she was breathless.

"Of course you can stay," she quipped with a cheeky smile, tapping an index finger against her empty glass. "You have to stick around to buy me another drink!"

Out of the corner of her eye, Maya spotted her girlfriends from Lyrical Soul on the dance floor, doing the electric slide with gusto, and smiled to herself. To celebrate the success of their ten-city European tour, which had wrapped up three days earlier in London after a month away from home, they'd booked the presidential suite at the hotel. Closer than sisters, Maya loved Liberty Clark, Eliza Neves, and Aquarius Davidson with all her heart, and valued their friendship. Last year, when her engagement imploded, her girlfriends had dropped everything to be at her side on Christmas Eve, and their support had meant the world to her.

Painful memories flooded her mind. Getting engaged had been the biggest mistake of her life, and although Maya knew her ex wasn't the right man for her, his rejection still hurt like hell. This was her first Christmas without him, and every time she heard

"Jingle Bells" or saw mistletoe hanging in a doorway, sadness consumed her.

"Do you have any special plans for the Christmas holidays?"

Hearing Marc's deep, panty-wetting voice in her ears, Maya surfaced from her thoughts, and swallowed hard to clear her throat. Conversation flowed smoothly and freely, and no topic was off limits. Over cocktails and decadent desserts, they chatted about pop culture, movies they were dying to see, and the worst blind dates they'd ever been on. The ballroom was crowded and noisy, filled with spirited partyers, and the festive atmosphere put Maya in a playful, flirtatious mood.

An R & B group took the stage, and when Marc asked Maya to dance, she rose to her feet and strode confidently onto the dance floor. He took her into his arms, holding her close to his broad, muscled chest, and they moved as one body to the sultry, sensuous music. It amused her to see people watching them—even her girlfriends—but Maya draped her arms around his neck, pulling him even closer. With his handsome face and muscled physique, it was no wonder women everywhere were making eyes at him. His caress was as dreamy as his smile, and as his hands stroked her arms and hips Maya imagined herself kissing him, but conquered her desires. They danced to so many songs, Maya lost count. Hot and thirsty, they returned to the bar for another drink.

"You're an incredible singer and dancer," Marc said, helping her onto the barstool. "Have you ever wished you were onstage instead of behind the scenes?"

"No way. I'm not cut out for show business."

He wore a pensive expression on his face. "How do you know if you've never tried?"

"I've been with Lyrical Soul since they won the first season of *Chicago's Got Talent*, three years ago, so I've seen it all and then some. Trust me, the music business is brutal."

"Care to elaborate? In what way?"

"Because Lyrical Soul are full-figured divas, and not Barbie-thin, they're routinely passed over for bookings and TV appearances. The girl who was second runner-up doesn't have half their talent, but she's a perky blonde with a killer body, and music execs love her. She recently signed a record deal, and is presently on tour with a country music legend."

"Beauty comes in all shapes, colors, and sizes, and it's sad that in this day and age we're still judging women by stupid, superficial standards."

"I agree, but take it from someone who knows. Thin is in, and curvy isn't."

"Not to me. I care more about a woman's heart than her physical measurements, but I'm not going to lie. You're a perfect ten, Maya, and your inner beauty shines through."

"Thank you. That's very sweet of you to say—"

Hearing loud noises, Maya broke off speaking. She saw guests exiting the ballroom through the open doors, servers clearing tables and stacking chairs, and the R & B group packing up their instruments. The lights came on, and the female bartender left the bar.

As she checked the time on her cell phone, her eyes widened, and a soft gasp escaped her lips. She'd been hanging out with Marc for three hours? More shocking still, Maya didn't want their conversation to end, wanted to talk and flirt for hours more.

Marc must have read her thoughts, because he

said, "I'll give you a ride home. We can make plans for our first date, and discuss the New Year's Eve black-tie party further. I think we should coordinate our outfits. Power couples always do."

"Smooth, Mr. Man," she teased, with a laugh. "*Very* smooth indeed."

"Is that a yes?"

"I'm spending the night here at the hotel with my girlfriends, but thanks for the offer."

"What a coincidence. I'm staying here, too."

"If you live nearby why are you spending the night in the hotel?"

"Because I deserve it. It's been a hell of a week, and I could use some R and R."

"And you're *sure* you don't have a wife and kids waiting up for you in the suburbs?"

"I'm positive," he said, his tone strong and convincing. "The party's winding down, but I want us to continue talking, so why don't you join me in my suite for a nightcap."

"What kind of girl would I be if I followed you to your suite at this time of night?"

"The kind of girl who's fun and spontaneous."

His words tickled her funny bone, and Maya giggled. "Fill me in on the joke. What's so funny?"

"This is such a cliché. Guy meets girl at the bar, takes her home, and they hook up—"

Marc made his eyes wide, wore an innocent expression on his face. "Who said anything about hooking up?" he asked, wiggling his eyebrows. "Maya, get your mind out of the gutter. No one's hooking up tonight. I'm not that kind of guy. I'm saving myself for marriage."

Maya laughed long and hard. "What are we going to do in your suite?"

"Share a bottle of wine, watch *Sex and the City* reruns, and make out."

"I like," she said, meeting his gaze.

Marc took her hand in his and kissed her palm. "Me too. So, what do you say? Are you coming upstairs for the after-party or not?"

His touch and the sound of his husky voice was her undoing. Her temperature rose, and adrenaline coursed through her veins. Maya had never had a one-night stand before, but Marc was every woman's dream, and the thought of spending the night with him excited her. Her mind made up, she pushed her doubts to the furthest corner of her mind. "Sure, Marc, I'd love to, but first I have to talk to my friends. If I don't tell them where I'm going, they'll worry."

"No problem. I'll meet you in the lobby in ten minutes." Marc grabbed his suit jacket, put it on, and brushed his lips against the curve of her ear. "Don't keep me waiting."

His cologne washed over her, exciting her body. Watching Marc leave the ballroom, Maya wet her lips with her tongue, couldn't wait to finally be alone with him. Anxious to see him again, she swiped her clutch purse off the bar counter and stood.

Turning around, she bumped into her girlfriends. Of mixed heritage, Eliza was proud of her Mexican roots and her full-figured shape; Aquarius was the lead singer of the group, and the unofficial manager, and Liberty was a social butterfly, with an energetic personality.

"Hey, you guys! I was just coming to find you."

"Likely story," Liberty quipped. "I'm surprised you even remember us."

Eliza nodded, and her gold chandelier earrings

swished back and forth. "I know, right? You were sitting at the bar, all hugged up with Mr. Tall, Dark, and Fine, flirting and laughing like there's no tomorrow, completely ignoring us."

"No, I didn't. You guys sounded amazing tonight, and at the end of your set I cheered louder than anyone." Refusing to feel bad for hanging out with Marc, she gave her friends a pointed look. "Marc's a great guy, and I really enjoy his company. Is that a crime?"

"Marc," they sang in unison, their angelic voices filling the air. "Marc, the herald angels sing. Glory to the newborn king . . ."

Maya laughed. "You guys are ridiculous, you know that?"

Liberty bumped Maya's hip with her own, Aquarius kissed her cheek, and Eliza gave her a one-arm hug. "We know. That's why you love us."

Exiting the ballroom, the women critiqued their performance, discussed the guests they'd met and liked, and argued about what movie to watch in their suite.

"I'm going to have a drink with Marc, so I'll meet you guys at the room later."

"I'll come, too." Liberty linked arms with Maya. "I love the hotel lounge, and besides, we want to meet your sexy new friend. Handsome, successful men usually travel in packs, so I know Marc probably has a friend or two who's exactly my type."

"We're not going to the hotel bar. We're going to his suite."

Gawking, their mouths open wide, her girlfriends stopped dead in their tracks. "He didn't invite you to his suite to have a drink," Liberty said, her tone matter-of-fact. "That's a cover. Marc invited you up-stairs to hook up with you."

"We're just going to talk."

Eliza snorted. "Right, *chiquita*, and I'm a natural blonde!"

"Girl, don't do this," Liberty pleaded. "It's not worth it. I know. I've been there."

"This isn't you, Maya. You're a relationship kind of girl. Not a floozy."

Snickering, Aquarius propped her hand on her hip. "Eliza, delete that hideous word from your vocabulary. You're twenty-eight, not eighty-eight, so act like it!"

Maya bit down on her bottom lip. Were her friends right? Was she making a mistake? Playing with fire? Maya didn't want Marc to think she didn't respect herself or her body, but she wanted to be alone with him. Wanted to kiss him, to touch him, wanted to be in his arms again. Her breakup had taken a toll on her, affecting her confidence and self-esteem, and hooking up with Marc was the perfect antidote for her holiday funk.

"Maya, don't listen to them. This isn't the Dark Ages," Aquarius argued, rolling her eyes to the ceiling. "Having a one-night stand doesn't make a woman easy. It means she's a confident, liberated woman who knows what she wants and isn't afraid to go after it."

"Exactly!" Maya nodded in agreement.

"Girl, do you," Aquarius advised, patting her shoul-der. "Or better yet, *do* that tall, dark, and handsome hottie with the bedroom eyes, and tell me all about it in the morning."

Maya gave her friends a one-arm hug. "See you later. Don't wait up."

"Like hell we won't!" Eliza raised an index finger in the air. "You have one hour. I mean it. If you're not back at the suite at midnight, we're coming to find you!"

Chapter 3

The elevator doors slid open on the tenth floor of the Peninsula Hotel, but Maya was laughing so hard she couldn't move. Water filled her eyes, blurring her vision, and her jaw ached. From the moment she'd reunited with Marc in the lobby he'd been cracking jokes, and he was so funny and entertaining Maya couldn't stop giggling. "You're lying. There's no way that happened."

"I'm serious." Sliding an arm around her waist, Marc led Maya out of the elevator and down the dimly lit hallway. "Last winter, I bet my boss Chicago would beat Philadelphia in the Basketball Winter Classic, and when they lost I had to dress up as Mrs. Claus for the holiday office party. Needless to say, it was the longest three hours of my life."

"I can't even picture you in a dress. You're so big, and tall, and you have huge feet."

"Tell me about it. I *still* have nightmares about those red, pointy-toe shoes!"

Marc stopped in front of suite 1012, reached into his pocket, and retrieved a key card.

Hearing noises, Maya's ears perked up. Frowning, she glanced around the hallway. Someone was whispering. Calling her name. Peering over his shoulder, Maya spotted Liberty, Eliza, and Aquarius at the other end of the hallway, waving frantically, and glared at them.

Annoyed her friends were spying on her, Maya gestured for them to leave, but they didn't. Dread filled her stomach, and heat flooded her body. What the hell? What were they doing? Were they planning to camp outside Marc's suite until she left?

Marc pushed open the door and stepped aside. "After you, mademoiselle."

Spacious, with oblong lamps and designer furniture, the suite had all the comforts of home—a gourmet kitchen equipped with stainless steel appliances, a living room filled with comfy couches, and floor-to-ceiling windows that offered striking views of Michigan Avenue. Snowflakes were falling from the sky, but stars twinkled bright.

"What would you like to drink?" Marc asked. "Wine, tea, or coffee?"

"A glass of wine would be great."

"One glass of Riesling coming right up."

Making herself comfortable on the couch, Maya opened her purse, took out her cell phone, and composed a group text message to Liberty, Eliza, and Aquarius. Typing furiously, she threatened them with bodily harm if they embarrassed her, and hit the Send button.

Using the remote control, Marc lowered the lights and turned on the stereo. The air smelled fresh and clean, as refreshing as the ocean breeze, and the jazz music playing in the background gave the suite a romantic ambience. "Are your friends giving you a hard time for joining me in my suite?"

Nodding, Maya fiddled with the gold Cartier bracelet on her wrist. It was a gift from her brother, and every time she looked at it she remembered how far they'd come. Taking a deep breath didn't help calm her nerves. At the bar, she'd been her usual loud, chatty, opinionated self, but now that she was alone with Marc in his hotel suite, her tongue was twisted inside her mouth like a pretzel, and she couldn't think of anything smart or witty to say.

Crossing the room, holding two glasses, Marc flashed a boyish smile. *God help me*, Maya thought. Her heart beat louder, faster, and threatened to explode out of her chest. It turned out her girlfriends were right. They knew her better than she knew herself. This wasn't her. Maya liked being in a relationship, enjoyed having one special man in her life, and even though she was attracted to Marc, she couldn't have sex without a commitment. *What was I thinking?* She'd let the music, the slow dancing, and the festive atmosphere at the charity event go to her head, but it wasn't too late to change her mind. *I'll have one drink*, she decided, taking the glass Marc offered. *Then I'm out of here*.

Marc sat down beside her on the couch. "I'm glad you're here, Maya."

Why? So you can lure me into bed? she thought but didn't dare ask. The less she said the better. They'd had their fun and it was time to go, but Maya didn't want to do anything to upset him. Her ex had had an explosive temper, and Maya knew how quickly a situation could spiral out of control. Thankfully, Marc was the polar opposite of her ex. He wasn't a hothead. He was a gentleman—polite, courteous, and charming—and Maya felt safe with him.

"You're friendly and down-to-earth and you tell great stories," he continued, his tone filled with warmth. "It's the craziest thing. We just met, but I'm so comfortable with you it feels like I've known you for years."

His words resonated in her soul. Having lots of guy friends, Maya knew every trick in the book, but Marc sounded so genuine and sincere, she believed him. "I agree, and since we exchanged numbers earlier in the elevator, I hope we'll be able to keep in touch."

"Of course we will. We have a date tomorrow night."

"We do?" she questioned, arching an eyebrow. "That's news to me."

"I'm taking you ice skating at Tribune Plaza," he said with a wink and a smile. "After we've worked up a sweat, we'll have dinner at Everest. The food is outstanding, the service is second to none, and the ambience is perfect for a delicious meal with a very special woman."

Pleased that he'd planned a romantic date for them, she said, "I look forward to it."

"So do I. Meeting you has been the highlight of my week. Hell, my year!"

Giggling, Maya picked up her wineglass and raised it in the air. "To friendship."

Marc scoffed, and Maya wondered why his gaze was narrowed and dark.

"I have lots of friends. I don't need another one."

Her head spun, but she asked the question that filled her mind. "What do you need?"

"Someone I can be myself with," he confessed, locking eyes with her. "Someone smart and witty and vivacious who stimulates my mind, my soul, and my body."

Oh, my, she thought, wetting her lips with her tongue. The silence was deafening, so loud Maya could hear the distant sound of female voices and hoped her friends weren't hanging out in the hallway, waiting anxiously for her to emerge from Marc's suite.

Taking her glass, Marc set it down on the coffee table. He reached out and drew his fingers across her cheek, slowly caressing it with his hands. "You're so appealing, I forgot about everyone else in the ballroom tonight—even my mother!" he joked, a grin curling his lips. "I know something valuable when I see it, Maya, and that's you."

Lost in the moment and the sensuous sound of his voice, her eyes fluttered closed. Turned on by his confession, Maya listened intently to what he had to say, found herself hanging on to every word that came out of his mouth.

"You are, without a doubt, the most beautiful woman I have ever met—"

Desire exploded inside her, overtaking her mind and body, and she crushed her lips to his mouth. It was the boldest, most shocking thing Maya had ever done, but kissing Marc felt right. Perfect. The kiss was so passionate she moaned into his mouth. Since her engagement ended, she hadn't even been on a date, let alone had sex, but her body responded eagerly to his touch. Wanted more. Needed more. Longed to make love. And when his hands slid up her thighs and under her dress, Maya shivered.

After she abruptly ended the kiss, the sound of their heavy breathing filled the air.

"Maya, baby, what's wrong?" Marc asked, a concerned expression on his face.

"I've never had a one-night stand," she blurted out, dodging his piercing gaze.

Her cell phone buzzed, cuing her she had a new text message, but Maya ignored it.

"That's not what this is. I'm going to see you tomorrow, and the day after that, and the day after that, and the day after that . . ." Trailing off, he kissed her forehead, the tip of her nose, and the corners of her lips. "'Tis the season for fun and merriment, and I can't think of anything better than spending the rest of the night talking and laughing with you."

Maybe I'm not ready to leave after all, she thought, moving closer to him.

"The moment I saw you, all I could think about was making love to you, but now that I've gotten to know you better, I know it would be a mistake for us to sleep together."

Her eyes widened, and her mouth dropped open. *You do?*

"This isn't about sex, Maya. I like you a lot, and I don't want you to think I'm only interested in one thing. I'm not. I'm deeper than that . . ."

Like his words, his soft kisses along her neck thrilled her. No one had ever made her feel so special, and as he whispered in her ears, Maya couldn't think of anything *but* making love. She needed a distraction from her busy life, someone to help her forget her miserable, holiday blues, and the tall, chiseled hottie was just what the doctor ordered.

Pressing herself flat against him, Maya massaged Marc's body with her own. The warmth of his skin and the scent of his cologne were intoxicating. Her undoing. What pushed her to the brink. Kissing him, she playfully nipped at his bottom lip and raked her hands through his short, thick hair. Holding his tongue hostage with her teeth, Maya tickled and sucked on the tip of it, as her hands undid the buttons of his dress shirt.

Turned on, her flesh quivering with need, her body ached desperately for him. Maya loved his touch, couldn't get enough, and kissed him deeply to let him know she liked what he was doing with his mouth and hands. Leaving was out of the question. Screw decorum. Maya wanted to make love to Marc, and for the first time in her life, she was going to live in the moment without second-guessing herself.

Kissing and caressing him, Maya enjoyed being in his arms, but soon it wasn't enough. Wanting his hands all over her body—in her hair, on her breasts, between her legs, squeezing and spanking her ass—Maya stood, unzipped her dress, and let it fall to the floor.

Gripping her hips, Marc swirled his tongue around her navel, kissing and sucking it into his open mouth. His touch was electrifying, more powerful than a lightning bolt. Her thighs quivered, her knees buckled, and the floor fell out from under her feet. Cradling the back of his head in her hands, Maya held him close to her body, eager for more of his caress.

He unhooked her bra, slid it down her arms, and tossed it in the air as if it was confetti. Maya giggled, couldn't believe they were making out on the couch like a couple of teenagers. He cupped her breasts, squeezing and rubbing them, turning her out with each flick of his thumb.

"Your body is exquisite, especially your breasts. They're so big and beautiful," he praised, his voice full of awe. Stroking them, he swirled his tongue over her erect nipples.

Knowing that he desired her, that he appreciated her curves, drove Maya wild. Made her soul sing, her heart dance, and a girlish smile overwhelm her mouth.

"Maya, tell me what you want me to do, what you need. I want to please you."

Wanting him to feel her wetness, she guided his hand between her thighs and slid his finger inside her sex. A moan fell from her lips. Then another one. Maya leaned against him and gripped his shoulders. "I need you inside me now. Please." Shocked to hear the desperation in her voice, her tone sounded foreign to her ears, but she didn't hide her feelings. They bubbled up inside her and spilled out of her mouth. "This is incredible, like a wonderful dream, and I want to make love to you."

"Baby, are you sure?"

His question confused her, and she took a moment to consider his words.

"It's a huge step, Maya, and I don't want you to hate me in the morning."

As he rose to his feet, she noticed his gaze was filled with uncertainty, and sought to put his fears to rest. "Marc, I won't. I'm a twenty-eight-year-old woman with needs and desires and wants, and I *want* you."

"We don't have to make love tonight. There'll be plenty more opportunities."

"I've never been more sure of anything in my life." To prove it, Maya kissed him hard on the mouth, then sashayed confidently toward the bedroom. "Are you coming?"

"Hell, yeah," Marc said with a lopsided grin. "Don't start without me!"

Warm and cozy under the blanket on the king-size bed seconds later, Maya watched Marc undress.

She drooled as her eyes slid down his ripped physique. Everything about his body was a turn-on, made her wet. His chiseled pecs and biceps, six-pack abs, and his firm, hard ass. Built like a superhero, he was the perfect physical specimen, and Maya couldn't wait for him to join her in bed.

Marc grabbed a packet from his wallet, took off his boxers, and rolled the condom onto his erection. Swallowing hard, Maya felt her body warm and her pulse race. It was a sight to behold. A thing of beauty. The staggering width and length of his erection made her mouth water, and Maya was so eager to make love she tossed aside the sheets, draped her arms around his neck, and pulled him down on top of her.

Giggling, she grabbed his ass and clasped her legs around his waist. Marc kissed her, and she sighed in contentment. He made love to her mouth with his lips, and Maya squealed when he tickled her earlobe with his tongue. They laughed, rolling around on the bed, their voices drowned out the jazz song playing on the stereo system. Marc gave her everything she needed, what her body wanted. Maya tightened her hold around his shoulders. She liked feeling his hard body against her soft, supple skin, and couldn't stop caressing and stroking his muscles.

Ravishing her mouth with kisses, Marc slid a hand between her thighs, positioned his erection against her clit, and eased it inside her. It was a tight, snug fit, but Maya spread her legs wide open, urging him deeper still. Squeezing her pelvic muscles, she moaned and cursed and whispered naughty words in his ears. Their wild, frenzied lovemaking excited her, had Maya saying and doing things she'd never said or done before.

Planting her feet flat on the bed, Maya used the

leverage to thrust her hips toward him. The missionary position had never felt so good, and she was so blissfully and ridiculously happy, she wanted to pinch herself to prove she wasn't dreaming. It was hard to believe this was the first time they'd ever had sex. Comfortable with him, she yearned to unleash her inner sex goddess. Wanted to please, and be pleased. Marc was not only every woman's dream, he was a thoughtful, considerate lover who put her needs first. He took his time with her, and seemed to derive great pleasure from making her moan. Reading her body as if it was a book, Marc knew how to please her, and Maya loved how fun and playful he was in bed.

Skin to skin, their hands and legs intertwined, they moved as one body. Maya didn't know lovemaking could be like this. Erotic. Passionate. Sensuous. No wonder she was losing it. Bucking against him, licking his earlobe, twerking his nipples, rubbing and slapping his ass.

Panting, her mouth unhearably dry, Maya thrust her hips back and forth, hard and fast. It took every ounce of her self-control not to scream out in ecstasy. At the point of no control, she arched her back and gripped his shoulders. The speed and depth and intensity of his penetration made it impossible for her to think or speak. Maya didn't want to come, wasn't ready for their lovemaking to end, but she had no choice but to ride out the delicious wave flowing through her body.

"My turn. I'm right behind you, baby." Hiking her leg in the air, Marc pressed his eyes shut, and threw his head back. He increased his pace, pumping his hips hard and fast, thrusting and swiveling. He groaned and his body went completely still.

As they basked in the afterglow of their lovemaking,

a slow smile crept across Maya's lips. Marc was an attentive and passionate lover, the best she'd ever had, and she'd never forget him.

He stretched out beside her, his feet dangling over the edge of the platform bed. He pulled her into his arms, and Maya snuggled against his chest. *Did that just happen?* she thought. *Did I actually have a one-night stand? And if so, why do I suddenly feel giddy and excited?*

"That was incredible," she whispered, speaking her thoughts aloud. Her head was in the clouds, full of happiness and romantic ideas, but Maya knew baring her soul to Marc after only one night together was a mistake. If she did, she'd scare him off, and she wanted to see him again tomorrow night. Her hopes were high—maybe too high considering they'd just met—but Maya sensed he was a good guy who wouldn't hurt her, and she was looking forward to their first official date at Tribune Plaza. "Thank you for a *very* memorable evening."

"You think that was good? Wait until you see what I can do with a can of whipped cream!"

"Why tell me when you can show me?"

Chuckling, he kissed the top of her head. "I didn't realize you were so naughty."

"There are a lot of things you don't know about me."

"I know you like this," Marc whispered, brushing his lips against her ear.

Her breath caught on a moan, sending shock waves through her flesh.

"You like this, too, don't you?"

He cupped her breast in his hand, lowered his face, and eagerly licked it.

She felt her nipples harden. Her mouth dried, and her sex tingled.

"And I know for a fact that you love this."

Marc slid a finger between her legs, and swirled it around her sex.

"Please don't rush off," he whispered, his tone silky smooth. "I want you to stay."

Aroused, Maya tried to focus her gaze on Marc's face, but everything in the room was a blur. It was hard to think when he was tweaking her nipples and stroking her hips, but she surfaced from her sexual haze and nodded in response. He'd seduced her with poignant words and tender caresses, and as they made love for the second time, Maya decided to put the past behind her and embrace the holiday season. With that thought in mind, she rolled on top of Marc, pinned his hands to the bed, and kissed him hard on the mouth.

Chapter 4

Marc walked into the media room inside Javonte's gated Northfield mansion on Saturday morning, noticed the footballer's entourage were already chugging beers at the wet bar, and shook his head in disgust. Framed football jerseys were displayed along the fireplace mantel, flat-screen TVs were mounted above the pool table, and glass shelves held trophies, plaques, and autographed footballs. The patterned wallpaper and bronze table lamps gave the space a masculine but elegant feel, but the air reeked of weed, and Marc suspected the men were smoking more than just cigarettes.

Put off by the odor, Marc wiggled his nose. He hoped the stench didn't saturate his clothes, and decided to speak to Javonte again about his "friends," once they were finished talking business. Though Marc doubted anything would change. For the life of him, he didn't understand why Javonte insisted on hanging out with guys from his old neighborhood. Didn't he realize they were bad for his image? His brand? Didn't he care about landing endorsement deals?

Releasing a deep sigh, he took off his sunglasses and slid them inside the pocket of his black leather jacket. A picture of Mya flashed in his mind, and his scowl morphed into a smile. Nothing was going to spoil his good mood. He'd met an angel, a smart, spirited beauty he'd instantly connected with, and Marc was looking forward to seeing her tonight. Couldn't wait. Since his divorce, he'd dated one woman after another, but the celebrity stylist was the only person to ever capture his attention. There was a lot to like about her—her sharp wit, her confidence, her wild, exuberant laugh—and he'd been taken with Maya from the moment he'd laid eyes on her. Everyone else in the room had disappeared, and the music had faded into the background. Successful in every area of his life, except love, Marc was tired of playing the field, and wondered if Maya was a Christmas fling or someone he could settle down with. Deep down, Marc hoped it was the latter. Last night in bed, they'd talked for hours, and he'd opened up to her in a way he couldn't with anyone else.

Marc shook his head, forced himself to pump his breaks. As usual, he was thinking too much, getting way ahead of himself. At heart, he was a relationship guy, the kind of person who thrived having a loving, committed partner, but this time around he had to be smart. Careful. Had to make better choices, or he would get hurt again, and Marc didn't want history to repeat itself. "Hey, Javonte," he said, abandoning his thoughts. "What's up?"

Grumbling, the defensive lineman cracked his knuckles.

Marc took off his jacket, hung it on the wooden coat hanger beside the window, and took a seat beside

Javonte on the tan couch. Stocky, with broad shoulders and large hands, he was one of the most explosive players in the National Football League, and coaches, teammates, and fans loved his tenacity out on the field. "How's my favorite client doing?"

"Did you call Coach Schneider?" he asked, using a face towel to mop the sweat dripping from his face. "What did he say? Did he believe you?"

"Javonte, I'm not going to lie for you."

"Why not? Everyone else does."

Marc swallowed hard. He loved sports, had since he was in elementary school, and although he specialized in baseball, basketball, and football, he represented several Olympians as well, but no one was more challenging than Javonte Malone. Still, he remained calm, didn't let his frustration show. "We've talked about this before. I'm your agent, not your manager—"

"I know, but Coach likes you. He said you're a loyal, stand-up guy and encouraged me to sign with your agency. Coach said you'd take good care of me. Was he wrong?"

Marc met his gaze, didn't flinch when the football player's eyes darkened. Javonte was trying to intimidate him, to bully him into doing what he wanted, but it wasn't going to happen. A month earlier, Marc had negotiated the largest contract in the agency's history, and three weeks later his boss was still celebrating. Landing Javonte "Bone Crusher" Malone as a client was the biggest accomplishment of his eight-year career, but Marc wasn't going to let the defensive lineman push him around. "What's going on? Last week, you were fired up about the New Orleans game, and now you're running scared. What gives?"

Hanging his head, Javonte leaned forward in his seat and rubbed at his eyes.

To lighten the mood and encourage the defensive lineman to confide in him, Marc clapped him good-naturedly on the back and said, "What's going on, man? Talk to me."

Seconds passed, and just when Marc had given up all hope of ever getting a straight answer, Javonte spoke in a low, pained voice.

"It's my knee. It's acting up again, and the pain medication isn't working."

"Have you met with the team doctor?"

"Yeah. I saw him yesterday, and he said everything looks good, but it's not."

Nodding in understanding, Marc wore a sympathetic expression on his face. Having worked with professional athletes for years, he understood why Javonte was upset, and why he didn't want to play in the nationally televised game. For all their toughness and bravado, a lot of athletes had self-esteem issues and feared being rejected by their coaches, teammates, and fans.

"If I play on Thursday night I'm risking further injury, and if I don't suit up I could be benched indefinitely." His shoulders drooped. "It's a no-win situation. Either way, I'm screwed."

"When are you supposed to leave for New Orleans?"

"Tuesday." Javonte glanced at his Rolex wristwatch. It was ostentatious and flashy, just like his diamond stud earrings, and chains, but he enjoyed showing off his wealth. "But I'm supposed to be at the stadium this afternoon to study film, and practice drills."

"I'll call Coach Schneider."

Sighing in relief, he lobbed his arm around Marc's shoulder and hugged him. "My man!" he shouted, pumping a fist in the air. "Thanks, Marc. This means a lot to me."

"I'm not making any promises, Javonte. I'll call Coach and tell him about your knee, but as a show of good faith you should attend practice today, and also travel with the team. It will prove you care about the game, your reputation, and your teammates."

"Sure, no problem. I can do that. I love the Big Easy!"

A short, lanky guy in a Lakers baseball cap wandered into the media room and gestured with his chin to the door. "J, can I holler at your sister? I bumped into her upstairs, and she was looking *real* nice. Like a video vixen!"

"Not if you value your life."

"Come on, bro. I'll be on my best behavior. You can trust me—"

Javonte spoke through clenched teeth. "We talked about this already, Chauncey. Don't even think about it. My sister is off limits, and that will never change. Got it?"

Marc felt his cell phone vibrate, and took it out of his pocket to read his latest text message. In the distance he heard someone singing "Christmas with You," and the woman's soft, melodious voice filled the air. "I didn't know you had a sister," Marc said.

Shrugging a shoulder, Javonte wore a crooked grin. "You never asked."

"Do you have any other siblings?"

"Nope. It's just me and Maya . . ."

Frowning, Marc cranked his head to the right. Stared at Javonte as if he was speaking a foreign language. *Maya?* Panic rose inside the walls of his chest, but he conquered his emotions. No way. It couldn't be. Had to be a coincidence. But when his one-night stand strode into the media room, his fears returned with a vengeance. His eyes were broken. Deceiving him. Playing tricks on his mind, because there was no way in hell Maya—*his* Maya—was at Javonte's estate.

Maya wet her lips with her tongue, and sweat soaked Marc's white knit shirt. The snowball-size lump in the back of his throat threatened to choke him, and his pulse was drumming so loud in his ears a headache began to form in his temples.

To regain control, Marc took a deep breath, but his temperature continued to climb. There were millions of smart, attractive women in Chicago, but he'd slept with his client's kid sister last night—done things with her in his suite that would make a groupie blush—and now he was living a nightmare. Dead, if Javonte ever found out. Still, despite the risk of being caught, he lusted after her. She looked delectable in a burgundy off-the-shoulder dress and black suede boots. Marc couldn't stop himself from admiring her full, curvy hips and supple thighs—thighs he'd stroked and massaged and licked last night.

"Maya, don't be shy. Come over here and meet my new agent," Javonte called.

Fear flashed in her eyes, but she nodded, and cautiously approached the couch.

His legs felt heavier than fifty-pound weights, but Marc stood and smoothed a hand over the front of his shirt. God help him. He was a mess. Couldn't stop staring at Maya if his life depended on it—and it did. She must have just gotten out of the shower because her hair was damp, her skin was glowing, and she smelled of perfume and lotion.

"What happened to Ike?" Maya asked, a frown bruising her glossy lips. "He's been with you for years and you guys have a great relationship."

"Not anymore. I found out he was bad-mouthing

me behind my back, so I fired his ass, and signed with
Marc Cunningham of Titan Management," Javonte
explained.

"I didn't know you and Ike were having problems.
Why didn't you say anything?"

"Because you were on the road with Lyrical Soul in
Europe and I didn't want you to worry. You know how
you get."

Javonte winked at Maya, and the siblings shared a
knowing smile.

"Marc, this is my sister, Maya. She's the stylist for
the a capella group Lyrical Soul, and also a budding
fashion designer. One day soon, she'll be a household
name. I know it."

Maya extended her right hand. Like playing tag in
rush-hour traffic, Marc knew touching her was dan-
gerous, but since he didn't want to make Javonte sus-
picious, he forced a smile and shook her outstretched
hand. Electricity rippled across his flesh, but Marc
maintained his composure. Kept his game face on.
"It's a pleasure to meet you."

"Same here." Fiddling with the gold thumb ring on
her left hand, Maya shifted and shuffled her feet. "I'd
better get back to the kitchen. The wings are in the
oven, and I don't want them to burn."

Maya turned and walked away, and Marc tracked
her every move. The woman had it all. A winning personality. A dazzling, Chiclet-white smile. Curves
galore. He was drooling, but noticed the other guys
in the room were slobbering all over themselves, too.
His eyes narrowed. Marc didn't like Javonte's friends
gawking at her, but there wasn't a damn thing he
could do about it.

Tearing his gaze away from her backside, Marc
swiped his cell phone off the coffee table and shoved

it into his pocket. It was time to go. Before he lost it. After his unexpected run-in with Maya, he needed a shot of vodka to calm his nerves, and a cold shower. "Javonte, I have to go, but I'll be in touch." Marc yanked his jacket off the coat hanger and shrugged it on. "I'll call you once I talk to Coach, but try not to worry."

"Stay for lunch. My sister is a culinary genius, and her recipes have won contests."

"I thought you had a personal chef."

"I do, but Batista only works when Maya's out of town."

Marc closed his gaping mouth. "She lives here with you? Why?"

"Why not?" Glancing around the room, Javonte flung his arms wide open. "I have tons of space, I love having her around, and best of all she's an outstanding cook."

The savory aroma in the air caused his stomach to groan and grumble, but Marc ignored his hunger. Staring at his watch, he tapped the glass with his index finger. "I have a one o'clock meeting with a golf prodigy in Gold Coast, and I don't want to be late."

"Don't sweat it. You have plenty of time."

Marc thought hard, but he couldn't think of an excuse to get out of lunch. And when he remembered his quickie with Maya in the shower last night—how she'd turned him out with her tongue a million different ways—his life flashed before his eyes, and dread filled his stomach.

"Now, let's eat. I'm hungrier than a sumo wrestler on a no-carb diet!" Javonte joked, with a hearty chuckle. The matter decided, he clapped Marc on the shoulder and steered him out of the media room, with his eight-man entourage in tow.

Chapter 5

Christmas music was playing on the stereo system, a lively, upbeat song by the reggae group Boney M., but Marc's thoughts were filled with guilt, not good-will to all men. Sliding his hands into the pockets of his dress pants, he admired his surroundings. The simplicity of the cathedral ceilings, granite counter-tops, and tiled floors in the gourmet kitchen were a stark contrast to the adjoining great room. It had chandeliers, ten-foot-long sofas, and the gold and black color scheme was striking. Just like Maya. She glanced over her shoulder and smiled at him, but Marc pretended to admire the framed photographs hanging on the walls. He'd been to Javonte's estate several times before, but he'd never been in the great room. If he had, he would have known about Maya. There were pictures of her everywhere.

"J, be a good host and get Marc something to drink," Maya advised.

Their eyes met, and desire scorched his skin. His heart was beating so loud, he feared everyone else could hear it, too. It was stressful being in the same room as his favorite client and his one-night stand—the woman who'd given him the best sex of his life—and if he was going to survive lunch, he had to stay far away from Maya. Avoid her at all costs.

Dodging her gaze, he accepted the wine cooler Javonte shoved into his hands, and nodded his thanks. It wasn't a shot of Grey Goose, but it would suffice. A creature of habit, Marc pulled out Maya's chair and waited until she was seated before he sat down beside her. *So much for keeping my distance,* he thought, wanting to kick himself for not sticking to his plan. His body yearned for her, but Marc kept his hands to himself and off her sinful curves.

The walnut table, which seated twelve, was covered in silverware and round serving platters. Poinsettias were positioned between the red, scented candles. Starving, Marc picked up the bowl of short ribs, prepared to fill his plate to the brim, but froze when Javonte spoke up.

"Hold up, man. We have to say grace first."

Marc thought he was joking and laughed out loud, but no one else did.

"Don't let the chains and tattoos fool you," Javonte said, clasping his hands together, his expression solemn. "I was raised in the church, and I'm a very spiritual dude."

To Marc's surprise, everyone at the table bowed their heads and closed their eyes. Maya took his hand, and his thoughts flashed back to last night. They'd made love in the shower, and after a midnight snack courtesy of room service, he'd escorted her to the presidential suite. Though he didn't leave. They'd remained in the hallway, talking and laughing and kissing, and if her girlfriends hadn't opened the door and dragged her inside, they probably would have returned to his suite to make love for the fourth time.

"God, we bow our heads to honor you," Javonte prayed, sounding as dignified as a bishop. "Thank you for this meal, and for the gift of good friends and family. Amen."

Marc couldn't speak. His tongue was frozen inside his mouth, and his lips were glued together. Worst of all, he felt like Judas. Breaking bread with Javonte, knowing now that Maya was his kid sister, troubled his conscience, and Marc couldn't look at the defensive lineman without being consumed with guilt and regret. And the more he tried to delete the images of last night from his mind, the more vivid they were.

In good spirits, the group chatted about the weather, their old neighborhood, and their plans for the Christmas holidays. Marc dished himself some food, took two bites, and put down his fork. He couldn't eat it. Not because it didn't taste good but because his stomach was in knots. He couldn't recall ever being this nervous, not even when he'd proposed to his ex-wife, and hoped he didn't make a fool of himself in front of Maya during lunch.

"What are you going to do with your signing bonus from Nike?" Chauncey asked.

"Buy a Rolls Royce Phantom for me and all of my boys."

A cheer rose up from the table, and Marc rolled his eyes to the ceiling. Couldn't believe Javonte was planning to spend his seven-figure check on his friends, even though he'd foot the bill for the group to travel to Brazil two weeks earlier. "Javonte, why don't you invest it, or donate it to your favorite inner-city charity?"

The grin slid off of his mouth. "Because I want a Rolls Royce Phantom."

Swallowing a curse, Marc stabbed a baby tomato with his fork. He wanted to remind Javonte that he had ten luxury cars and motorcycles in his garage, but changed his mind. Why bother? The defensive lineman spent money faster than he earned it, but since he'd rather listen to his friends than sound advice, Marc held his tongue.

"J, Marc's right," Maya said, a concerned expression on her pretty face. "You don't need another sports car. You need to save. You can't play football forever—"

Rap music filled the air, and everyone at the table checked their electronic devices. "I have to take this call," Maya explained, rising to her feet. "I'll be right back."

Maya left the table, but this time Marc kept his eyes on his plate and off her shapely ass.

"Hey! Knock it off!" Scowling, Javonte gave the guy in the Lakers jersey a shot in the chest with his fist. "Maya's not one of those chicks you like messing with at the club. She's classy and sophisticated, so stop staring at her butt or I'll gouge your eyes out."

The guy gave a nervous laugh and wiped the sweat from his brow. "J, relax. I wouldn't disrespect you like that. I wasn't checking out your sister. I was, ah, looking out the window."

"That better be all you're looking at, or you'll be sorry."

Conversation turned to boxing, and everyone spoke at once, but Marc tuned them out. He wanted to talk to Maya alone before he left for his meeting, and sensed this was his opportunity. Marc finished his wine cooler, wiped his mouth with a napkin, and pushed away from the table. "Javonte, thanks for lunch. You were right, man. It was delicious."

"You can't leave. We haven't had dessert yet—"

Chauncey sucked his teeth. "Let Preppy Boy go," he snarled, his lips curled into a sneer. "He doesn't want to be here. He thinks he's better than us."

I don't think *I'm better than you*, Marc thought, glaring at the full-time jerk and part-time barber. *I* am *better than you. I don't mooch off my friends, and I always pay my own way.*

"Javonte, I'll call you once I talk to Coach."

"Sounds good."

They bumped fists, and Marc exited the kitchen. Lunch had been the longest hour of his life, and he was anxious to return to his car, but he wasn't leaving the estate until he spoke to Maya.

Marching through the main floor, listening for the sound of her voice, he glanced around in search of her but couldn't find her anywhere. The door at the end of the hallway creaked open. Maya poked her head out and waved him inside. Entering the bathroom, he noticed the bright and airy space had limestone countertops, mother-of-pearl wallpaper, and sports-themed artwork.

"I can't believe you're here. What a wonderful surprise." Resting a hand on his chest, she gave him a sweet, soft kiss on the lips. "I almost fainted when I walked into the media room and saw you sitting on the couch with my brother."

"Why didn't you tell me you're Javonte Malone's sister?"

"Because it never came up," she said, shrugging a shoulder. "Why are you mad?"

"If Javonte finds out we slept together, he'll go ballistic."

"He won't find out. It's our little secret." Maya pressed a finger to his lips. "I won't tell a soul, and neither will you. See? Problem solved."

Irked by her easy-breezy attitude, Marc paced the length of the room to blow off some steam. Maya chatted excitedly about their plans for the evening, but Marc wasn't listening. He was thinking about Javonte. In his mind's eye, he saw the defensive lineman tackling him to the floor and beating him to a pulp. Instinctively, he wiggled his nose and jaw to make sure everything was still intact.

"In light of everything that's going on with Javonte right now, it's probably best we keep our relationship under wraps," she said. "So I'll meet you at Tribune Plaza at seven o'clock. I can't wait. I haven't been ice skating in years."

"Maya, we can't go out tonight, or any night, for that matter."

She raised her eyebrows in a questioning slant, and puckered her lips.

"Javonte will kill me if he finds out we hooked up, and I can't lose him as a client."

"Then don't say anything," she whispered, draping her arms around his neck.

Taking her arms from around his neck, he took a giant step back. He had to keep his distance or his resolve would crumble, and Marc didn't want to disrespect Javonte in his home by kissing his kid sister. "We can't hide our relationship from him forever."

A mischievous expression covered her face. "Are you planning to be around forever?"

"Maya, this is serious. It's not a laughing matter."

"But I cancelled my plans with my girlfriends tonight so I could see you."

Hearing the sadness in her voice pierced his heart. He thought he was doing the right thing by cancelling their date, so why did he feel worse, not better?

Silence descended on the room, and the air was colder than the North Pole. The walls were closing in, and the distant sound of voices reminded Marc what was at stake. What he could lose if the truth got out. So he unlocked the door and took his car keys out of his pocket.

"I have to go," he said, with a sad smile. "Happy holidays, Maya, and all the best in the New Year. I hope you find great success as a fashion designer."

She laughed, realized he was serious, and slid in front of him, stopping him mid-stride. "You told me I was special, and that we had a strong connection. Did you just say that to get me into bed? Was that just a slick line to seal the deal?"

"No. I meant everything I said last night. You're an incredible woman, Maya, the complete package, and I'd be lying if I said I didn't have feelings for you. I do."

"If that's true, you wouldn't be blowing me off."

Maya gave him a hopeful look, but when she touched his forearm Marc's body tensed.

"My brother is an NFL star. Big deal! Why does it matter?"

"Because I'm his agent. If I'd known you were Javonte Malone's sister, I wouldn't have slept with you last night. I would have gone home alone instead of inviting you to my suite."

Her face fell, and a murderous expression darkened her big brown eyes, but she spoke in a quiet tone, as if she was feeling peaceful and Zen. "You're right." Her hoop earrings swung back and forth as she fervently nodded her head. "Last night was a mistake."

Mad at himself for upsetting her, he rested a hand on his chest to convey his regret and wore an apologetic smile. "Maya, I'm sorry. That came out wrong. That's not what I meant."

"Yes, it is. That's *exactly* what you meant."

"You're putting words in my mouth."

"No, I'm not. I'm quite skilled at reading between the lines, and it's obvious you regret sleeping with me, but don't worry. It will *never, ever* happen again."

Maya blew past him, but Marc grabbed her arm and pulled her into his arms.

"I didn't mean it."

"Yes, you did, but that's okay. Don't sweat it," she said, breaking free of his grasp. "You're not the only handsome, successful guy in Chi-Town. There are plenty of other men who'll be proud to call me their girlfriend, and treat me like the queen I am. "

Brushing past him, Maya yanked open the bathroom door. Marc couldn't stomach the thought of her with another man, and called out to her, asking her to stay so they could talk. Deaf to his pleas, she flew down the hallway, and Marc felt like a jerk for hurting her feelings.

Chapter 6

Water Tower Place was the most exclusive shopping area in the city, and Maya's favorite place to shop. A tourist attraction, with upscale stores and restaurants, it had a chic, contemporary design and a vibrant atmosphere. Packed with holiday shoppers clutching coffee cups, shopping bags, and unruly children, Maya couldn't move without someone bumping into her.

Swaying to the beat of the music, Maya sang along with her friends and snapped her fingers. Lyrical Soul had been hired to perform at the mall during the Christmas season, and as Liberty, Aquarius, and Eliza belted out the chorus of "Jingle Bells," Maya noticed people were cheering, whistling, and clapping. Her friends were having fun onstage, and it showed. They were blowing kisses and dancing with people in the audience, and the crowd ate it up.

Impressed with the huge turnout, Maya knew their afternoon show was going to be a hit, and hoped it would lead to more bookings for Lyrical Soul. Santa's Magical Winter Wonderland was on the main floor of the mall, near the Jolly Express Train, and the bright, colorful set looked like something out of a Christmas book. Blue crystal snowflakes hung from the ceiling, ten-foot trees were elaborately decorated, and Mrs. Claus handed out candy canes to the children in the audience. The air smelled of pastries and apple cider, and the mouthwatering scent made Maya hanker for a sweet treat.

A couple walked by, holding ice skates, and the smile slid off Maya's lips. Last night had been a bust. Another boring, uneventful evening at home. Instead of going out on a date with Marc, she'd stayed home with Javonte and his friends, eating junk food and watching videos. Outgoing and friendly, her brother was more popular than a teen heartthrob, and every time Maya returned from a road trip with Lyrical Soul, his entourage was bigger. Everyone loved Javonte and wanted to get close to him—especially people from their old neighborhood. Unscrupulous characters were always popping up on their doorstep, and Maya had a feeling Chauncey Matthews was up to no good. Sure, he was athletic and attractive, but he mooched off her brother, which was a turnoff. Add to that, he lacked ambition and flirted with anyone in a skirt. Why couldn't he be more like Marc, and less like himself?

At the thought of her dreamy one-night stand, her temperature rose and her nipples hardened under her plaid DKNY sweater dress. Being with him had felt right, as natural as breathing. Maya wished Javonte wasn't controlling, and overprotective of her. Wished he treated her like a twenty-eight-year-old woman instead of like a teenager. If he wasn't so stubborn and hardheaded, she'd tell him she was romantically interested in Marc, but experience had taught her not to confide in her brother about her love life. He couldn't handle it. In his eyes, she was still a little girl, and although Maya hated it when he babied her, she loved him dearly, and she couldn't have asked for a better brother.

Maya felt someone tug on the sleeve of her dress, and turned around.

A boy with short black hair and dark brown skin rubbed at his eyes. "I'm lost," he said, shifting and shuffling his sneaker-clad feet. "Can you help me find my uncle?"

Concerned, she crouched down and smiled sympathetically at the distraught child. "Sure, I can help you. What's your name?"

Tears spilled down his cheek, but he wiped them away. "Tyson Daniels."

"How old are you?"

He held up his hands. "Six. I go to Legacy Charter School. My teacher's name is Mr. Villanueva, but we call him Scrooge because he never gives us candy . . ."

Maya smirked. The boy was so articulate and well-spoken, she found it hard to believe he was in the first grade. To hear him over the noise of the crowd, Maya moved closer, and rested a hand on his shoulder. "Tyson, when did you last see your uncle?"

"I-I-I don't remember," he stammered, scratching his head. "We were looking at games in Toys'R'Us, and when I turned around he was gone. Poof! Like a puff of smoke."

Swallowing a laugh, Maya gestured to the escalators. "Let's go upstairs to the customer service desk. They'll be able to help us find your uncle."

"I'm hungry." Tyson licked his lips and patted his stomach. "Can I please have some milk and cookies first? I haven't had lunch yet, and I'm starving."

Clasping his hand, Maya led the first-grader over to the snack table, and introduced him to Mrs. Claus.

He filled his plate with cookies and grabbed a juice box. Tyson was polite and courteous, and Maya laughed as he chatted excitedly about his plans for the Christmas holidays.

"Did you write your list, and mail it to Santa at the North Pole?"

"Yes. I've been a *really* good boy this year, and now it's time for Santa to pay up!" Tyson guzzled down his apple juice, then helped himself to a fourth cookie. "I want a tablet, a new PlayStation, a Spiderman desk, some WWE action figures, and a treehouse."

Amused, Maya asked Tyson what his parents thought of his Christmas list, but when she heard a deep, male voice behind her she broke off speaking and glanced around.

"There you are. I've been looking all over for you."

Tyson took off running, and launched himself in the air at a tall, muscled man with short black hair and chiseled features. Her tongue froze inside her mouth. Marc, the guy who'd romanced her on Friday night, then insulted her hours later at Javonte's onsale, appeared out of nowhere. *Talk about a stroke of bad luck*, Maya thought.

As she stared at the pair, a lightbulb went off in her mind. This was no coincidence. No chance encounter. Maya smelled a setup, and when Marc approached her, holding Tyson in his arms, her frown deepened. His gaze held her captive, but she rolled her eyes to the ceiling to prove she was immune to his charms. Though, when he spoke to her, her body quivered.

"It's great seeing you again, Maya. You're looking as lovely as ever."

His voice tickled her ears, and goose bumps exploded across her arms. *What's the matter with me?* she thought, swallowing hard. *Why are my knees knocking together?* Her makeup was impeccable, every hair was in place, and her fit-and-flare dress accentuated her curves, but her confidence withered under his smoldering gaze.

"Thanks for finding Tyson. I was worried sick."

Marc was insanely hot, with a body made for sin, and her hands longed to reunite with his toned physique. Phew. So much sexy. Dressed in a wool jacket, black turtleneck, and dark blue jeans, it was no surprise the women standing nearby were ogling him, too.

"Is Tyson actually your nephew, or did you rent him for the day?"

The first-grader giggled. "Uncle Marc didn't rent me!" he argued, fervently shaking his head, his eyes big and wide. "I'm his favorite nephew."

"Of course you are. You're my *only* nephew."

Chuckling, Marc put him down and gave him a one-arm hug. "My sister, Kingsley, is engaged to Tyson's dad, and now we're all one big happy family."

"No, we're not. My mom hates your sister, your mom hates my dad, and Grandma Phyllis said it'll be a cold day in hell before she lets them get married—"

Marc cupped a hand over the first-grader's mouth. "Kids. They say the craziest things sometimes, especially this one. He has absolutely no filter."

Maya laughed, but remembered Marc was the enemy and clamped her lips together. *Damn him. Why does he have to be so funny?* she thought, mad at herself for letting her guard down. *Doesn't he know I'm mad at him? That I want nothing to do with him?*

Her friends appeared at her side, and introduced themselves to Marc. He complimented them on their performance and their fashionable dresses, but his eyes never left Maya's face. His piercing gaze put her on edge, and her palms were damp with sweat.

"Tyson and I are going to the food court to have lunch," Marc announced. "Would you lovely ladies care to join us?"

"We'd love to!" Liberty stepped forward and linked arms with Marc. "I worked up quite an appetite during our set, and all I could think about was a cheeseburger!"

Laughing, the group meandered through the mall toward the escalators. It amused Maya to watch Marc with her friends, and although she kept her distance from him, she was dying to know what he was saying. Was he talking about her? Was he sorry about yesterday? Had he come to the mall to see her?

As they passed a specialty store, Marc stopped and gestured to the front window. "My dad used to have a telescope like that, and we'd look at birds, and stare at the sky for hours. I lost interest in the telescope when I was a teenager, but I never forgot those times with my dad."

Her girlfriends stared at him with stars in their eyes, and Maya knew they were touched by his confession, too. To keep her mind off Marc and the conversation he was having with her friends, she chatted with Tyson. He was a sweet, likable kid, and by the time they reached the food court, Maya knew all about his love of video games, Pokémon, and hockey. After much debate, the group decided to eat at a fusion-style restaurant, with large tables and low-hanging lights, and bubbly, friendly staff decked out in elf costumes.

Conversation around the table was lively, and the

Christmas music playing in the restaurant created a festive mood. Having fun with her friends and Marc, she answered his questions about her fashion line, Luxe Designs, and her long-term goals for the business.

"Have you ever considered buying a fashion truck?" Marc asked.

"A fashion truck?" Maya repeated. "I've never heard of it. What is it?"

"Like a food truck, but with clothes instead of sandwiches and cold drinks. I've seen them in Montreal and London, and they seem to be real popular with millennials. With your personality and your unique, eye-catching designs, you'd make a killing if you had a fashion truck downtown or at one of the tourist hot spots."

"Wow, Marc, what a great idea," Eliza praised, flashing a thumbs-up. "I love it!"

Maya took a sip of her apple cider. Marc had certainly given her something to think about, and the more she considered his suggestion, the more excited she was about the idea of owning a fashion truck. First thing tomorrow, she'd call the Better Business Bureau to inquire about it, and she hoped someone would be able to point her in the right direction.

"I finished my burger, and I drank all of my water." Tyson tapped Marc's shoulder, then shook it with all his might. "Uncle Marc, I'm done. Can we go to Dairy Queen now?"

"Not now, buddy. I'm talking to Maya—"

"But you said if I helped you find her you'd buy me chocolate ice cream," he whined.

Maya smirked behind her napkin. *Out of the mouths of babes!*

"We'll take you," Aquarius offered. "Let's go."

"Come on, Tyson. Follow me." Standing, Eliza fluffed her honey-blond curls and tucked her clutch purse under her arm. "You too, *chiquita*."

Liberty shook her head. "No way. I'm staying here. I'm tired."

"You're not tired. You're nosy," Aquarius quipped, tapping her stilettos impatiently on the floor. "If you don't come, I'm telling everyone about your mishap on the escalator yesterday."

"Coming!" Liberty surged to her feet and dragged Aquarius away from the table.

Alone with Marc now, Maya didn't know what to say, and stared down at her cranberry spinach salad. It was so much easier to talk to him when her friends were around. They were fun, and chatty, and kept the conversation going when her nerves got the best of her. Like right now. "Tyson is a great kid."

"Yeah, when he's not running his mouth!"

Laughing, Maya picked up her glass, raised it to her lips and sipped her cider.

"I promised myself I'd stay away from you, but I can't get you out of my mind . . ."

His hands skimmed her knee, warming her all over.

"Is that why you bribed Tyson to trick me?" she asked.

"Yes. I couldn't risk Chauncey, or one of your brother's teammates, making a move on you. Not when I have strong feelings for you."

Maya pressed her lips together to trap a gasp inside.

"I can't stop thinking about you," he continued. "And I'm mad at myself for hurting your feelings yesterday. I was angry, and upset, and I wasn't thinking straight. Do you forgive me?"

Yes . . . No . . . I don't know. I'm confused, Maya thought, biting her bottom lip. At a loss for words, her mind reeling from Marc's jaw-dropping confession, she slowly nodded her head. "Marc, what are you saying? What do you want from me?"

"I want to date you."

His cell buzzed, but instead of picking it up off the table, he moved closer to her.

"I want to take you ice-skating, and dancing, and out for dinner at fancy French restaurants I can't spell, or pronounce."

The sound of his deep, hearty chuckle made Maya laugh. Her smile returned, and the butterflies in her stomach disappeared. Weighing the pros and cons of dating Marc on the down-low and telling Javonte the truth about her relationship, she decided to trust her gut. As much as she wanted to confide in her brother, she knew she couldn't—not if she wanted Marc to live. Javonte had an explosive temper, and Maya feared what would happen if he knew she'd hooked up with Marc at the Peninsula Hotel.

"Marc, I'd like that," she said, a shy smile tickling the corners of her lips. "I enjoy your company, and I want to get to know you better."

"How do you think we should handle things with Javonte?" Marc asked, as if reading her mind. "I can talk to him before he leaves for New Orleans, or I can wait until he gets back. What do you think is best?"

"None of the above. The less Javonte knows about us the better."

"Are you sure? He's one of my favorite clients, and I don't want to deceive him."

"I'm positive. It would be a huge mistake coming clean to him now. We just met."

Marc raised an eyebrow. "What does that have to do with anything?"

"In my experience, most men would rather play the field than commit."

"Not me. My grandparents got hitched after dating for a year, and my mom and dad eloped for their six-month anniversary. Both couples were happily married for decades, so I know that true love exists," he said, meeting her gaze. "Cunningham men are bold and decisive, and when we find the right woman, we waste no time committing to her."

Moved by his words, Maya leaned forward in her seat. His voice was as soothing as a gentle caress, drawing her in, holding her captive. Her heart and mind were telling her that Marc was special, the kind of man she could grow old with, but after a disastrous dating history and a broken engagement, Maya knew she had to be wise. Couldn't fall hard and fast. "Let's give it some more time," she proposed. "If we're still going strong in the New Year, then we'll sit Javonte down and talk to him together."

Marc kissed her, catching her off guard, but it was a wonderful surprise. His lips brushing against hers caused shivers to careen down her spine. "I have big plans for you this week."

Happiness ballooned inside her chest. "Well?" she prompted, playfully batting her eyelashes. "Don't keep me in suspense. What are we doing?"

"Tomorrow we're going to Winter WonderFest, for tobogganing, winter mini-golf, and ice-skating," he explained, taking her hand in his and giving it a light squeeze. "On Tuesday we're going to Brew Lights, and on Friday we're going to the Mistletoe Bash."

Feeling warm and giddy inside, Maya beamed.

His smile was dreamy, his excitement was contagious, and this time when Marc brushed his mouth against her lips, Maya melted in his arms. His tender caress, along her shoulders and hips, put her in an amorous mood, and it took every ounce of self-control she had not to climb onto his lap, hike up her dress, and ride him until he exploded inside her.

"I can't get enough of you," he whispered, nipping at her bottom lip. "You're addictive."

His grip tightened around her waist, and Maya sighed inwardly. She loved his closeness, his warmth, couldn't get enough of him. Eager to create wonderful new memories with the only man to ever capture her heart with just one kiss, Maya surrendered to the needs of her flesh, and devoured his mouth.

Chapter 7

Titan Management was a stone's throw away from the United Center, and as Marc entered the attractive brick building on Monday morning, the first things he noticed were the extravagant Christmas decorations in the lobby. Icicles dangled from the ceiling, miniature trees were adorned with colorful ornaments, and velvet stockings lined the windowsill. The scent of cinnamon was so heavy in the air, his mouth watered and his stomach growled.

Pressed for time, Marc grabbed his messages from the blue-eyed receptionist and marched through the lobby. Sultry lights, leather bucket chairs, and mounted flat-screen TVs made the room look more like a sports bar than a reception area. Clients played video games, scarfed down sugar cookies, and were gathered around the espresso station, shooting the breeze. Seeing the framed photographs, autographed jerseys, and Business of the Year plaques hanging on the sable-brown walls gave Marc a rush of pride. He'd been with the award-winning agency for years, and if during the holidays he signed another superstar athlete worth millions, he was confident he'd be named vice president in the New Year.

Marc heard his cell phone ring and fished it out of his jacket pocket. His eyes narrowed. Why did Sloane keep calling him? Couldn't she take a hint? A text message from Maya popped up on the screen, and Marc grinned. Great. She'd cancelled her plans with her girlfriends for tonight. Pleased Maya wasn't going to a house party in her old neighborhood, he sighed in relief. She was spending the night with him, not on the South Side, and Marc couldn't wait to see her.

Sunlight splashed through the windows, filling the corridor with warmth and light, instantly brightening his mood. That morning at his breakfast meeting, one of his clients had given him tickets for the movie premiere of *Christmas in Monte Carlo*, and he'd asked Maya to be his date. He was going to go all out tonight—flowers, a chauffeured limo. Afterwards, they'd have dinner at a Greek restaurant, then return to his house for a nightcap—and more. Just the thought of her excited him. Maya was a passionate, sensuous woman, and making love to her was his new favorite pastime. Forget meeting his boys at the pub after work for beers, wings, and basketball; he was going to the theater with his girlfriend, and there was nowhere else he'd rather be. They'd been inseparable for the past two weeks. They'd attended local events, driven around the city checking out fashion trucks for sale, and hung out at his house, baking, watching Christmas movies, and making love whenever the mood struck. And, since Javonte was out of town with some of his teammates, frolicking in the Cayman Islands, Maya could spend the night at his place without her brother grilling her about where she was.

Thirsty, Marc stopped in the staff room for a drink. Fitness magazines covered the tables, potted plants filled the air with a refreshing scent, and the stainless steel refrigerator was stocked with everything from sandwiches to fruit, and beer.

His cell rang, and Marc glanced down at it. Damn. Why was Sloane blowing up his phone again? How many times did he have to tell her they were through? That he had a girlfriend? Before meeting Maya, he'd dated a bevy of beauties, but after he and Maya had spent a romantic three-day weekend in Rockford, he'd cut everyone else loose. Had told his friends and family he was officially off the market. Maya was the only woman he wanted, and even though his boys teased him mercilessly about being whipped, he'd never been happier. He'd found everything he'd ever wanted in a partner in Maya, and he wasn't going to lose her by screwing around, or playing mind games. She was it for him, and he needed her in his life.

Marc grabbed a banana from the fruit bowl and finished it in seconds. As he poured himself a cup of coffee, his eyes caught sight of the TV, and his mouth dried. ESPN was doing a segment on the NFL, and when Javonte's image filled the screen, guilt pricked his conscience. Tonight, he'd talk to Maya about coming clean to her brother. It was time. He was too old to be sneaking around with her, and he hated deceiving his favorite client. More importantly, he wanted the world to know—especially Javonte's entourage and teammates—that Maya was taken. Proud to have her on his arm, he wanted to take her to industry events and work functions, and hoped after he spoke to the footballer man-to-man he'd give them his blessing.

Encouraged by his thoughts, Marc picked up his

mug and exited the staff room. Passing several of his colleagues in the hallway, he nodded and smiled. He didn't have time to chitchat. Not when he was booked solid. Marc had a full day ahead of him, and there was no way in hell he was working late tonight. He had plans with Maya, and nothing mattered more to him than spending time with his girlfriend.

Dumping his leather satchel on a padded chair in his office, Marc glanced up and was shocked to see his boss seated behind his desk, puffing on a cigar. Thirty pounds overweight, with tinted eyeglasses and salt-and-pepper hair, the Brooklyn native bore an uncanny resemblance to Samuel L. Jackson, and had the attitude to match. Marc felt like an intruder in his own office, but Mr. Frederick waved him inside and said, "Get in here, son. We need to talk."

"Sure, sir, is everything okay?"

"That depends. Who is she, and how serious are you about her?"

Eyes wide, his mouth ajar, he felt a cold chill flood his body. Marc wouldn't have been more surprised if an elf had popped out of the closet, singing "Santa Baby." *How does Mr. Frederick know I have a girlfriend? Who told him I'm dating Maya?* He'd been discreet, hadn't told anyone about her except his family, and couldn't figure out how his secret had gotten out. Marc coughed into his fist, but the lump in his throat remained.

"Out with it," Mr. Frederick snapped. "Who is she?"

"Sir, I don't know what you're—"

"Don't *sir* me, and quit playing dumb. You know exactly what I'm talking about."

Annoyed, Marc swallowed a curse and slid his hands into his pockets. He didn't like Mr. Frederick's tone. His attitude. His pissed-off vibe. But he didn't wither under the New Yorker's cold, dark stare. "I give a hundred percent to my clients, day in and day out."

"True," he conceded with a nod. "But you haven't been to happy hour in weeks, and you don't answer your cell phone in the evenings anymore . . ."

That's because my evenings are for Maya now, he thought, as images of his girlfriend filled his mind. She challenged his way of thinking, made him laugh out loud, and brought out the best in him. Her thoughtfulness and compassion had not only renewed his faith in the opposite sex, but changed him for the better. Life was about more than making money and partying with his clients, and these days he'd rather spend time with his family than hit the clubs. He valued Maya's opinion, appreciated her sound advice, and couldn't recall ever being this smitten with a woman, not even his ex-wife, and they were together for years.

"Worst of all, Alexis Ray said she invited you to her penthouse for drinks on Saturday night, and you shot her down. What's *that* about? Have you lost your everloving mind? She's stunning, with a body that doesn't quit, and a three-time Wimbledon champion."

His boss was a riot, unintentionally entertaining, and Marc had to swallow a laugh every time Mr. Frederick wagged his finger in the air and rubbed his round, protruding belly.

"Alexis Ray is the highest paid tennis player in the world, and I want her to sign with Titan Management, so quit blowing her off, and close the deal before one of our rivals swoops in and steals her away."

"I don't believe in mixing business with pleasure."

"Since when?" Mr. Frederick barked a laugh, and his double chin quivered. "You didn't mind mixing business with pleasure to sign Olympic gymnast Dominique Rowe."

Embarrassed by his past transgressions, Marc wished he could turn back the hands of time. His ego had taken a hit when his wife filed for divorce, and he'd foolishly hooked up with a client. A year later, he still regretted the choices he'd made in his career.

"You've dated other clients on your roster as well," his boss pointed out.

"People change."

"You don't. You're a player, and women love you, especially our female clients."

"Mr. Frederick, I have a girlfriend now, and I'd never do anything to disrespect her."

The grin slid off his boss's face, and his bushy eyebrows climbed up his forehead.

Marc noticed Mr. Frederick was gripping the armrest, and straightened to his full height. He wasn't going to let his boss intimidate him. Not when he'd done nothing wrong. He wasn't going out with Alexis Ray, and if his boss didn't like it that was too damn bad. He was 100 percent committed to Maya, and he wasn't going to blow things with her by hooking up with a potential client—not even a woman his colleagues drooled over.

"Date whoever you want, but whatever you do, don't fall in love."

His boss's words gave him pause, something to think about. Three months ago, he never would have considered settling down with one woman, let alone getting married again, but Marc liked the idea of spending the rest of his life with Maya, and couldn't picture himself with anyone else. Crazy, considering he'd been burned by love before, but everything about Maya appealed to him, and every day she taught him something new. On Friday, it was how to make the perfect omelet, on Saturday it was how to do the Downward Dog while they did yoga in his home gym, and yesterday she'd helped him finish the *New York Times* crossword puzzle. In three short weeks, she'd become his best friend, and when they were apart Maya was all he could think about. Like right now. His boss was talking, but his thoughts were a million miles away and his girlfriend was the reason why.

"Love's bad for business," Mr. Frederick said, taking a puff of his cigar.

"Bad for business? But you've been happily married for years."

"That's because Rosa-Ann is one in a million. She loves me, in sickness and in health, and there's nothing in the world she wouldn't do for me, or our three sons . . ."

A grin overwhelmed Marc's mouth. Listening to his boss gush about his wife, he realized Maya and Mrs. Fredcrick were cut from the same cloth. That's why he wanted to spend all of his free time with her, why he thought about her nonstop, and why he'd cut loose every other girl weeks ago. Maya was it for him, and he was ready to introduce her to his family. In his mother's eyes, no one would ever be good enough for him, but he wanted a future with Maya and hoped his mother would welcome her into the family with open arms.

"Sir, I don't mean to be rude," Marc said, noting the time on the wall clock. "But I have a conference call within the hour with Adidas, and I need to review my notes before I speak to the president about a potential endorsement deal for Javonte Malone."

"Fine, I won't keep you." Standing, his cigar dangling from his thin lips, he strode around the desk and clapped Marc on the back. "One more thing. I want you to plan the anniversary bash."

"But I plan it every year," he pointed out. "It's time I give someone else at the agency the opportunity to shine. If I don't, everyone will hate me!"

His joke fell flat, and the scowl on Mr. Frederick's face deepened.

"Why mess with a winning formula? You're the most popular agent at Titan Management, and when our clients hear you're throwing one of your legendary parties, they'll come out in droves, *and* bring their rich friends and teammates. Cha-ching!"

"Sebastian has tons of great ideas for the event—"

His face hardened. "Sebastian's no longer with the agency."

Shock reverberated through Marc's brain. "He quit? Why? Sebastian loves it here, and his clients practically worship the ground he walks on."

"He didn't quit. I canned his sorry ass."

Marc's eyes widened and his ears perked up.

"Insubordination is something I won't tolerate at Titan Management, so I fired him."

At a loss for words, Marc leaned against his desk to support his shaky legs.

"If you sign Alexis Ray, you could be my new VP. Wouldn't that be something?"

"Yes, sir," he said, reclaiming his voice. "That would be an honor."

"Good, then plan a kick-ass party that makes me the envy of all my competitors . . ."

Marc heard his cell ring, knew it was Maya calling from the sound of the Rihanna ringtone, but he didn't take his iPhone out of his pocket. He couldn't think, let alone talk, and knew he'd have to splash some cold water on his face before his one o'clock conference call. Torn between pleasing his boss and following his heart, Marc struggled over what to do. His job was on the line, and his reputation, and if he wanted to be vice president of Titan Management, he'd have to find a way to sign Alexis Ray without compromising his integrity.

"I want it all." Talking with his hands, Mr. Frederick spoke with an animated expression on his face. "Champagne, celebrities, exotic dancers, and fireworks. Spare no expense, son. Go all out."

"What date do you have in mind?"

"New Year's Eve, of course."

Bewildered, Marc closed his gaping mouth and shook his head. "I can't plan the anniversary bash in three weeks. This will take months of planning."

"You can, and you will. I have complete faith in you, son."

Marc groaned inwardly. Damn. Could this day get any worse? Tugging at his shirt collar, he hid his frustration by speaking in a lighthearted tone of voice. "What's the rush? Our anniversary isn't for another month."

"I know, but those jerks at Sports for Life are throwing a New Year's Eve bash at Clinique Nightclub, and I won't let them outshine me. Anything they can do, *I* can do better."

Marc's shoulders sagged and his spirits plummeted. He had plans with Maya on New Year's Eve. Big plans. He'd bought tickets for the New Year's Eve black-tie party, booked a limo and the presidential suite at the Peninsula Hotel. In honor of the event, Maya was making her own gown, and Marc knew she'd be disappointed if he cancelled on her, which is exactly what his boss wanted him to do. Drop everything for work. It felt as if a pinecone was stuck in his throat, and heartburn spread through his chest like fire. Marc was bummed that he couldn't spend his favorite holiday with his girlfriend, but he said, "I'll get right on it."

"That's just what I wanted to hear." His boss chuckled. "And remember, this is an exclusive event. No wives, no kids, and absolutely no girlfriends. What happens at Titan Management on New Year's Eve stays at Titan Management. Understood?"

Marc nodded, but guilt troubled his conscience. Watching Mr. Frederick march out of the office door, he couldn't shake the feeling that he'd just made a deal with the Devil.

Chapter 8

Maya sat in the darkened auditorium of the Rosemont Theatre, listening to the soul-stirring music, riveted by the performers dancing across the stage. Marc clasped her hand, squeezing it, and Maya snuggled against him. Hours earlier, he'd picked her up at home and greeted her with a kiss that instantly made her wet. Horny. Aroused, she'd considered dragging him inside the house for a quickie, but she remembered they were going to see *The Hip Hop Nutcracker* and had broken off the kiss. After a year of being single, it felt great having someone to spend time with on her days off, and Marc was everything she'd ever wanted in a boyfriend, and more.

Escorting her to his car, he'd showered her with compliments, telling her repeatedly how stunning she looked in her gold backless dress. Being with Marc was a heady, mind-blowing feeling. Quick to laugh, Marc was always the most popular person in the room, and although his cell rang nonstop, he never made her feel insecure or jealous. He doted on her, and thanks to Marc she'd fallen in love with the holiday season all over again.

As the musical ended, her thoughts returned to their dream date last Saturday. They'd driven to a popular downtown restaurant that attracted a young, chic crowd. Sophisticated, yet inviting, Jerk Hut was Maya's favorite Caribbean restaurant in the city. Filled with dark wood, colorful paintings, and candlelight, the décor evoked feelings of calm, and live jazz music and poetry readings added to the romantic ambience. They'd shared a bottle of wine, and Maya's entrée had tasted so good she'd eaten with a smile on her face. Even better than her three-course meal was her conversation with Marc. A great listener, with a quick smile and a calm disposition, he was easy to open up to about her hopes and dreams for the future.

Stroking his forearm, Maya studied his handsome profile. It was hard to believe they'd only known each other for a month; it felt like they'd been dating for years. He was never too busy to call her or text her, and Maya beamed every time his name and number popped up on her screen. She looked forward to their dates, never knew what to expect when he picked her up after work, but was guaranteed a good time with the hunky sports agent. One night he took her bowling, the next to the opera, or they'd hang out at his house, cooking, playing board games, and watching old Christmas movies. Yesterday, they'd donned their ugliest, flashiest sweaters and headed to Portage Park to take part in the five-mile charity run. Marc had won, and they'd celebrated his first-place win with their friends at a nearby pub. They'd laughed at the same jokes, finished each other's sentences, and had fed each other dessert. Liberty had teased them for acting like an old married couple, but Maya didn't take offense and had laughed louder than anyone. It was true. She was smitten with Marc, and proud to be his girlfriend. Marc knew when to let go, when to take charge, and he was impressed—not intimidated—by her strength.

"Are you having a good time?" he whispered, glancing at her.

"The best. The music is incredible."

His eyes brightened, and a proud smile curled his lips. "I knew you'd like it. My sister got us tickets for the show last year, and we danced and rapped all night."

The performers took a bow, and the lights came on in the auditorium, but the young, energetic crowd continued to sing and dance. The audience cheered long after the cast left the stage, and Maya giggled when Marc pulled her into his arms and dipped her, drawing the attention of every woman in the room. Seeing their envious looks, Maya felt proud.

Exiting the auditorium, hand in hand, they strolled outside into the crisp winter night, talking and laughing about their favorite parts of the ninety-minute show. Starving, they decided to have dinner at one of the restaurants along Park Place, and ducked inside Seven Lounge.

At Seven Lounge, the hostess escorted them to a booth positioned in front of the window. The restaurant had an elegant black and gold color scheme, and Maya loved the holiday décor, the vanilla-scented candles on the table, and the comfy red cushions in their corner booth.

Snowflakes fell from the sky, blanketing the streets in snow. The wind howled, and it looked like a winter wonderland outside, but thanks to the fireplace Maya felt warm and cozy. They placed their orders with the blond, suit-clad waiter, then chatted about their day while they waited for their appetizers to arrive.

"Guess what?" Maya said, feeling as if she'd burst with happiness. "Lyrical Soul's been added to the list of performers for the New Year's Eve black-tie bash. Isn't that awesome? Thousands of tickets have been sold, and tons of A-list celebrities will be there."

"Baby, that's great. The more people who see outfits from your fashion line the better." Marc kissed her forehead. "This is the big break you've been waiting for. I can feel it."

"You sound like Javonte."

"Your brother's right. You're talented, creative, and hardworking, and it's just a matter of time before you're a household name in the fashion world."

"Thanks for the vote of confidence."

"I meant what I said earlier, Maya. If you need financial help, just say the word and I'll write you a check. I believe in you, and I'll do anything to support your vision."

"Marc, I appreciate the offer, but I can't take your money. I want to make it as a designer by my own merit, not because my brother or my boyfriend paid my way."

"Ripping up that check Javonte gave you took a lot of guts, Maya."

"My friends think I'm crazy, but it was the right thing to do. Javonte's been giving me money for years, and it's time I quit living off him and stand on my own two feet," she said, speaking from the heart. "I want to get my own place, purchase a fashion truck, and maybe even live in Paris for the summer."

The light went out in Marc's eyes, but he wore a broad smile. "Why not? You only live once, right?" His voice was flat, and his expression was wary, full of concern. "What does Javonte think about your plan? Is he on board?"

"No," she said, fiddling with the silver bangles on her wrist. "I mentioned it to him a few days ago, while he was packing for his trip, but he totally brushed me off. He said I wasn't savvy enough to travel alone, but I am, and I will."

"Maybe I should come with you. You know, to make sure everything's copacetic."

"Yeah, right. As if. You're a big-time sports agent with dozens of superstar clients."

"I'll take a leave of absence, and we'll travel together next summer." Marc took her hand, lowered his mouth, and kissed her palm. "I've always wanted to see the City of Lights, and there's no one else in this world I'd rather go to Paris with than you."

Maya wanted to throw herself in his arms and kiss him passionately, but she tamped down her excitement. Was this for real? Was Marc serious? Maya studied him for several seconds. He looked serious, but his offer was too good to be true, and Maya didn't want to get her hopes up. She loved the idea of traveling with him, but she knew it would never happen. How could it? He had clients to manage, and millions of dollars to make for his agency.

"After dinner, we'll go to my place and discuss it further," Marc suggested.

"Baby, I want to, but I can't stay out late tonight. Lyrical Soul is performing at Covenant Nursing Home tomorrow, and I still have to plan their hairstyles and select their wardrobe."

Moving closer to her, he draped an arm around her shoulders. "Maya, I understand."

His voice was soft and soothing, causing her to instantly fall under his spell.

"I won't keep you out late. When you're ready to go, I'll drop you home. Promise."

Her cell phone chimed, and Maya took it out of her purse. She had three new text messages from Javonte, and cracked up when she read them. He'd left for vacation in the Cayman Islands after a season-ending injury, and even though Maya missed him, she loved having the house to herself. Finally, some peace and quiet. Tired of her brother's massive entourage and his raucous, midweek parties, she'd made up her mind to move out in the New Year, and was busy house hunting with her friends.

A picture of Javonte, buried neck-deep in sand, popped up on her cell phone, and Maya burst out laughing. He was her best friend, the person she trusted most, and she couldn't have asked for a more loving or supportive brother.

"What's so funny?"

"Javonte." Maya raised her cell in the air so Marc could see the picture, and shook her head. "He's the biggest goofball ever, and his messages always make me crack up."

"Have you guys always been close?"

"Yeah, Javonte really stepped up after our mom passed, and if not for his love and support, there's no telling where I'd be. I was a headstrong teenager who was angry at the world, but Javonte never gave up on me. He was there for me, and I'll always be grateful for everything he did, especially when my engagement ended."

"What happened with your ex?" Marc asked. "Why did you call off the wedding?"

"I didn't. He did—"

The waitstaff arrived, carrying trays filled with appetizers, entrées, and drinks, and Maya broke off speaking. Thankful for the interruption, she picked up her fork and tasted her beef Wellington. Maya needed a moment to gather her thoughts, and hoped Marc wouldn't press her for details about her broken engagement. No such luck.

"Please don't shut me out," he said. "I want to know more about you, Maya."

Thirsty, she picked up her glass and sipped her eggnog. Flavored with rum, ginger, and nutmeg, it was the most delicious drink she'd ever tasted. Maya hated talking about her ex-fiancé, always got choked up when she did, but she honored Marc's request and pushed the truth out of her mouth. "Landon got cold feet, but instead of manning up and telling me he didn't want to get married, he was a no-show at our Christmas Eve wedding."

"Damn, Maya, that's brutal."

"It was the most humiliating moment of my life, but thank God I survived."

"I can't imagine what you must have gone through."

"Deep down, I knew Landon wasn't the right man for me, but it didn't lessen the pain of our breakup. I thought I was going to die of a broken heart, but my brother and my girlfriends stepped up and rallied around me. They contacted everyone so I wouldn't have to, and Javonte entertained the out-of-town guests for the entire weekend."

"Did you ever get a chance to speak to your ex? To find out why he bailed?"

Nodding, Maya wore a sad smile. "He called that afternoon, and I actually begged him to come back. Isn't that pathetic? I told him I would do anything to make him happy—lose more weight, and quit my job so I could take better care of him—but Landon said I wasn't the right woman for him. Apparently, I don't know how to be submissive."

"That's a damn lie. You're the most subservient woman I know."

"Shush," Maya quipped, trying hard not to laugh. "No one asked you!"

Marc grinned. "You're strong and feisty and opinionated, but that's what I love most about you. You're not afraid to speak your mind, and I always know where I stand with you."

Maya blinked, leaned forward eagerly in her chair. Her ears weren't working. Were playing tricks on her. Deceiving her. Did Marc just use the word *love* in a sentence?

"You move to the beat of your own drum, and that's damn sexy." Taking her hand in his, Marc winked, then kissed her palm. "I'm one very lucky man."

"You sure are," Maya agreed. "And if you ever forget I'll be sure to remind you!"

An hour after leaving Seven Lounge, Marc pulled into the three-car garage of his Barrington home, put his Range Rover in Park, and took off his seat belt. They'd eaten so much food, and danced to so many songs in the swank VIP lounge, he felt tired and sluggish. "We're home," he said, taking her hand in his.

Glancing at Maya, he saw the troubled expression on her face, and wondered what was on her mind. During dinner, he'd planned to tell her he couldn't be her date for the black-tie New Year's Eve party, but after she'd confided in him about her broken engagement, he didn't have the heart to disappoint her. Moved by her story, he'd considered opening up to her about his divorce, but got cold feet. He wanted to, but couldn't bring himself to tell her the truth. Marc was worried that she'd judge him—or worse dump him—and he didn't want to lose her. Not when they were closer than ever. A good woman was hard to find, and Maya was a great woman. The best. One in a million. Everyone said so—her brother, her girlfriends, her customers who filled her social media pages with compliments, praise, and good wishes, and even Tyson was smitten with her. He didn't want to say or do anything to jeopardize their relationship.

An idea formed in his mind, materialized as he intertwined his fingers with hers. Maybe he didn't have to cancel their plans. He could go to the anniversary bash, shake hands and pose for pictures, then duck out when the exotic dancers started their routine. That way, he'd make his boss happy, spend time with his clients, and still see Maya. He'd meet her at the Peninsula Hotel before midnight, and they'd celebrate in style. Marc didn't know what he was going to do about Alexis Ray, and wished she'd stop blowing up his cell phone, but he'd think of something. He had to, or he could lose everything he'd worked hard for.

His cell phone buzzed in the center console, and Marc glanced down at it. It was Esmerelda, a woman he'd briefly dated over the summer, but he had zero desire to talk to the aspiring model; he let the call go to voicemail. "Ready to go in?"

"No. Not yet. This is nice. I love sitting outside, staring at the stars."

Marc turned up the heat, then lowered the volume on the stereo system. Holding her hand, listening to the music on the radio, was a great stress reliever. All week, he'd been running around getting things ready for the anniversary bash, and thanks to his colleagues, he'd completed everything on his to-do list. He hadn't told Maya about the event yet, and didn't plan to. She wouldn't understand why she couldn't be his date, and he didn't want to argue with her about it. "You still haven't given me an answer about Javonte. What's the verdict?"

Maya nodded, but he saw the fear in her eyes, her unease, and kissed her cheek to comfort her. "You have nothing to worry about. I won't leave your side. We'll do it together."

"We agreed to wait until the New Year."

"I know, but I hate sneaking around behind Javonte's back. I want us to date publicly, without fear of getting caught, and I think the longer we wait to tell him, the more upset he'll be. If I was in his shoes, I'd want to know sooner rather than later."

"Okay, let's do it. We'll tell Javonte we're dating when he returns from his trip."

"Maybe I should come by on Christmas Day. What are you guys doing to celebrate?"

"Nothing. Javonte won't be back from his trip until January third, and since my girlfriends will be busy with their families, I'm going to make myself a big breakfast and spend the rest of the day on the couch, watching my favorite movies."

"You can't be alone on Christmas Day. That's depressing."

"No, it's not. It's relaxing and peaceful. I did the exact same thing last year and—"

"Last year you were nursing a broken heart, but this year you have me."

"How can I forget when you keep reminding me?" she teased, batting her eyelashes.

"Don't blame me. It's not my fault I'm *totally* into you. You're the one with the model good looks, the effervescent personality, and the outrageous laugh. I'm helpless to resist you."

Her smile turned to a laugh, and the sound of her girlish giggle made him chuckle, too.

"My mom is hosting Christmas Day dinner at her house. We eat too much, drink too much, and exchange gifts, and a good time is had by all. Please say you'll come."

"Marc, are you sure about this? Meeting your relatives is a huge step."

"I know, but I'm ready. You're the only woman I've invited home since my divorce, so this is not only a big deal for me, but also my family."

"Did your mom and your ex get along?" Maya asked, turning in her seat to face him.

A knot formed in his throat, and his stomach lurched. Where did *that* come from? Why was she asking about his ex-wife? Instinctively, he reached for the door handle, but Maya grabbed his forearm, preventing him from escaping the car.

"Marc, talk to me . . ."

I'd rather spend a year in solitary confinement, he thought, releasing a deep sigh.

"I want to know more about your past relationships, starting with your marriage."

"My mom thought Brielle was a gold digger, and it turned out she was right."

"How long were you married?"

Marc shrugged. "A while."

"What's a while?"

"Give or take three years."

"Was it an amicable divorce?" Maya tucked a leg under her bottom, as if she was sitting on a couch watching a movie. "Do you miss her? Would you take her back if she asked?"

"No, no, and hell no."

The car was quiet, except for the sound of the

radio, and hearing his favorite Christmas song, "Mary's Boy Child" by Harry Belafonte, brought to mind happy memories of his dad. His father would have liked Maya. No doubt about it. Bright and bubbly, she was a ball of positive energy, and would have easily charmed his old man. She didn't have an agenda, or any ulterior motives. Unlike his ex-wife, Maya cared about him as a person, not how much money he had in his bank account, and he admired how independent she was.

"I confided in you about my broken engagement, even though I hate talking about it, and I wish you'd do the same about your divorce . . ."

Hearing the hurt in her voice, Marc noticed the pained expression on her face. It bothered him that he'd upset her, and he realized if he didn't open up to Maya about his past, he could lose her. Needing a moment to collect his thoughts, he pressed his eyes shut and searched his heart for the right words to say.

"We're supposed to be a couple, but how can we grow together if you won't open up to me about your past relationships?"

Marc winced. *Ouch.* Supposed *to be a couple? We are!* Hanging his head, he raked a hand through his hair. Mustering his courage, he spoke in a calm tone. "I met Brielle Williams my freshman year of university," he said, with a sad smile. "After four years together, I popped the question, and we tied the knot in sunny Maui. Returning home, we both found jobs in our respective fields, then bought our dream house in Gold Coast."

"It sounds like you guys were living the American dream."

"We were, until Brielle got fired from the advertising firm she worked at. Instead of looking for another position, she'd spend hours on the Internet, blowing money on designer clothes and other crap she didn't need. The more money I made, the more Brielle spent, and in three short months she'd raked up thousands of dollars in consumer debt."

"Is that why you guys broke up? Because of her out-of-control spending?"

A bitter taste filled his mouth. "No, my dad had a stroke, and she wasn't there for me when I needed her most. She was too busy shopping."

"People cope in different ways, Marc. There is no right or wrong way to grieve—"

"Don't make excuses for her," he snapped, speaking through clenched teeth. His hands tightened around the steering wheel as he stared out into the dark winter night. "She was my wife. She should have been with me at the hospital, not at the mall with her stupid friends."

Silence engulfed the car, and tension filled the air, suffocating him. There was more to the story—a lot more—but Marc struggled, couldn't get the words out. He didn't know how to tell Maya about the mistakes he'd made in his marriage, so he kept his mouth shut.

"Are you mad at me?"

"No. Why would I be mad at you? You didn't bail on me in my time of need, my ex did."

Maya moved in close and brushed her lips against his. One kiss. That's all it took. One slow, tender kiss, and his mood changed. His scowl morphed into a smile, and his frustration melted away. Just like that. As she massaged his shoulders and made love to his mouth, turning him out with her tongue, his chest inflated with pride. Overflowed with happiness. Knowing she desired him as much as he desired her gave Marc an adrenaline rush. Made him feel ten feet tall. Maya had a way of making everything better, of proving that she was everything he could ever need or want in a woman, and when she ended the kiss and pulled out of his arms, his disappointment was so profound his heart ached.

"Thanks for opening up to me about your past. I know it wasn't easy."

"My divorce is a painful chapter of my life that I hate talking about, but I trust you and wanted to confide in you," he said quietly. "You're important to me, Maya. That's why I want you to meet my family."

"The last time I met a guy's family, he left me stranded at the altar."

"I'm not that guy, Maya. I'm not going to bail on you."

Her smile returned, exploded across her face, and happiness twinkled in her eyes.

"Baby, this time will be different. I promise." Reaching out, he caressed her cheek with his thumb, then slowly kissed the corner of her mouth. "If I thought, even for a minute, that we didn't have what it takes to go the distance, I wouldn't invite you to my mom's house for dinner, but you're the only one for me, Maya, so quit stalling and say you'll be my date, or I'm taking your Christmas gift back to the store!"

"You're *so* romantic. How can I refuse?"

Cupping her face in his hands, he stared deep into her eyes. "Meeting you at the Peninsula Hotel last month was a wonderful, unexpected gift," he said, taken aback by his confession. This wasn't him. Not by a long shot. In past relationships, he'd always struggled to share his feelings, but not tonight. He wanted Maya to know what was in his heart, and didn't hold back. "Thanks for making me smile again, for making me laugh, and for reminding me what matters most this holiday season. Love."

Maya didn't speak, stared at him as if she was seeing him for the first time. Her eyes watered and her nose twitched, as if she was on the verge of tears. "Compliments will get you everywhere," she quipped, draping an arm around his neck. "If you want me to spend the night with you, just ask. You don't have to sweet-talk me."

"I'm not. You mean the world to me, and I'll always cherish you."

They kissed, feasting hungrily, desperately, on each other's lips. The car warmed, the windows fogged up, and their moans and groans consumed the air. Unbuckling her seat belt, she climbed onto his lap and snuggled against him. "Baby, you taste so good," she said, between kisses. "I want to make love to you so bad it's all I can think about."

Her sultry voice tickled and teased his ear, and a grin filled his mouth. Maya was giving him an early Christmas present, and when she stroked his chest, Marc hoped she was going to be naughty, not nice. And, just when he thought the night couldn't get any better, she licked the rim of his ear, and Marc knew all of his R-rated dreams were about to come true.

Chapter 9

Maya stood in Marc's kitchen on Christmas Day, dicing vegetables for the spinach-mushroom omelet she was preparing for brunch. They were going to his mother's house in the afternoon, but Maya was starving, and she wanted to eat something before they made the hour-long drive to Mrs. Cunningham's Lincoln Park estate.

Nestled in a suburban community, the attractive, four-bedroom home in Barrington had it all—high ceilings, decorative chandeliers, Ralph Lauren furniture, and gleaming marble floors. The kitchen was open to the living room, giving the main floor a warm and inviting feel. Sculptures and glass vases filled the space, candles perfumed the air with their floral scent, and the framed photographs prominently displayed along the bookshelves proved how much Marc loved his family, his clients, and his community.

Picking up the cutting board from the granite countertop, Maya tossed the vegetables into the pan, added a pinch of salt, and cranked up the heat on the stove. The Bing Crosby classic "I'll Be Home for Christmas" played on the radio, and Maya thought about her mother. Bitter memories consumed her mind, and pain stabbed her chest. Filled with an overwhelming sense of loss, she braced her hands against the breakfast bar to steady her quivering limbs.

Maya dabbed at the corners of her eyes with the sleeve of her V-neck dress. Her mother was gone, but life was good. Better than it had ever been. She had Javonte, her girlfriends, her fashion line, and now Marc—the best boyfriend she'd ever had.

Her gaze landed on the sapphire bangle on her left wrist, and the smile in her heart spread to her mouth. They'd agreed not to exchange Christmas gifts, choosing instead to make monetary donations to one another's favorite Chicago charity, so when Maya woke up that morning and saw the red, glitzy gift bag on the side table, she'd gasped. Inside was a handwritten card, two tickets for *Love Jones: The Musical*, and the bangle. It was ridiculously expensive, and although Maya loved the unique, eye-catching design, she never would have dipped into her savings to buy it. Not when she had plans to move out in the New Year.

Questions had consumed her mind. How did Marc know she wanted the bracelet? Who told him? Pressed for answers, he'd admitted to going shopping with Liberty at Water Tower Place days earlier. The words *faith*, *hope*, and *love* were inscribed on the bangle, and when Marc slid it onto her wrist she'd felt like the happiest woman alive. Overcome with emotion, she'd pulled him down on top of her and kissed him passionately on the lips. Tossing her negligee aside, she'd climbed onto his lap and ridden him until an orgasm exploded inside her body.

Burning up inside the kitchen, Maya fanned her face with one hand and opened the window with the other. The wind battered the trees, dogs barked, and the family across the street was building a snowman. Carolers, decked out in candy-cane-themed toques, scarves, and sweaters, wandered the streets, spreading holiday cheer. Impressed with their beautiful, melodious voices, Maya wanted to record them but remembered she'd left her cell in her purse last night, and didn't feel like going into the foyer to get it. "*'Feliz Navidad,'*" she sang along with the carolers. "*'Feliz Navidad, prospero año y felicidad.'*"

"Are those the words? All these years I had no idea what José Feliciano was saying!"

Marc came up behind her and slid his arms around her waist. His aftershave tickled her nose, and his touch warmed her all over.

"Good morning, handsome." Resting her head against his bare chest, Maya caressed his arms and hands. He had on black silk pajama bottoms, and feeling his erection against her bottom made her mouth dry, and her body tingle. "Merry Christmas."

"Merry Christmas, baby," he whispered, nibbling on her earlobe. "I've gotten a lot of great presents over the years, but you're the best Christmas gift I've ever received."

"Marc, I feel the same way about you. These last few weeks have been a dream."

"Let's go back to bed. I have something to show you."

Maya giggled. "I bet you do, but you have to wait. Brunch is on the stove."

Groaning as if he was being physically tortured, Marc backed her up against the wall, slid his hands under her dress, and stroked her flesh. If Maya hadn't had food on the stove, she would have made love to him right then and there, but since she didn't want their lunch to burn, she gave him a peck on the lips and returned to the stove.

"Marc, can you grab me a bag of flour from the pantry?" she asked. "I want to make your mom a homemade maple-nut pie, and if I don't get started now, it won't be ready in time."

Pouring the batter into the sizzling frying pan, Maya pretended not to notice the sour expression on his face, and gestured to the wall clock. "Babe, you have to hustle. It's already one o'clock, and I don't want to be late for your mom's family dinner."

"Sure. No problem, babe. Anything for you."

Watching him cross the room, Maya yanked off her oven mitts, chucked them on the counter, and tiptoed across the kitchen. Marc opened the pantry door, flipped on the light switch, then stopped abruptly. Didn't move. Appeared to be in shock. A Celestron NexStar 6SE telescope, swathed in red ribbon, with a gigantic bow, was in front of the upright freezer, and Marc stared at it with wide eyes.

"Maya, what is this?" he asked, rubbing a hand along the back of his neck.

"Your Christmas gift, of course. Merry Christmas, baby. I hope you like it." Wrapping her arms around his waist, she gave him a peck on the lips, and held him tight. "You like star gazing almost as much as I do, and I figured you'd enjoy having a telescope again."

He kissed her forehead and patted her hips. "I love it, baby. Thanks for—"

The doorbell rang, and he broke off speaking.

"Are you expecting someone?" Maya asked, glancing down the hallway.

"No, but it's probably my mom."

"Your mom?" Maya repeated, bewildered by his

words. "Why would your mom come here when we'll be at her house in a few hours?"

"Because she's *super* anxious to meet you. You know how moms are!"

The doorbell rang, buzzed over and over again.

Steering Marc out of the kitchen, she gestured to the staircase. "I'll get the door and you go get dressed," Maya said, glancing at the wall mirror. She'd planned to curl her hair and do her makeup, but there was no time. His mom was outside, banging urgently on the door, and Maya didn't want to make Mrs. Cunningham wait. "If your mom comes in here and sees you half-naked, she'll think less of me, and I want to make a good first impression."

"Don't worry. I already told mom I'm your sex slave."

Laughing, Maya gave him a shot in the arm, then playfully stuck out her tongue. "Go get dressed, Mr. Man. I don't want your mom to think I'm using you for your body."

A devilish grin curled his lips. "You're not? But I'm dreamy!"

"Yeah, a dreamy pain in the ass," she teased. "Hurry up, babe. Take a quick shower, then meet us in the great room. We can all eat brunch together. There's plenty."

"As you wish." Marc kissed her cheek, then jogged upstairs, whistling "Feliz Navidad."

The knocking stopped, then started up again, and Maya flew down the hallway. "Coming! Be right there!" In the foyer, she took a deep breath to steady her nerves. Opening the door before panic set in and she lost her nerve, she spoke with confidence. "Merry Christmas, Mrs. Cunningham! I'm Maya, and it's a pleasure to finally meet you—"

Paralyzed with shock, Maya lost her voice. Mrs. Cunningham wasn't standing on the welcome mat; Javonte was. Her first impulse was to run, but her feet were rooted to the floor.

Unable to speak, Maya stared at her brother in disbelief. His eyes were narrowed, his chin was set in a stubborn line, and his hands were balled into fists. He looked exhausted, as if he hadn't slept in days, and reeked of vodka. Peering over his shoulder, she noticed his entourage standing in front of his black Cadillac Escalade, and strangled a groan.

"Where is he?" Anger oozed from his pores, and his eyes were dark with hate.

"Javonte, what are you doing here? You're supposed to be in the Cayman Islands."

"I cut my vacation short to confront Marc. He's playing you, Maya."

"Calm down," she said, bracing her hands against his chest to stop him from entering the house. "You're wound up for nothing, and you're blowing things way out of proportion."

"Am I? Chauncey was at Seven Lounge last night, and guess what he saw?"

Heat flooded Maya's cheeks, and her pulse pounded in her ears, wailed like a siren.

Raising his cell in the air, Javonte pointed at the screen. "What were you thinking? Are you trying to embarrass me? Do you want my friends and teammates to rag on me?"

Maya stared at the screen, shocked to see pictures of her with Marc at Seven Lounge—dirty dancing, French kissing at the bar, making out in their corner booth, slipping into the coat-check room for a quickie—and imagined herself strangling punk-ass Chauncey.

To make things right and soothe her brother's feelings, Maya apologized. "J, I'm sorry I didn't tell you the truth. Marc wanted to, but I asked him not to."

Lines wrinkled his forehead, and his frown deepened.

"I didn't want to add to your stress," she continued. "You're worried about your knee, and I knew you'd be upset if we told you about us—"

"Damn right, I'm upset! You have no business dating Marc. He works for me, and furthermore he's not good enough for you. He's a player, and you deserve better."

"J, stop. You're shouting. Someone will hear you, and call the police."

"Good," he shot back, rolling up the sleeves of his gray Nike sweatshirt. "I hope the paramedics come, too, because Marc's going to need medical attention after I whoop his ass."

Storming into the house, Javonte shouted, "Get down here, Marc! I need to talk to you!"

Thinking fast, Maya grabbed her purse off the glass table and stuffed her feet into her shoes. "Javonte, let's go. We'll discuss this at home. Not here."

"Is this why you want to move out? Because you want to live with Marc?"

"No, Marc has nothing to do with it," she said, struggling to hide her frustration. "I need my own space. I've lived with you long enough, J. It's time."

Javonte shook his head. "It's a bad idea. You're safer at my estate. I can protect you."

Appearing in the foyer, Marc stood behind her and rested his hands on her shoulders. His touch was needed, reassuring, and when Maya glanced up at him he nodded, as if to say everything was going to be okay. Was it? Deep down, she feared what would happen if her brother made good on his threats. Known in the NFL for his explosive temper, Javonte had been suspended by the league twice, and had also lost lucrative endorsements deals as a result, and Maya didn't want history to repeat itself on Christmas Day.

"Javonte, I know this looks bad, but it's not what you think."

He made his eyes wide. "Oh, so you're *not* screwing my sister behind my back?"

Maya winced but spoke up. "Javonte, we want to be together. We're in love."

His loud, bitter laugh pierced her eardrum.

"Yeah, right," he spat, his tone thick with sarcasm. "The only thing Marc loves is hooking up with different women every day of the week."

Her heart plunged to the bottom of her feet, and the room flipped upside down on its head. *What women? Marc's dating other people? But he's committed to me!* Surprise must have shown on her face, because Javonte answered the question that popped into her mind.

"That's right, Maya. You're not the only one."

Marc squeezed her shoulders. "Yes, she is. There's no one else."

"Bullshit!" he raged, folding his beefy arms across his chest. "What about Mercedes in West Town? Sloane in Avondale? And Caitlyn? No way you stopped seeing her."

A cell phone rang, cutting through the noise, but no one moved.

"Sis, don't fall for his bullshit lines. I know what's up. I've seen him in action."

Maya spun around and faced Marc. Was it true? Was he cheating on her?

Javonte said, "You think I'm a player? Well, I'm a saint compared to your lover boy. He's so charming and persuasive, women throw themselves at him twenty-four seven."

Her temperature soared, making her head woozy. It felt as if her cheeks were stuffed with cotton, but she found her voice. "Marc, is it true? Are you hooking up with other women?"

Hurt covered his face. "How can you ask me that? Don't you trust me?"

"I do . . . I did . . ." Maya shook her head. "I don't know what to think anymore."

"It's true. I was dating around when we first met," he confessed. "But I cut everyone else loose weeks ago. I swear. You're the only woman in my life."

"Don't believe him. He's a master manipulator with no conscience," Javonte warned. "He cheated on his ex-wife, and he'll cheat on you, too."

What? The words exploded in her ears like a bomb, and Maya struggled to catch her breath. Needed a moment to compose herself. She thought she could trust Marc, but he'd been playing her all along. *How could I have been so stupid? Why didn't I notice the signs?*

Marc started to speak, to plead his case, but Maya interrupted him.

"Did you cheat on your ex-wife? Is that why your marriage ended?"

"My marriage ended because my ex wasn't there for me when I needed her most."

Javonte snarled. "Quit lying and tell my sister the truth, or I'll kick your ass for real."

"Marc, I'm going to ask you one more time, and this time I want the truth," Maya said, ignoring the tremble in her voice. "Did you cheat on your wife? Yes or no?"

Marc opened his mouth, then closed it, and Maya knew he'd lied to her about his past. He'd played the role of the victim to gain her sympathy, and it turned out Marc wasn't who she thought he was. He was a fraud, an imposter.

Emotions flooded her body—sadness, regret, and confusion—and although her knees buckled, she didn't drop to the floor. She willed herself not to cry, but tears pricked her eyes, blurring her vision, and a sob rose in her throat.

Javonte grabbed her hand. "Let's go, before I do something I regret."

In the distance, Maya heard carolers singing "O Holy Night," but their angelic voices made her feel worse, not better. Her relationship with Marc was over, and her heart hurt so bad Maya feared she'd never be whole again. In a haze, she allowed Javonte to lead her through the foyer and out the front door. The air was cold, and snowflakes were falling from the sky.

"Baby, please don't go. We can work this out." Sounding desperate, like a man who had everything to lose, Marc pleaded for understanding. "I'll tell you everything you want to know. Just don't leave. I need you, and I want to be with you."

"Yeah, right, and I've never smoked weed!" Tightening his grip on her forearm, Javonte led Maya down the steps. She didn't argue. Couldn't. Didn't have the strength.

"One more thing," Javonte said, glancing over his shoulder and glaring at Marc. "You're fired. Stay the hell away from me and my sister, or you'll be sorry."

At a loss for words, Maya ducked inside the SUV and stared out the window. She saw Marc standing in the doorway, heard him shouting her name, and dropped her gaze to her lap. As Javonte sped through the neighborhood, blasting rap music on the stereo system, tears slid down her cheeks, and this time Maya didn't stop them.

Chapter 10

"This is the worst New Year's Eve *ever*," Liberty complained, hurling her empty soda can at the garbage inside the washroom off the lobby of the Peninsula Hotel. Missing by a mile, she flipped her hair over her shoulders and released a long, dramatic sigh. "If I didn't need the money from this gig to pay for our Bahamian singles cruise next week, I'd be at home in bed, watching *Dick Clark's New Year's Rockin' Eve* with that cute little Ryan Seacrest . . ."

Biting the inside of her cheek, Maya blinked back tears. The last time she'd been at the Peninsula Hotel, she'd met Marc, and memories of that fateful, wonderful night warmed her all over. Tuning her friends out, she opened her leather makeup trunk and selected the items she needed to finish Lyrical Soul's glamorous looks.

Tilting Aquarius's chin up, Maya reapplied the lead singer's mascara, blush, and lipstick. A spritz of Chanel No. 5 perfume, some hairspray, and her friend was ready to hit the stage. Conversation swirled around her, but Maya didn't join the discussion. It was hard to concentrate when all she could think about was Marc. They hadn't seen or spoken to each other since she'd walked out on him on Christmas Day, and six days later, Maya was still broken up inside about their argument. Over and over again, his words played in her mind. *You're the only woman in my life . . . I want you more than anything . . . Baby, please don't go. We can work this out . . .*

To break free of her thoughts, Maya shook her head and pressed her eyes shut. He'd called her every day since their breakup, but she'd let his calls go to voicemail. She wasn't ready to talk to him, needed more time to process her feelings, and wanted space to clear her head.

As she was straightening Eliza's hair with the flat-iron, her mind wandered. After Javonte showed up at Marc's house, and practically dragged her out the door, Maya hadn't known what to think. How to feel. The drive to Northfield had been long and strained, but once they got home she'd sat him down and had an honest talk with her brother about her relationship with Marc. Several minutes had passed, then he'd reluctantly apologized for his actions that afternoon. Maya was glad they'd cleared the air, but the accusations Javonte made about Marc tormented her. Were they true? Did Marc have a roving eye? Was she one of many?

Her gaze landed on the pink, glossy flyer sitting on the countertop, and a sad smile curled her lips. It was for the grand opening of her fashion truck next week. Yesterday had been a big day for her. She'd purchased her own fashion truck, and although Javonte and her friends had been there to celebrate with her, she wished Marc had been at her side. Sure, he'd gone with her before to look at the truck, but it wasn't the same without him. Nothing was. He meant the world to her, and every day without him was a painful reminder of the love she'd had, and lost.

Hours earlier, as Maya was getting ready for the black-tie New Year's Eve party at the Peninsula Hotel, Marc had emailed her, explaining why he didn't tell her the full story about his divorce, but vehemently denied cheating on Maya with other women. She'd fallen head over heels with the suave, dashing sports agent, but after everything her ex had put her through, she didn't have the strength to deal with another wishy-washy man. Furthermore, it was New Year's Eve, and she wanted to celebrate with her girlfriends, not fret about Marc.

"As usual, you're exaggerating. There are plenty of eligible, successful men at the party." Staring at her reflection in the mirror, Eliza pulled on her white satin gloves and fluffed her beehive hairstyle. "Liberty, you are *such* a drama queen."

"No, I'm not. No one's asked me to dance tonight, or bought me a drink, and I look hot in this vintage polka-dot dress that Maya made for me." A frown stained her ruby lips. "Thank God Big Mama bought me a new vibrator for Christmas or I'd *really* be depressed."

A giggle bubbled up in Maya's throat. Leave it to Liberty to make her laugh. All night, she'd been complaining about the lack of available suitors at the party, and when she wasn't grumbling about being single on New Year's Eve she was downing flutes of champagne.

"Quit stressing about your love life, and focus on nailing your solo during 'Happy New Year,'" Aquarius advised, glancing up from her bejeweled cell phone.

"We're performing in front of a sold-out crowd full of music execs and celebrities, and this could be our big break."

"Or not." Liberty shrugged a shoulder. "I don't know about you guys, but I need a break. I'm sick of touring and rehearsing, and I'm so anxious to leave for our trip, I packed weeks ago."

Finished styling Aquarius's hair, Maya stepped back and assessed her work. It had taken hours to create Lyrical Soul's fifties-style ensemble, but her efforts had paid off. They'd looked and sounded amazing during their set, and after their closing song they'd received a standing ovation. Impressed with their performance, the hotel event planner had asked them to do another song, and they'd jumped at the chance to sing again in front of the hometown crowd.

Due on stage in ten minutes, the women gathered their things and exited the bathroom. Linking arms, they sashayed through the lobby, rehearsing their final song. Entering the grand ballroom, Maya saw guests in top hats and feathered boas, waving glow sticks and blowing noise makers. Out on the dance floor, couples moved and grooved to Prince. A silver-lettered banner was suspended above the stage, and glitzy lanterns hung from the ceiling. Round tables were decorated with fine china, and the gold candle-holders made the room sparkle and shine.

Standing at the bar drinking cocktails with her friends, Maya noticed a slim, dark-haired man watching her, and dodged his gaze. Feeling like a goddess in her flowing chiffon gown, she adjusted the bold red sash draped around her waist. Sequins were sprinkled across the bodice, and the floral-print design along the hem was eye-catching and unique. All evening, she'd been receiving compliments from women, and dinner invitations from wealthy older men, but since none of them excited her the way Marc did, she'd turned them all down.

"The Spanish guy in the white tuxedo is staring at you so hard, he's probably going to pop an eye vessel," Aquarius joked. "Want me to go over there and get his number for you?"

Liberty waved a hand in the air as if she was a queen on a throne. "Don't bother. Pretty Boy doesn't stand a chance. Her heart is with Marc, always will be, and that will never change."

"If she's in love with Marc, then why is she shutting him out?" As she cocked her head to the left, a confused expression marred Eliza's delicate facial features. "Why won't she talk to him?"

"Hello? I can hear you," Maya quipped. "I'm right here. Quit talking about me like I'm not."

Aquarius piped up, "Is this about Javonte not liking Marc? I hope not, because your brother hates anyone who even looks at you, let alone anyone who tries to date you, so Marc is fighting a losing battle. He can't win when it comes to Javonte, so cut the guy some slack."

"This isn't about my brother." Feeling cornered, Maya defended herself. "Marc lied to me about his divorce, among other things, and I don't know if I can trust him."

"Call him and talk things over. That's what couples do."

"Liberty, you make it sound so simple . . ." she complained, her voice fading into silence.

"It's New Year's Eve, Maya, one of the most romantic days of the year," Eliza pointed out. "Wouldn't you rather spend the night with Marc than with us?"

"Yes, but—"

Aquarius cut her off. "But nothing, Maya. If you don't call Marc, I will, because I'm sick of seeing you mope around. It's depressing. You've been sad all week, and the longer you shut Marc out, the harder it's going to be for you guys to resolve your issues."

"And, it would be a shame if you lost your true love because you were afraid of getting hurt again," Eliza added, giving her a one-arm hug. "Take it from someone who knows. I've been there, and if I could turn back the hands of time, I'd still be happily married."

With a heavy heart, Maya stared down at her cocktail glass. Were her friends right? Should she reach out to Marc? Was their relationship worth fighting for? Was he?

"Welcome back to the stage, Chicago's favorite a capella group, Lyrical Soul!"

To the sound of thunderous applause and whistles, Liberty, Eliza, and Aquarius strode confidently onstage, and stood in front of their microphone stands. The lights dimmed, and silence fell across the room. "This song is dedicated to our favorite couple," Liberty said, with a smile. "We love you, Maya and Marc. All the best in the New Year."

Heat flooded Maya's cheeks. *What an odd thing for Liberty to say*, she thought, taking a sip of her Mistletoe Martini. Marc wasn't there; he was at the Titan Management anniversary bash, living it up with groupies and exotic dancers, no doubt. She'd learned about the party from Javonte that afternoon, and was shocked to learn Marc had planned the exclusive event. It sounded like an excuse for his clients to get drunk, and even though they were no longer a couple, Maya hoped for Marc's sake that the party was a success.

Her friends began singing "Christmas with You,"

and Maya frowned. Raising her eyebrows, she stared at the trio in disbelief. What were they doing? Had they had too many cocktails to drink? Were they drunk? They sounded amazing, and their harmonies were bang on, but that wasn't the song they'd practiced in the bathroom for the past hour.

Looking out on the dance floor, at all the kissing couples, made her heart sad. Liberty was right; this was the worst New Year's Eve ever. Without Marc, her nights were long and lonely, and Maya would do anything to see him one more time.

Her gaze dropped to her wrist, and she admired her sapphire bangle—her most treasured gift. In that moment, Maya realized what she'd done, recognized what was at stake. It was time to reunite with Marc. Once her friends were finished singing, she was going to take a cab to Titan Management. Maya didn't know where his office was, but it didn't matter— she was going to go get her man. She'd find him and apologize for walking out on him

Standing in the shadows, Maya swayed to the beat of the music. "'Christmas with you, is a dream come true,'" she sang, touched by the lyrics of the song. "'The only place I want to be is nestled in your arms, holding you close. Christmas with you, is a dream come true . . .'"

In her peripheral vision, Maya caught sight of someone marching through the ballroom doors, and glanced at the dance floor to see who the new arrival was. The crowd parted, and Maya's mouth fell open. Time stopped, and all she could do was stare.

Her eyes weren't deceiving her. It was Marc. *Her* Marc. Her soul mate, her one true love, the man she loved with every fiber of her being. He looked devilishly handsome in his all-black attire, and when their eyes met her body warmed. His hair was neatly trimmed, his tailored suit jacket hugged his shoulders, and he moved with a wealth of confidence, as if he could have anything in the world—including her.

Hope surged in her heart. Eager to speak to him, Maya put her glass on the bar and shouldered her way through the well-dressed crowd. She hadn't seen him in days, and although she acted tough in front of her friends, every minute without him was torture. Several times, she'd considered calling him, but she'd lost her nerve. *Not tonight*, Maya thought, weaving her way around a portly waiter holding a tray of desserts.

His cologne wafted over her, and butterflies swarmed her stomach. Maya didn't know what to say, or how to greet him, and wondered what Marc would do if she threw her arms around him. She yearned for him, and longed to touch him more than anything.

As if reading her thoughts, Marc answered her unspoken request. He wrapped her up in his arms and held her tight. His hands stroked her hair, caressed her shoulders and hips. Maya didn't know how long they stood there, holding each other, but it felt like hours passed. It didn't matter. Marc was back, and everything was right in the world again. He released her, and they stared at each other for a long, quiet moment.

"How was the anniversary bash?" she asked, breaking the silence.

"Uneventful." His eyes twinkled with mischief, and a boyish smile claimed his lips. Five minutes after I got to the party, I told Mr. Frederick I was leaving, and drove straight here."

"You did? Why?"

"Because I had to see you. I was dying a slow death without you, and I wasn't going to let another day go by without seeing your beautiful face."

The music stopped, the crowd erupted into applause, and Lyrical Soul took a bow. Proud of her friends, Maya whistled and cheered. A local rock band rushed the stage, strumming their electric guitars, and their fans shouted and screamed in wild excitement.

"Let's find somewhere quiet to talk." Clasping her hand, Marc led Maya out of the ballroom, and through the corridor. Finding a padded leather chair at the end of the hallway, he sat down and pulled her onto his lap. "Congratulations on your fashion truck, Maya. I'm proud of you, and I'm confident Luxe Design is going to be a hit."

"Thank you. If not for you, I wouldn't be fulfilling my dreams."

They intertwined fingers, and Marc kissed her palm.

"I can handle losing Javonte as a client, and Mr. Frederick cursing me out about it, but I can't lose you. I feel fortunate to have you in my life, and I don't want anyone else."

"I'm so glad you're here. I've missed you so much—"

"Then why didn't you call? You had to know that I was going crazy without you."

"I was scared," she confessed, dropping her gaze to her lap. "I thought you were playing me, and I didn't want to get burned by love again."

"I'm sorry for not telling you everything about my past, but I was ashamed about the mistakes I'd made in my marriage, and I was afraid if I told you the truth you'd leave me."

Maya felt a twinge of disappointment. "How could you think that? Don't you know how I feel about you? Isn't it obvious? You're important to me, and I want to be with you."

"I know, but life hasn't always been kind. Once women find out I cheated in the past, they usually run for the hills, and I didn't want history to repeat itself."

"What happened? Why did you cheat on your ex?"

"I'm not trying to make excuses for what I did, but I was upset with my ex for bailing on me when my dad got sick, so to get even I hooked up with one of her friends." He spoke in a solemn tone. "We were legally separated at the time, but it was wrong, and I still feel a lot of guilt and shame about it."

"Everyone has a past, Marc, even me, but the mistakes I've made don't define me. I learned from them, moved on, and became a better person, and I know you've done the same."

Wearing a pensive expression on his face, he slowly and tenderly caressed her hands.

"How was Christmas Day at your mom's house?" she asked with a heavy heart. "I hope your family isn't mad at me for being a no-show, but I was a wreck after I left your house."

"They were surprisingly understanding *until* I told them what happened. Then my mom and sister went off on me!" Shivering, as if freezing cold, he expelled a deep breath. "Kingsley said it'll be a miracle if you forgive me, because she wouldn't, and my mom reamed me for being secretive and deceitful. She said I'm better than that, and I am."

Go, Mom! Maya thought, but when she saw sadness flicker in his eyes, she squeezed his hand and gave him a peck on the cheek. "Don't sweat it, baby. It's in the past."

"From now on, I'll be honest about everything, and you'll never have to worry about me hiding things from you. Maya, I want us to work, and we will . . ."

Lowering his head, he brushed his nose against hers, and she giggled. Being with Marc would never grow old, and Maya was looking forward to spending the rest of her life with him. "I love you, Marc, and I always will, as long as we both shall live."

It was the first time she'd bared her soul to him, the only time she'd ever said those three magic words. Walking out on Marc on Christmas Day had been a mistake, but Maya knew what to do to make things right. "Tomorrow, I'm going to cook New Year's Day dinner for all of our friends and family, so call everyone up and tell them to be at my house at six."

Marc raised an eyebrow. "What about Javonte? The last time I saw him he was pissed, and I don't want to set him off again. I'm not his agent, but I still want the best for him."

"Leave my brother to me. He'll be a gracious host tomorrow night, or he'll have me to answer to, and trust me, Javonte doesn't want to get on my bad side."

"Then count me in. I'll be there." Marc cupped her chin. "Baby, you're my number one girl, and I love you with all my heart. You are, and always will be, the only woman for me."

Marc brushed his lips against her forehead, and Maya melted in his arms. He made her feel like the most beautiful woman alive, and she reveled in their newfound love. And, when he tightened his hold around her waist and kissed her passionately on the lips, Maya realized Marc was the best Christmas gift she'd ever been given, and she was going to cherish him forever.

DON'T MISS

The Betting Vow

by K.M. Jackson

Leila Darling is past done with the supermodel thing, especially the mega-parties and high-profile flings that have done nothing but leave her alone and jaded. She's got the talent to be a serious actress, but the industry sees her as a high-maintenance, impulsive party girl with a reputation for leaving men in the dust—especially TV producer Carter Bain.

Carter's had his eye on Leila for years, so when a bet gives him a chance to get close to her, he accepts. With the goal of getting Leila the image makeover she needs and Carter the star he desires, the game is on. Get married and stay married for six months. If Leila lasts, she gets her pick of his A-list roles. If Carter wins, she'll take the hot sidekick part he's offered.

But as their "I do" turns up all kinds of heat, Leila and Carter find they have more in common than they ever imagined. Are these two prepared to put business aside and surrender the ultimate prize, their hearts?

Enjoy the following excerpt from
The Betting Vow . . .

Chapter 1

Balancing on the hood of a sports car while slickly oiled up was a lot harder than most people imagined. Add to that doing it one-handed, because you've got your hands wrapped around a fully loaded burger. Plus, you are in a bikini and are wearing six-inch stilettos. Well, then, you've got yourself a straight-up high-wire act.

Leila Darling tried her best to suck in her stomach, push out her behind, while simultaneously "making love" to the camera by puffing out her lips into a sultry, come-hither pout. She narrowed her eyes ever so slightly, as if extending a welcome invitation to wanton sex, while still appearing approachable with her version of the ever popular smize. Why it took this much sex to sell a hamburger still baffled her, but hers was not to reason why, since she was getting paid a small ransom to sit on the shiny car, be extra shiny herself, and make the Barn Burger the most lusted-after burger in fast-food history.

"Give me more. Give me more!" yelled Matteo, the famed photographer, fighting to be heard over the blaring bass of the heart-thumping rock music in the studio. If you could call the rented garage space in a rather sketchy part of East LA a studio. The tips of Matteo's dark hair, what little he had left, were bleached and spiked so that they stood up at odd angles, and he wore an excessive amount of kohl around his eyes, making his deep under-eye bags all the more pronounced.

"That's right, Leila. Just like that. Oh, darling, you are selling it. Those eyes, those breasts . . . I'm getting hungry just watching you. You're a sexual beast, *darling!*"

Leila pushed back a sneer at the way the word *darling* rolled off his tongue. Though it was her last name, in her case the word could be used as a proper noun, an adjective, or sadly, as of late, a verb. "Pulling a darling" was, now thanks to social media, used for all sorts of things, and none of them good. Such as wild clubbing until the wee hours of the morning. Though, for the life of her, Leila didn't understand what was wrong with blowing off a bit of steam. Or it was used when one threw a fit. Though in Leila's eyes, demanding respect, even if it was in a forceful tone, was essential in her business.

But worst, in her eyes, was that now—thanks to her ex, well, her third ex-fiancé, Miles G, and that crappy song of his, "Darling Leila"—"pulling a darling" was synonymous with being a man-eater who used men, made them fall in love, but never committed to them. Of course, it didn't matter that in all her terminal relationships, it was the guys who'd failed her, making promises they ultimately had no intentions of keeping. Giving her perfectly valid reasons to bail on the so-called relationships.

So today, with Leila's nerves already frayed, Matteo's use of the word *darling* slid over Leila in a way that was too slimy and too personal and had her questioning his usage altogether. In the end, the sneer won out, and Leila went with it, her top lip curling as she looked at the photographer. Besides, the "sexual beast" comment had got to her, too. Especially now, when Leila considered herself in a career transition. She couldn't just let a comment like that go unchecked.

Sure she knew she should be happy and feel accomplished as one of the few African American top models in the business, though her current position of burger eating slash car hood bikini balancing would bring one to question that fact. Still, most would think Leila had it all and was living on top, but in reality, she felt something was sorely lacking. Respect. Leila wanted so very much to be seen as more than a sexy body that could sell anything, be it fast food or French couture.

Leila inwardly sighed as she recalled, while balancing herself precariously, one leg cocked up, the other pushing hard into the hood of the sports car, that a little over a month ago she'd been in Cannes, being celebrated as a breakout star in a less than breakout movie. Sure, she might have had only a few actual lines in the movie, and yes, she'd been brought on for her looks. However, she'd taken that part and ran with it. Showing she had chops, and for that she'd been rewarded for something besides the way she filled out a bikini top. Leila wanted more of that.

But here she was, back home in the States and back to the same grind. *Stand. Sit. Turn this way. Tilt that way.* Was it any wonder she was on edge? Add to it the fact that taking an early flight back from Cannes had resulted in the demise of yet another high-profile relationship when she caught Miles, in his words, "just doing what he do," horizontally with the skank du jour. Well Leila was officially done with her life as usual.

"Now take a bite. We want to see you eat it," Matteo said, his voice piercing Leila's musings and pinging her nerve endings with its raw excitement, so much so that Leila didn't quite know if he was talking about the burger or something else that she didn't want to touch.

Leila let out a low breath and went in for the burger, but then, as if on cue, the music in the studio changed and on came the familiar first thumps to the song Leila was fast growing to hate: "Darling Leila." Would she ever escape Miles or that damned song? And really *Darling Leila*? Talk about an unoriginal name. The jerk didn't have an original bone in his overly hyped body let alone thought in that little brain of his.

"Oh yeah!" Matteo yelled, now smiling wide and circling her with his camera as he clicked, clicked around her. Each click of the shutter felt like a tiny prick to her skin.

Leila shot Matteo a death stare but then forced her features to soften as she glanced over to the side of the room and saw the group of execs from Burger Barn huddled in the corner, looking at her expectantly. Bills needed to be paid, and for that to happen, the customer was always right. Leila reminded herself of this tried-and-true mantra as she let out a sigh and further softened her features, going on automatic pilot as she mentally blocked out the song that mocked her and Miles's now failed relationship and, worse, all her relationships before that. She took a hungry bite of the burger, imagining for a moment that it was the head of the photographer.

Method acting. Zone it out, woman. Use that anger.

Just then her agent and longtime friend, Jasper Weston, stepped into her side view as he went over to glad-hand the Burger Barn folks. Leila took another bite of the burger. This time it was Jasper's head she was biting off, as she remembered it was he who had told her that taking this job would be a good idea.

"That's it, Leila," Matteo finally said. "Though, maybe next time you could go at it with just a little less enthusiasm?" He lowered his camera and turned toward his group of assistants. Leila noted that they were all young and all blond, whether male or female, with slightly vacant eyes. It would seem Matteo had a type and stuck to it through and through.

"We're going to need another burger on set," he said to no one in particular before turning back to Leila. She hoped that the actual food handlers picked up on his query and that it wouldn't be one of the Stepford blondes who handed her the next burger. "How about we get ready for the next set and wardrobe change, but before that we'll do the rain sequence?"

Rain sequence? Since when is a rain sequence on the shoot list? Leila thought as she looked around for a rain machine. She saw none. It was then that another on-set blond assistant came over and took the burger missing two bites from Leila's hands and scurried off into the background. Then another young blonde came toward her with a large hose and a dubious look in her eyes. Instantly, Leila stiffened.

"No way, honey," Leila said with a sharp look at the young woman. "You come at me with that hose, you'd better be prepared to eat it." It was as if the whole garage had got put on mute, as all heads swiveled Leila's way. She saw Jasper smile uncomfortably at the Burger Barn people and take a step forward.

"Aw, come on now, Leila, darling," Matteo began.

"We need a shot with you wet on top of the car. You moving around for me. Doing a little dance. Selling those burgers as only you can." And with that, the damned near geriatric photographer standing in front of her, holding his camera at his side, mimed his version of sexy dance moves, rubbing his hands over his body, bringing them up and, to Leila's revulsion, licking his fingers.

Leila looked at him in horror and then blinked her way out of the shock of it all and leveled him with a hard glare. "Like I said, little Miss Assistant of the Corn here is not coming near me with some dirty-assed water hose. Now, if you want to try, you can, but I warn you, you won't like where the hose ends up in the end."

And with that, Leila slid her oiled body off the car as gracefully as she could and walked off set toward her makeshift dressing room, Jasper following quickly behind.

"You almost had a grand slam with this one, Walker. Almost."

Carter Bain watched Greyson Hill, the CFO of Hillibrand Inc., give his critique of their weeklong schmooze fest. All he could hear was the admonishment in the loaded word *almost*. Screw almost. He'd wanted to hit it out of the park. He hadn't come all the way out to California to take on the launch of Sphere, World Broadcasting's new nightly station programming, for an "almost."

Carter's boss and mentor, Everett Walker, shook Greyson's hand and nodded. "Don't worry. You just get your ads ready. By the time we're in place for pilot filming, all will be perfect and vendors will be clamoring for spots. You'll want to be in on the ground floor with this one."

Greyson raised a skeptical bushy gray brow. "I hope so, because I see a lot that we think may have potential, with the right players. Especially that *Brentwood* concept, but you have to get bang-up talent behind it. All that deep thinking programming may be fine for cable and those O channel guru–loving ladies, but we can't forget the males from eighteen to twenty-four while still capturing the thirty-five-plus moms. We want the kind of shows that are worth them streaming on their tablets, as well as getting the ladies checking in and tweeting live.

"The way we see it, the moms are the destination watchers, and they are harder to pull away from the shows they're already loyal to. So it's new viewers you're going to have to scramble for. And to get the young males, there is only one tried-and-true way, and that is to pull them in with sex. Give them something to come for, and keep them coming so they stay." With that statement, Greyson gave a pointed turn of the head toward Carter's assistant, Karen.

To keep his job in place and the potential ad revenue still in play, Carter chose to ignore the look, but still he stepped into Greyson's field of vision. "Thank you, Mr. Hill. Your insight is very much appreciated. But believe me, you don't have to worry about *Brentwood* or any of our upcoming shows. We have a long line of A-listers fighting for casting consideration." Carter feigned a humble look. "Unfortunately, due to some contractual obligations and the way the press works, we're not at liberty to share them yet. I'll just say, be prepared to be wowed at our next meeting." He gave Greyson a wink and a pat on his shoulder.

Greyson looked over at his brothers, the Hill Pack, and gave a short snort. "I sure hope so," he said before turning back to Everett. "You've got a real go-getter in this one," he said, indicating Carter. "He's hungry. I like that."

Everett looked Carter's way and gave a nod. "That he is. Carter is one of the best. When there is a job to be done, I can always count on him. Like he said, there's no need to worry. You all just get your ads lined up. Let us handle the programming."

Carter shook Greyson's hand a final time. "I'll have my assistant e-mail yours with all the details of our meeting and the kits."

Carter then turned his attention toward Greyson's brother Waymon. Next to him were Bret and Cliff. It would seem the rumor about the Hills traveling in packs had officially been confirmed. At least when it came to getting off their property in Tennessee and coming out to California to do business with the so-called "city folk." They all had thick accents, but Carter had no doubt it was more for show than anything else. You didn't run a multinational company with businesses in the food, media, and technology industries, not to mention exert political influence that went deep, or so the rumors said, while being country bumpkins. But, hey, Carter could play along. Anything to seal the deal. If he had to, he'd chew tobacco and don a pair of overalls to bring in their ad commitment.

Still, it was with relief that Carter stood beside Everett and Karen outside World Broadcasting's California studios and watched the limo take the Hill clan away, their expressions all nearly frozen in place as they waved their final good-byes. The next car to pull up was Everett's. No limo this time. It was a not so understated Mercedes convertible. Everett turned to the duo and shook Karen's hand first.

"You did an outstanding job this week, Karen. I know a lot was thrown your way, but you stepped up to the plate. Carter's lucky to have you on his team."

Karen smiled as she returned the handshake. "Thank you, sir. Just doing my job."

"You do it well. Never sell yourself short."

He turned to Carter, sobering. "You both did very well. But Greyson is right, there is room for improvement. I want this account. If we get Hillibrand, then more vendors will follow suit. Don't make a liar out of me. I expect to have a short list of names ready by next week to consider for *Brentwood*."

Carter fought to stay cool and keep from frowning. He had known this would come up with Everett, but he had thought he'd maybe get a five-minute congratulatory breather. Hell, who was he fooling? This was Everett Walker. He wasn't into pats on the back, and he definitely wasn't into giving breathers. It was part of the reason Carter admired him. Carter had always respected Everett's no-nonsense business manner and drive. It was so different from his upbringing, where his business sense and appreciation of capitalism were considered a fault. Coming from a working class family, you'd think his accomplishments would be celebrated, but to his bohemian parents, they were more of an embarrassment.

Still, he couldn't complain all that much on the parental front. Though he'd been poor, Carter counted himself lucky having grown up with both a mother and a father in the home. His father, Malcolm, was an artist who was a jack-of-all-trades and a master of none, and his mother, Faye, was a woman with an obsession for helping those less fortunate, second only to her obsession with trying to manage her only son's life.

"Don't worry, sir," Carter said. "I have some ideas in the works. We'll discuss them next week."

Everett pulled off, leaving Carter and Karen standing together, once again with plastered-on smiles, as they mumbled behind clenched teeth and waved. Karen let out a grumble before she spoke aloud.

"I'm so glad this week is over. I've had enough California sunshine to last me a while, thank you very much. And I swear, if that little perv Cliff Hill took one more leering look at my boobs, I was going to gouge his eyes out. It wasn't only the older Hill who couldn't keep his eyes to himself."

Carter's smile wavered ony slightly as he gave Karen a quick glance and continued to wave at Everett's car. Part of him couldn't blame the Hills. His assistant, Karen Woodley, was a good-looking woman, he supposed. But it didn't matter, since Karen was a part of his staff, which put her in the off-limits category. And since she was his assistant, in a weird sort of way, Carter felt that put her under his protection. He knew it wasn't entirely true, and was clearly overstepping on his part, but still he wouldn't have her messed with or in any way disrespected.

Despite word on the street about his slick reputation, he did have a conscience. It was that same conscience that kept every woman on his staff off limits in his book. Sex was one thing, but it didn't trump money in the bank.

"Thanks for not gouging his eyes out," Carter said, addressing Karen's comment about Cliff. "At least not just yet. Let's get all the signatures we need from them and seal this deal first, and then you can gouge away. Metaphorically, of course. Hell, I'll do it for you. Hey, at least you didn't have Waymon breathing down your neck. The man was looking at my package like I was fresh crab legs just put out at Caesar's buffet."

At that comment, Karen pulled a face, and he couldn't help laughing. The car turned out of sight, and they both put their hands down and shook their heads.

"You think his wife knows?" Carter asked.

Karen nodded. "Probably so. Believe me, even if she says she doesn't, she has a clue. The wife always knows . . . something."

Carter shrugged. Given that she was twice divorced, he figured Karen knew what she was talking about, so he just deferred to her on such subjects. Besides, he steered clear of romantic attachments. Nobody was ever on the up-and-up. At least not when it came to matters of the heart. His parents were the rare exceptions and he was sure last holdouts of a bygone era. And he wasn't swayed in the least by his best buds falling so hard that they both went the commitment route. Hell, part of him felt bad seeing them as whipped as they were.

Not him, though. No way. That was why he'd rather stick to business. At least across a board room table, a man looked you in the eye before stabbing you in the back. Not that he didn't love women and indulge in his fair share of them. It was just that he wasn't foolish enough to believe in the fallacy of true love, trust, soul mates, forever, and all that bull. He'd had his fair share of women who'd been with him for what he could do for them and then hit the road when he'd taken them as far as his position would go. So yeah, he had learned his lessons about love and found it best to leave the fiction for what he was producing for the small screen.

Carter let out a breath and tugged at his collar before looking up at the blazing sun. "How can something so beautiful be so torturous? What is with this freaking heat?"

Karen shrugged. Her sleeveless white blouse and black skirt had remained unwrinkled. "Well, it would help if you dressed a little less for New York and a lot more for California. You could practically choke on that tie of yours. You look like you're ready for fall in London instead of spring in California." She arched a brow. "And is a bow tie necessary?"

Carter's brow rose. "Yeah, it is. Besides, it won over ole Greyson. We were matching."

Karen let out a snort. "Matching. Ah, now I get it. Knowing you, you did that on purpose."

Carter grinned, and Karen's eyes went skyward. "I swear, is there anything you won't do to make a deal?"

Carter put his finger to his temple and feigned thinking. "Not that I can come up with."

Karen shook her head. "That's what I'm afraid of."

Carter let out a snort. "Tell that to your holiday bonus."

With that, Karen held up a hand. "You win. The tie is a perfect touch." She pointed to her feet and looked down. "Somebody has to keep me in these fancy shoes."

Carter laughed, relieved to have the dog and pony show over, as they walked back inside the studio. The lights had been dimmed, and the stars—what few they had and what few they could call stars—had all left, as had the live studio audience for the last taping.

Today they had tested a pilot for a family comedy with quintuplets that so far had received high test ratings. It was risky, but they were using actual quints to star in the key roles. Carter knew it was a big gamble, but each time he'd had *The Morning Show* broadcast an update on "miracle babies," their ratings had gone through the roof. Why not try to re-create that magic in prime time?

So as not to be considered too far off his rocker, though, Carter had been smart enough to cast actual actors in the lead parental roles. This was much to the chagrin of the quints' mother, but the blow was softened by the fact that her sub was a very well-known blond beauty who in her heyday had turned quite a few heads by being the lead in a top lifeguard dramedy.

But that was just one of the shows they'd gotten settled. There was still plenty to do back in New York, where most of the productions would take place and where World Broadcasting was headquartered. Carter knew he'd be spending a little time in LA, but he was thankful that shooting was moving east and he wouldn't have to upend his life completely. California was nice, but all this sunshine could turn a guy's brain to mush. Hell, this week alone had put him halfway there. The Hills liked to party, and hard. They might be older, but they came with stamina to spare, both natural and, he suspected, in some cases pharmaceutical. Each night he and the rest of the network's team had taken them to a different hot spot, where they'd been wined and dined in the VIP lounge. Due to the company going liberal with the tipping and bottle service, and the Hills heavily greasing the right palms at the after parties, they had never been without arm candy as they made their way back to their hotel villas.

But the partying only got so hard for Carter. He knew that keeping a clear head at all times was paramount on this trip. He was there for the clients. His pleasure would come when the deal was inked. Getting a woman to warm his bed, well, that was easy. All he had to do was make a call, but he didn't need any distractions or possible entanglements. These next few months—hell, the next year—were too important. Everett had put a lot in his hands this time, and it was up to him to pass or fail this most important of tests.

And Carter was sure many were expecting him to fail. Maybe even wanting him to fail. Sure, he'd heard the watercooler talk of how he'd gotten as far as he had only because he'd been close friends with Everett's son, Aidan, all these years. And yes, being friends with Aidan had maybe gotten him in the door. But Everett didn't play when it came to his money or his business. It was Carter's hard work and determination that had kicked the door down, and it was that same determination that would take him to the very top.

If he'd learned anything from his parents, who worked hard on their respective endeavors but didn't have his same drive, it was that hope and a righteous cause didn't pay the rent. The lights got left on due to cold, hard cash. As a family, they had had their lean years of living hand to mouth and had even endured the embarrassment of living off the mercy of the system. Coming home from his fancy Upper East Side school, where he was on a scholarship, and being hit by a red eviction notice on his door had taught him early on that the streets were paved with promises and good intentions, but it was cash that made the world go around and kept a roof over one's head. Not that Carter had any animosity or regrets. He considered his past nothing but a supersize classroom, one that had taught him that when opportunity knocked you hurried up and opened the damned door.

That was what he was doing with this new network, Sphere. It would be a hit if it killed him. Still, the wrinkle in this week's dog and pony show was *Brentwood Drive*, a sort of retro nod to *Three's Company*, but flipped, with two guys and one girl rooming together. So far the male leads, a couple of up-and-coming comedic actors, seemed solid, but the female leads that had been tested had left the focus groups with low feedback numbers. For the female spot, they needed someone with real star quality, but honestly, the network didn't have the budget or the cachet to warrant an actual star.

They couldn't even get any big names to come in and test during this off season. All the real stars were off vacationing, doing feature films, or taking up off-season DJing. Either way, no one was out to risk their career on a possible disaster of a pilot comedy on an obscure no-name station. But Carter had to make this work. Getting these pilots off the ground could turn this germ of a side network into something, and possibly something big. He needed this. There was only so much hard news he could do and still compete with the other two networks. He'd taken mornings as far as he could.

Making a bit of a splash with his more reality-based pieces had awakened him to the fact that viral scripted content was the way to go. Everyone was leaning toward destination watching, and that was where the network needed to be, even if his old friend Aidan didn't agree. Let him handle the real life, and Carter would keep everyone suitably placated over in dreamland.

But for that to happen, he needed some certified hit shows. And there would be no hits without a few stars.

Connect with

Us

Visit us online at
KensingtonBooks.com
to read more from your favorite authors, see books
by series, view reading group guides, and more.

Join us on social media

for sneak peeks, chances to win books and prize packs,
and to share your thoughts with other readers.

facebook.com/kensingtonpublishing
twitter.com/kensingtonbooks

Tell us what you think!

To share your thoughts, submit a review,
or sign up for our eNewsletters, please visit:
KensingtonBooks.com/TellUs.